After a public health career in Peru, Spain and Scotland, Martin Donaghy became a volunteer with the Govan Stones, a community heritage project in Glasgow. A lifelong history afficionado, he learned there of the Vinegar Letters, a famous early 19th century scandal which embroiled the city. Fascinated by the conflict in mores, personality and class at a time of social and political unrest, he wrote this novel based on accounts of the affair.

To Ann, Dan, Sara, Isla and Ruby.

Martin Donaghy

THE VINEGAR LETTERS

AUSTIN MACAULEY PUBLISHERS™
LONDON * CAMBRIDGE * NEW YORK * SHARJAH

Copyright © Martin Donaghy 2024

The right of Martin Donaghy to be identified as author of this work has been asserted by the author in accordance with sections 77 and 78 of the Copyright, Designs and Patents Act 1988.

All rights reserved. No part of this publication may be reproduced, stored in a retrieval system, or transmitted in any form or by any means, electronic, mechanical, photocopying, recording, or otherwise, without the prior permission of the publishers.

Any person who commits any unauthorised act in relation to this publication may be liable to criminal prosecution and civil claims for damages.

This is a work of fiction. Names, characters, businesses, places, events, locales, and incidents are either the products of the author's imagination or used in a fictitious manner. Any resemblance to actual persons, living or dead, or actual events is purely coincidental.

A CIP catalogue record for this title is available from the British Library.

ISBN 9781035802241 (Paperback)
ISBN 9781035802258 (Hardback)
ISBN 9781035803620 (ePub e-book)

www.austinmacauley.com

First Published 2024
Austin Macauley Publishers Ltd®
1 Canada Square
Canary Wharf
London
E14 5AA

My thanks to David J Simons, novelist and mentor. His support was obtained through the Scottish Book Trust.

My thanks to the encouragement and guidance from Mr Frazer Capie and all at the Govan Stones.

Thanks to all at Austin Macauley Publishers.

Table of Contents

Chapter 1: The Hodge Podge   11

Chapter 2: The Printed Gown   16

Chapter 3: Mr Nip's Dinner   23

Chapter 4: Woes   29

Chapter 5: The First Is One Too Many   33

Chapter 6: The Best for the Best Alone   38

Chapter 7: Attention to Detail   43

Chapter 8: The Ball   48

Chapter 9: Vinegar   53

Chapter 10: Don't Tell   59

Chapter 11: George   66

Chapter 12: Blackball   71

Chapter 13: The Bankers' Tryst   74

Chapter 14: Vinegar's in His Bottle   79

Chapter 15: The Most Difficult Fight in the City of Life   81

Chapter 16: Arbitration   85

Chapter 17: Word Is Out   92

Chapter 18: The Moral Burning   97

Chapter 19: Apology   102

Chapter 20: Lily Patrick   107

Chapter 21: The Avalanche of Grudges   112

Chapter 22: The Financial World   117

Chapter 23: The Clawman	120
Chapter 24: Facedown	126
Chapter 25: Housewarming	130
Chapter 26: Mr Jeffrey	135
Chapter 27: The Summons	140
Chapter 28: Oswald's Betrayal	146
Chapter 29: Lily's Predicament	149
Chapter 30: Options	154
Chapter 31: The Theatre	158
Chapter 32: Lily's Escape	161
Chapter 33: Cover All Bets	165
Chapter 34: The First Day	169
Chapter 35: Lily Waits	175
Chapter 36: The Second Day	180
Chapter 37: Lily in Court	186
Chapter 38: The Verdicts	192
Chapter 39: By the Well	197
Chapter 40: Eager Was the Wait	201
Chapter 41: Salvation	205
Chapter 42: No, Not Again	210
Chapter 43: A Strange Visitor	213
Chapter 44: O'Neill	219
Chapter 45: Find Him	224
Chapter 46: A Murder	227
Chapter 47: Manoeuvres	234
Chapter 48: The Endgame	241
Epilogue	247

Chapter 1
The Hodge Podge

'We'd just ridden over the brig at the Calmachie Burn. Billy Orr and I,' said Kingan in the cheery lilt which he employed for his anecdotes. The light from the chandeliers played up the twinkle in his pale blue eyes. His fellow tipplers at the bar craned their necks towards him.

'It was then, I spotted a gig coming towards us at a furious rate, the horse's eyes rolling, its mouth foaming. We swerved to avoid it. Then I spied Mr Adam Aitken, the renowned banker, seated by a coachman, his face contorted like when he was short-changed at the Tontine.'

He paused, enjoying the sniggers.

'Danger was upon him! Then, just before the bridge, from a ditch at the side of the road, a cottar in tattered trousers and split boots leapt out.'

Kingan jerked forward; arms outstretched as if trying to catch the imaginary horse. A couple of the party took a step back.

'Forsaking all risk to himself, the poor man grasped the reins and dug his heels into the ground. The horse heaved to, then stopped. A simple cottar had saved the life of the most important banker in our dear, green Glasgow. By the time Billy and I had turned our horses around, Aitken's gig had moved on. Billy inquired of the rescuer whether he'd got anything for his courage. "Oh yes," said he. "I got a shilling." To which Billy replied, "A shilling for saving a life?" "Come away. John," said I. "That's quite sufficient. Every man bases the price of life on the value of his own."'

Laughter boomed through the warm evening air. Exulting in the mirth of good company, he smoothed his silver hair combed forward over his temples then straightened his red velvet frock coat.

He surveyed the stir in the grand assembly room at the George Inn, noting which select member of the Quality was mingling with whom. He returned his attention to his fellows, like him well practised in the art of spirited conviviality. He stilled when his gaze met a pair of raised eyebrows. He winked. He was about to ask his closest friend, James Oswald, what was up when the sharp crack of a wooden hammer on a gavel sounded.

The merry group moved to take their places at the long table set for thirty. On the starched white tablecloth, every measured three feet, stood a candelabra lighting up the tableware embossed with the club's name—Hodge Podge.

Kingan took his usual place beside Oswald. The two bachelors made a contrasting pair: Kingan wiry with a chiselled face and knowing eyes, Oswald corpulent with a ruddy face and bulging eyes. Kingan put his hand on his friend's shoulder. 'You didn't enjoy my little tale?'

Oswald leaned over. 'Your yarn'll get back to Aitken. You need to take care, bandying your scorn in public.'

'This isn't the public, James,' replied Kingan nodding to those seated at the table. 'These are Gentlemen. Even the bankers. Together in the privacy of our club. If you want rectitude, join the Club of the Knights of the Holy Sepulchre and moan for hours in masonic mystery. Or perhaps, you've already joined?'

Oswald's lips curled. 'You've been drinking too much again, John. You know what it does to you.'

Kingan shrugged. His gout had been in abeyance for months. His friend's sanctimony rankled. He had known him for thirty years since he had just entered the business. Oswald had been barely a boy. Even then, Kingan had poked fun at his aristocratic affectations. But in recent years, especially since Oswald had been made Captain of Honour for the King's visit to Edinburgh last year, the younger man had become more set in his assumed superiority and in equal measure, his ambitions as a Whig politician.

The hammer struck three times. At the far end of the table, Baillie James Dennistoun of Golfhill, High President of the Hodge Podge Club proclaimed in a clipped accent, 'Good evening, fellow members!' He turned to a middle-aged man on his left, 'The minutes, Mr Secretary.'

The tall stooping figure peered at the raised page and read out the minutes of the club's gathering on 6 August 1823. Few if any of those seated, scions of Glasgow's merchant clans, paid any attention until the last item, "Wagers".

'We have three bets outstanding,' said the secretary. 'Mr Peter Murdoch wagered Mr John Kingan two guineas that Justice Archibald Alison while on the bench, did not say, "Jesus Christ, an honest man, was nae reformer." Mr James

Bogle bet Mr William Stirling a bottle of rum punch that a magnum bottle of spirits holds more than ten pints. And lastly, the following members,' he listed the names, 'Bet in pairs on each other's weights, the lighter to pay the heavier a bottle of rum.'

Guffaws rang out. At the end of last month's deep potation, a dozen carousers had tottered through the streets to Mr Dunlop Donald's warehouse. After three attempts, he managed to unlock the door. The secretary had stood at the side of the scales to record the measurements.

'And the winners?' bellowed Mr Samuel Hunter, the corpulent editor of the Glasgow Herald.

'Mr Secretary proceed,' nodded the President.

'I have failed to obtain any independent verification of Sherriff Allison's alleged statement. The matter will, therefore, be held over. A magnum holds eight pints. A bottle of rum punch, therefore, is due to Mr Stirling. Now to the first pair, Mr Blair weighed seventeen stone and ten pounds, Mr Hunter nineteen and two.'

'He's been fasting!' shouted Kingan.

'Mr Henderson twelve and one,' continued the secretary, reading out the rest of the list until he reached, 'Finally, Mr Colin Dunlop Donald, no weight recorded due to extreme lassitude. Given that members bet against each other, I will leave it to them to settle their accounts. Any substantiated infraction should be reported to me.'

'Any objections?' asked the President. None came. 'Let us now turn to the discussion on our Quares. Who seek the opinion of the club on matters of interest to members, Mr Secretary?'

'Three have submitted cases. Mr Dundas on "With the current insurrection in Demerara, who is the greater risk to Glasgow's prosperity, the rebel slaves or the Emancipationists?".'

Oswald, a vocal abolitionist, stiffened as heads turned towards him. The secretary continued, 'Mr Allston on "men run into danger to get out of apprehension. We are apprehensive of being damned. Therefore, we should destroy ourselves."'

'Eh?' snorted Hunter, his buttocks spread over two chairs.

'Mr Kingan on "Don Quixote said 'the path of virtue is narrow and laborious and that of vice, wide and spacious.' But is not vice as laborious as virtue?"'

'Good one, John!' shouted Hunter. Kingan stood up and bowed.

As he sat down, the President announced, 'I have chosen Mr Allston.'

A prolonged groan filled the room.

A flushed Allston pulled out his text. He curtailed his droning to half an hour. His finale was greeted with polite applause.

After a nil reply to his request for comments, The President struck the gavel, pointed the hammer at the door and shouted, 'The Hodge Podge, please!'

Waiters, aprons covering their shirts and breeches, entered the dining room, each carrying a tureen of hodge-podge soup. The cloying smell of mutton filled the room. Others followed, struggling with large trays of boiled legs and fried chops of mutton interspersed with rolls of roasted sirloin beef, the oozing juices lapping the rims. They laid them carefully on the dining table. As some served the soup and carved the meat, other attendants retrieved from behind the bar, bottles of rum, rum punch, port and madeira (porter and beer were banned for being too lowly, claret for being French).

The meal began. Twenty minutes later, the plates cleared, the glasses filled, the hammer sounded once more.

'Gentlemen, the toasts!' The hubbub stilled. All stood and faced the President who cleared his throat, raised his glass and proclaimed, 'to the honour of Hodge Podgers past and present!'

As one, they yelled, 'May the companions of our youth be the friends of our age!'

They emptied their glasses and sat down except the President who continued, 'As you know, tonight is our club's sixty-second anniversary. At our last meeting, I, as your President, had the pleasure of inviting you to submit those of our city's most beautiful and virtuous, unmarried ladies deemed most deserving of our annual toast. You were limited to nominating twelve each. Our secretary received a bounteous list. In accordance with our club's settled custom, I counted the number of votes for each lady nominated. Our secretary subsequently verified the result.'

The secretary nodded earnestly.

'I now have the pleasure of leading the toasts to each of the five fair maidens elected, named in ascending order,' said the President. As he put on his spectacles and picked up a page, waiters spaced themselves around the table and filled the members' glasses. Once everyone had stood up, he declared loudly, 'Have the following ladies comported themselves during the year in a manner befitting the high position of being toasted by the Hodge Podge Club?' He paused then shouted, 'Miss Jane Buchanan of Ardenconnell!'

Each member, extending their glass to the President, replied, 'She has!' then drained his glass which was immediately refilled.

The call and chorus continued until the last of the five.

'Miss Georgette McCall of Ibroxholme!'

On the cusp of the throng's reply, Kingan shouted, 'She's fae Govan!'

Another wag shouted, 'Send her a letter!'

Aware of the scurrilous anonymous letters circulating in that Parish, all erupted in laughter.

'Mr Secretary will record the names for posterity,' announced the President grinning. He turned to the still standing members and boomed, 'And now, gentlemen, to whist!'

The scraping of chairs sounded against the wooden floor. Kingan downed the last of his madeira treasuring its sweet thickness on his palate. He leaned into Oswald, 'Enjoy the lamb?'

'Decent,' slurred Oswald. 'But not as good as McPherson's. Remember?'

'Where's he now?'

'Edinburgh, I heard. Mr Hope's residence.'

Oswald rose but a tad too quickly. Kingan caught his forearm and guided him back down into the chair.

'Sorry, John,' blurted Oswald. 'A bit the worse for a drink.'

'No, James. A bit the better.'

A footman entered the room and interrupted their sniggering. 'Mr Finlay is waiting for you in the upstairs room,' he announced. 'The rubber is about to commence.'

Leaning against each other, they exited the room leaving the waiters to wipe the table clear of the puddles of alcohol and grease.

Chapter 2
The Printed Gown

Two weeks later, Kingan followed Williamson the butler dressed in the Oswalds' yellow and black livery down the oak-panelled hall hung with Italian landscapes, of his friend's fifteen-roomed mansion on the Shieldhall estate in Govan Parish.

On entry into the drawing room with its Greek-style painted friezes and cream velvet-covered upholstery, he joined Oswald who stood hands clasped on stomach, looking out the bay window. In the courtyard, a wiry stable lad attempted to mount his Master's new prancing and twisting thoroughbred, the two friends guffawed until the red-faced youth eventually mounted the horse.

'Why did you request to see me before joining your mother and sisters?' asked Kingan.

'Let's sit.' Oswald led his friend to an armchair by the black-veined white marble fireplace and then sat facing him.

'It's Nancy. She's received one of these anonymous letters.'

'Really?'

The prospect of titillation immediately aroused Kingan's interest as did the mention of Nancy. He had always found Oswald's older sister fascinating. Baptised Agnes, she had insisted on being known as Nancy after her return from a two-year stay at Paris. Her joie de vivre gave her the attribute Kingan most treasured in life, good company. Nancy better fitted her character than the more prosaic Agnes.

Oswald's scowl removed Kingan's smile. Face suitably stern, he declared, 'How terrible! Is it bad?'

'I don't know. She hasn't let me read it. She, Margaret and my mother have been in a frenzy since it arrived yesterday. Even the spaniels.' He threw his hands up. 'It's something to do with a printed gown.'

'A printed gown?'

Oswald's eyes went to the roof. 'How would I know?'

Kingan wondered why, with the upset, they hadn't cancelled his invitation. The answer came.

'I tried to calm them down,' said Oswald. 'I told them about the anonymous letter you received last year. How you said it had been of little import and let it ride. And nothing more came off it.'

Kingan recalled the letter. It had initially worried him. With time, however, his anxiety had passed. Now, he considered it just another underhand barb, a coin in Glasgow's second currency, tittle-tattle. 'Did they calm?'

Oswald looked at the empty hearth. 'Unfortunately, no. My mother immediately wanted to hear more. Directly from you. To see if there's a connection.'

'But James,' whined Kingan. 'It was six months ago.' He was about to protest further but knowing Mrs Oswald's hold over her son realised it would be useless.

'Let's go,' said Oswald. 'They'll know you've arrived.'

They passed through the main hall to the conservatory. Light flooded through the glass panels which composed the outer half of the long room. Pink and yellow peonies adorned each sidewall, their fragrance percolating the warm air. In the inner half, under a tapestry of figures frolicking in a rococo garden scene, Margaret, the younger sister, thin, pale of face with a slight stoop, was sitting on a white floral-patterned sofa; Ruby one of the four King Charles spaniels in the room lay stretched out on her lap.

Facing her, sat Nancy, in a blue velvet dress, picking out stray threads from an incomplete tapestry, stretched on a frame in front of her, of a scene from Chaucer's the Knight's Tale. She looked up. Corpulent like her brother, with a handsome round face, her clear blue eyes met Kingan's. He smiled broadly and she returned his warmth, clearing a fallen brown curl from her high forehead.

He bowed to the widowed matriarch Mrs Elizabeth Dundas Oswald, who though wracked by arthritis, sat erect in the wooden armchair she had brought down from Perthshire on her marriage fifty years ago. He did the same to the sisters.

Mrs Oswald put down her knitting and focused her watery eyes on Kingan. 'You look well, Mr Kingan,' she said. 'Please be seated.'

Oswald ushered him to Margaret's side, facing the widow and Nancy then sat down in a chair to their side.

'Your gout?'

He nodded to Nancy's tapestry. 'Like Palamon, through courage and persistence, I've overcome it.'

They chuckled in harmony.

'The good always wins out,' cooed Nancy. She nodded to her brother. 'Although there are exceptions.'

Oswald pouted.

'Has James told you that we too have had our troubles?' asked Mrs Oswald.

'He did, Mrs Oswald.' He turned to his side. 'My sympathies, Miss Nancy.'

Cheeks reddening, Nancy began wafting a Chinese fan. Margaret ruffled Ruby's neck.

'We need your help, Mr Kingan,' said Mrs Oswald firmly.

Kingan looked at Oswald, who shifting in his chair, remained silent. With forced enthusiasm, he responded, 'You have it, Mrs Oswald.'

'You understand this is a private matter?' she continued.

'I do. It will remain with me.'

She nodded. 'Tell us about your anonymous letter.'

Kingan breathed in. 'It was about a dinner I held some six months ago. Full of slanders, mainly about me but also about Mr Hunter of the Herald, Dr Richard Smith and Mr James Murdoch. Most disconcerting were the quotes from our conversation.'

'It's often the case that what the author knows wounds more than what the letter says.'

'That caused me great upset. But it passed.'

'Did you suspect anyone?'

Kingan stiffened. 'We thought it might have been Mr Gilbert Watson, the Writer.'

Nancy and Margaret gasped. Eyes wide, they stared at him.

What have I said, thought Kingan. 'I invited him to dinner,' he continued. 'But' Mr Hunter objected. 'He's as dull as mud.'' He imitated Hunter's basso voice. 'I had to invent an excuse. I don't think it convinced Watson. I heard he felt most slighted.'

'And how would Mr Gilbert Watson have known about what you talked?'

'We discussed that at length over the weeks. I'd had servant problems and had had to dispatch one. We speculated that she had informed Watson. But it was highly unlikely.' He froze a moment at the intensity of the women's stares.

He glanced at Oswald, who nodded in support. 'Anyway, Gilbert Watson can't be the author of Nancy's letters. His right hand's been paralysed since his shooting accident.'

'Still a strong coincidence,' declared Nancy.

'Coincidence?'

Mrs Oswald cleared her throat. 'I and my family suspect that our neighbour, Mr Robert Watson of Linthouse is the author of Nancy's letter.'

'Gilbert's brother, the banker?' He recalled the small, bald man whom he had met a few times. Even more than the other banks, he kept away from his business. Watson had the reputation as the most ruthless of a rapacious lot. Even so, it seemed inconceivable that he would do such a thing.

Mrs Oswald turned to Nancy. 'Perhaps you could show Mr Kingan your letter so he can discern if the handwriting is the same as his?'

'Can't he show me his?' she challenged.

'I threw it out,' said Kingan softly. 'I'm sorry.'

'Just let Mr Kingan see the address on yours, Nancy,' commanded Mrs Oswald.

'You have it, Mother,' countered Nancy gruffly. She recommenced her fanning.

Mrs Oswald nodded to Margaret. 'Go check there's no-one by the door.'

Margaret placed Ruby's head gently on the sofa. She opened the door. The corridor was empty.

On her return, Mrs Oswald slipped her hand under the left lapel of her black linen gown and extracted a folded letter, which she handed to Kingan.

Kingan wished he could hide. He took his time scanning the handwriting. The only sound in the room was Ruby jumping down to join her siblings at the opposite end of the conservatory.

'I'm not sure,' he said. 'There are some similarities but I'm not sure it's the same.' He passed the letter back to Mrs Oswald.

'But it could be?' asked Nancy.

Her insistence unnerved him. 'Perhaps,' he replied in a wavering voice. 'But I'm really not sure. What reasons do you have for believing Mr Watson is the author of your letter?'

'It's what it says.'

'Read it to Mr Kingan,' cajoled her mother.

'But—' Kingan protested, not wanting to be thought of impugning a lady's honour.

The old lady put her hand up and then handed the letter to her son, 'You read it.'

Nancy snatched the page from his hand. 'I'll read out the relevant paragraph. Most of the others are atrociously obscene.'

Kingan couldn't help but feel cheated. He had a notion of what they might concern. Nancy, despite being well into her forties and unmarried, maintained a disregard for the expected constraints on her station. This left her open to ridicule, especially about her pursuit of fashion and entertainment but most of all, her fruitless dalliances with prospective spouses, about which there were sure to be several savoury allusions.

She began in a clear voice, 'This is the opening paragraph, Mr Kingan, to give you a flavour of the trash that follows.'

Madam

I hope that you have the goodness to take this as it is meant for your good but whether you take it well or ill, I don't care. I think you are either a fool or very stupid for no mortal in their course of mind would go on the way you do.

She paused. Kingan joined Margaret in loudly tutting.

'Here's the relevant part.

Who visits now with a printed gown? Nobody on earth. Get a good silk gown on your back, to put on when you go out to your dinner or tea. For even the expelled of an old family should keep up their dignity. Mind that.'

Kingan, although disappointed by the mildness of the insult, let rip, 'Disgusting twaddle! Disgraceful!' He leaned towards her. 'Who would think a lady of your taste would be seen in something printed? Something so common.'

'Exactly!' chimed Margaret. 'Printed cotton indeed. The gown is of the finest Chinese silk.'

'Thank you, Mr Kingan,' said Nancy. For a moment, her eyes turned coquettish. She handed the letter back to her mother.

Stirred by her agreeable look and relieved at having made the right response, Kingan grinned. He sat back, thinking, 'But, what's it to do with Robert Watson?'

'Two Mondays ago, after the Sacrament,' she continued. 'I met our Minister Reverend Matthew Leishman's sister, Elizabeth, on the riverside path. We conversed and she invited me to a dinner her brother was holding at the manse. I put on the silk gown. Not having a suitable headdress, I made a turban using the method I learned in Paris a couple of years back.'

Oswald's eyes rose to the ceiling.

'At the table, I was sat next to Miss Georgette McCall.'

'She was toasted at the Hodge Podge,' interjected Oswald.

Nancy glared at him and shook her head. 'She admired the turban and I showed her how to fashion one with a napkin. We then chatted about our dresses. I showed her the weave on mine. Miss Georgette commented that the needlework was so fine, it almost appeared that it had been printed. The letter to me arrived four days after that dinner. Whoever wrote it must have overheard our conversation.'

'The other guests were clergymen from far outside of Glasgow. The letter's postmark is the Glasgow Post Office. Reverend Matthew's mother, father and sister live in Paisley. That excludes them.'

'Miss Georgette is grossly libelled in the letter. Her brother, who accompanied her, is devoted to her. I can scarcely believe it was them. That leaves the only other person present, Mr Robert Watson. He sat close to us. I saw him at the corner of my eye listening to our conversation. I wasn't surprised. We call him Mr Nip. He needs to know everything about everything. Linthouse is the Office for Information.'

'He even talks to the servants on the road to Glasgow!' exclaimed Margaret.

Nancy continued, 'Yesterday, we went to the service at the Govan Kirk.' Her eyes shone. 'Such a fine sermon by Reverend Matthew! After the service, as always, I met with Miss Catherine Hutton for a brief conversation. You know her, Mr Kingan?'

He shook his head.

'She's Mr George Rowan's sister-in-law and housekeeper. Our boys play with her charges.'

Nancy's brother had died two years before. His wife had never overcome her grief. Oswald had dispatched her back to her birth family in England. Her children were being raised at Shieldhall.

'Miss Catherine told me that she had met Mr Watson at her brother-in-law's two days before. He had recounted the dinner at the manse, remarking that, "no lady nowadays visits in a printed cotton gown."'

'The same as in the letter,' squeaked Margaret.

There was a momentary silence before Mrs Oswald declared, 'You now understand, Mr Kingan, why we are of a view Mr Watson is the author.'

Chapter 3
Mr Nip's Dinner

Robert Watson stood in the entry hall at the bottom of the red-carpeted staircase, waiting for his guests. For tonight's dinner party, he had added a dash of colour to his customary garb of black frock coat and waistcoat, white shirt and collar, a bottle green cravat. The door to the kitchen creaked open. Mrs Iris Watson, a stout woman in her forties, walked towards him. His owlish eyes below a bald head and between greying mutton chop sideboards scanned her dark blue dress with a white frilled ruffler. Satisfied with her mix of splendour and propriety, his thin lips broke into a brief smile. Looking down, she flushed.

'The food is ready?' he asked.

She nodded.

'The table set?'

'Yes.'

'They polished it again?'

'I supervised it myself.'

'And that waiter?'

'As you ordered. We found a shirt for him.'

'Good!'

She smiled but not brightly enough for him. He decided to encourage her. 'Attention to detail. Iris! The secret of success. For us. For the Parish!'

Six years before, by dint of having bought the Linthouse Estate, he had become one of the heritors of Govan Parish, responsible for the Kirk's finances. For a few years, he had also been an Elder, a member of the Kirk session, monitoring the congregation's moral behaviour. Due to work pressures, he regretfully had to stand down. But he still maintained his contacts. Tonight, he was hosting the heritors' annual dinner.

The front door opened and the first guest came in, Miss Nancy Oswald of Shieldhall.

Watson suppressed a growl. *She's come alone,* he thought. *'Again. Draped in the same gauche finery of a gown she had on at the Manse. And that grotesque turban like some Hindoostan Rajah!'* He bowed. 'Miss Oswald! It's a pleasure to see you.'

'And you,' she said in a sparkling voice. 'Thank you so much for the invitation.'

'The pleasure belongs to the Parish.' He paused, thinking, *although the norm is for a replacement to be a man.*

'It's a pity, Mr Oswald's indisposed. I received his card.'

He knew her brother's excuse for illness was fabricated. His allegiance to Presbyterianism was tenuous (the mother remained a Jacobite Episcopalian). Nancy, as she ludicrously called herself, however, rarely missed a dinner. He decided to show the Oswalds, the richest heritors in a Parish in need of finance, what they expected. 'And your mother?' he asked deferentially. 'And Sister?'

'She was come over by a terrible lassitude this afternoon. I fear it may be a summer cold. Margaret is well.'

'And you? We haven't conversed since Reverend Leishman's dinner party.'

'I'm well,' she said tersely. 'All things considered.'

He stared, surprised by her answer and her curtness. Fortunately, his wife intervened with her welcome.

The next couple arrived. He welcomed Mr James "Dignity" Campbell of Moorepark and his wife Elizabeth warmly, proposing a later conversation about their recent prizes from the Glasgow Horticultural Society.

After his welcomes were complete, with Iris on his arm, he went to his ample drawing room. He looked over at the twenty guests, apart from Miss Oswald, all soberly dressed. Sitting facing each other on two light green striped sofas in front of the white marble fireplace with the gilt-framed mirror on top, the older women of the party chatted desultorily.

A glowing fire took the chill off the evening air. Strewn in small groups among the ottomans, easy chairs, occasional tables and screens, the others conversed earnestly. Waiters circulated with trays of drinks. A few mannered laughs floated through the room. He asked his wife to mingle with the women on the sofas, then looked around for a suitable haven.

He decided not to join his brother, Gilbert. Of more interest was the Minister Reverend Matthew Leishman, clad in his Geneva gown and collar, who was conversing with the Kirk Treasurer, Mr George Rowan of Holmfauldhead and his sister-in-law, the demure Miss Catherine Hutton. He wanted to assure himself that the theme of the evening's homily remained as they had agreed earlier that week.

As he approached, Leishman turned his six-foot frame. His keen blue eyes, below a high forehead, looked down on the banker. 'Mr Watson, we were just talking about children and the pleasure they give.'

'They're a heritage from the Lord, Reverend,' he replied flatly.

'And your boys?' asked Miss Hutton. 'They're not with us.'

'They're still young.' David and Henry were entering adolescence, but Watson preferred separating his family from his social life.

He was about to take the Minister aside when Nancy bustled into the group.

'Reverend Matthew!' she simpered, fluttering her fan to hide the flush ascending her neck.

'Miss Nancy!' Leishman exclaimed, eyes sparkling.

Watson stopped himself from tutting at their use of first names.

'What a beautiful gown, Miss Nancy,' declared Miss Hutton.

'Thank you,' cooed Nancy. She turned to Watson. 'I had it on at Reverend Matthew's dinner, Mr Watson. Don't you remember it? It's very fine, the weave. Some think it's printed.' She smiled but her eyes were cold.

Just like her. Obsessed with finery, he thought. 'It's lovely, Miss Oswald,' he said quietly.

'But you remember it?' she insisted.

He did but now exasperated, he shook his head to discomfort her.

She glared at him, then turned her back. Watson resisted an urge to tap her shoulder.

'I learned to wear a turban in Paris,' she announced to the Minster, playing with a ringlet of her brown hair. 'You visited there some years back, didn't you?'

'I did. In June 1818,' Leishman replied, smiling. 'It opened up a new world for me. The sights. The art. The literature. I remember my father's face when I returned home with a cargo of thirty volumes. My only problem was the heat. One hundred and three in the shade.'

'But the heat is essential,' she warbled. 'Domestic life there is in the open air. Unlike here, huddled round the hearth for months. The streets are full—'

Watson left them, scowling. From her, he had expected no more, but a Minister of the Kirk espousing that cesspit.

Before he could join another group, the gong for dinner sounded. He led his guests to the dining room.

He took his place at the head of the long table, gratified by the clear reflection of the chandelier playing on it. Leishman was on his right; Iris, on his left. After the diners quietened, he nodded to the Minister, who rose.

'Welcome heritors and good wives! My thanks to Mr Watson and his family for hosting this evening's dinner.' He breathed in. 'God, in the measure of restoring a degenerate world unto himself, hath set in operation the principle of gratitude.'

Watson smiled slowly. It was as agreed. Gratitude. To God, but as would be understood by all here, to the heritors.

'As soon as a man believes in God's love of kindness, so soon does the love of gratitude spring up in his heart. Some seem to look at the love of gratitude as having within it a taint of selfishness. They have confused the love that is felt for the benefit of gratitude, with that felt towards its donor. That second elevates gratitude to the rank of pure virtue, a worthy prospect deserving of our admiration.'

Watson nodded. He checked the table. All eyes were on the Minister.

Leishman finished the homily. 'And now, the blessing for our meal. Gracious God, we have sinned against Thee and are unworthy of Thy mercy; pardon our sins—'

Watson resurveyed the diners. All heads were down except for Miss Oswald, staring rapturously at the Minister. *Shameless*, he thought.

The meal began. Oyster soup made with cream was followed by the fish course (cod heads and shoulders) then the meat course (platters of roast beef, ham and veal pie, skinned boiled chickens, boiled ham, sliced tongue, chopped liver and sweetmeats were placed throughout the table).

After a pause, came the sweets (apple pie and cream, plum pudding, frushey and rhubarb tart) and lastly, an assortment of cheeses. Claret, port, sherry, madeira and Malmsey's for the ladies were imbibed. Watson kept an eye on the flurry of servants who carved, placed, cleared, wiped and poured. There was no need for admonishment.

After coffee, he rose. The gentlemen accompanied him to the drawing room. The women stayed around the dining table.

He passed around the cigars but desisted from lighting one himself. He accepted the compliments on the meal with grace, then praised Leishman for his "insightful and pithy discourse". The conversation started. What should they do with the Evangelicals who were calling evermore loudly for the Kirk to return to the rigour of the Auld Book? They had again disrupted the service last Sabbath. As they puffed, the concourse dwelt on the level of punishment merited, the least strident was the Minister. Watson kept his sympathy for the protests silent.

After a few minutes, he went to relieve himself. On returning, he heard a high-pitched tittering which he recognised as belonging to Mrs Galbraith of Greenhead. *The Malmsley's talking*, he thought to himself. The urge came over him. He went to the door.

Someone he didn't recognise was saying in a conspiratorial tone, 'Have you heard that Mr Robert Baillie has broken off his match with Miss Janet Smith and fled to London?'

To his disappointment, his wife's voice came in. 'Yes! And he left considerable debts.'

His lips curled on hearing Nancy. 'My brother met his father at William Armour's in the Trongate. Old Baillie was most upset. Particularly at the thought of having to pay off the debtors!'

On the giggles starting, he heard footsteps behind him. He hurried back to the drawing room.

On entering, Perry stood up and excused himself. He had to get back to his drysalters for the final two hours of business before closing at ten. The others who had their country residence in the Parish but their business in Glasgow followed. The butler went and called the women to the drawing room.

After the goodbyes, Watson and his wife joined those left in the drawing room: Mr Rowan, Miss Hutton, the Campbells, Mr Galbraith (his wife had gone to lie down), Reverend Leishman and Nancy.

As he sat down, Nancy asked, 'These letters, who do you think's writing them?'

'Why's she bringing this up at the Heritor's dinner?' he asked himself. *'Has she no decorum?'*

Mrs Campbell responded, 'Who knows, my dear? What type of misguided soul could do such things?'

'Not misguided,' barked Galbraith. 'He has chosen to be evil!' He turned to Leishman. 'What do you say, Minister?'

'Both, Edward. Free will frequently acts in concert with satanic possession. The author alone has decided to ally himself with Satan and then followed his malign guidance.'

'I think they indicate madness myself,' stated Rowan.

'I'm not sure, George,' said the Reverend. 'I've seen a few. They seem to follow a design, alluding to some fault in a person which they enlarge and distort. Self-doubt results. That shows intelligence.'

'I agree,' announced Dignity, shifting in his chair.

'What do you think, Mr Watson?' asked Nancy, peering at him. 'It must be someone among us who has the capacity to delve into our lives, don't you think?'

He had had enough of her. 'Perhaps you're right,' he snarled. He abruptly turned to face Dignity. 'How are your apples, Mr Campbell? Our Braeburns have been excellent this year. You must come and see them.'

After twenty minutes, Dignity announced that he had an early morning appointment in Glasgow. The others took the opportunity to give their apologies.

The group went to the hall, Mrs Galbraith supported by a footman, to give their goodbyes to the hosts. Watson accepted their compliments with grace despite a feeling of sourness eating at him. He girded himself for its cause. Nancy was last in the queue.

After she had thanked his wife effusively, he went to take her hand, but she didn't proffer it. Instead, she looked him in the eye and smiled brazenly. 'My gratitude for the evening, Mr Watson. I hope I haven't confused my love for its benefit from what I feel towards the donor.'

She raised her hand. Bristling at her mockery, he brushed it with his lips.

As she tried to extract her hand from his, he kept hold of it. Eyes cool, voice leering, he said, 'Today, I heard that Miss Jean Elizabeth Boag of Burntisland is coming to dine at the manse next week. She and Reverend Leishman have formed an attachment.' He dropped her hand and crowed, 'I hear she is a known beauty.'

Chapter 4
Woes

'Mr Kingan! How are you? It's been weeks.' Kingan smiled at Muir, his warehouse guard, still ramrod erect at sixty.

They shook hands.

'I've been drawing up my affairs,' said Kingan. 'I have a new house.'

'I heard.'

Kingan had grown dissatisfied with living by the river on Clyde Street. The restless bustle of the Broomielaw wharves and the fumes from the growing number of mills down river encroached more and more. Most of his peers had moved upwind and uphill to Blythswood on the outskirts of the city. There, life was elegant, spacious and quiet. A year ago, he had purchased land there. The builders were almost finished. He had begun to plan the decoration of the interior.

Muir led him into the main office with its shelves full of brown ledgers. He shouted, 'Look and see who's here!'

The three clerks simultaneously put down their pens onto the sloped desks and came down from the high stools. Kingan received their warm handshakes. After exchanging pleasantries, the Head Clerk Simson, his waistcoat showing the chain of the pocket watch Kingan had gifted on his thirty years of service, directed him to his Master's office, emptied now of much of its contents in preparation for his final leaving. Kingan sat in his old cane armchair with its curved armrests and green leather cushion at his mahogany desk.

His pleasure in trading had begun to diminish some five years before. There was more and more competition for slimmer profits. Before, merchants had controlled the banks but now the order was reversed. More and more, the real money was in manufacturing, but he had always been a canny middleman, import to export, order to sale, profit to capital.

He had ample funds set aside for a comfortable retirement. His share from the dissolution of this, his last partnership, however, would ensure that his house's ornamentation and trimmings were of the highest fashion. Then, he could entertain in style, a man of princely liberality.

'Where's Mr Walkinshaw?' he asked.

'I don't know,' replied Simson. 'He's been gone since morning.'

From the clerk's raised eyebrows, Kingan recognised that this wasn't unusual. 'Can I see the latest ledgers?'

Edward Walkinshaw was the last of the five partners he'd had. He'd had high hopes for him when he had taken him on as an apprentice, but they had been misplaced. He lacked judgement and, worse, openness.

Simson left after depositing the ledgers. Kingan's face turned to stone as he read the latest. He sat stewing for the next twenty minutes.

He exhaled at the sound of the doorbell ringing. Two minutes later, a tall thin young man with a sallow face, dull eyes, and a long, drooping nose appeared.

'Hello, Edward,' said Kingan in forced cheeriness. He looked over his partner's red velvet frock coat, which, contrary to its intended purpose, highlighted his ungainliness.

'John,' intoned Walkinshaw.

They shook hands, Kingan's firm grip on Walkinshaw's limp and sat down opposite each other at the desk.

'I didn't know you were coming,' said Walkinshaw.

'Some unfinished affairs.'

'Did Simson offer you some tea?'

'He did but I'm fine.'

Kingan tried fixing his eyes on Walkinshaw's but the other looked to his side. 'I suppose you're wondering why I'm here.'

'Is it to do with the Riga shipment?'

'Yes.' He scanned the young man's brazen expression. 'Your note told me it had been detained.'

Walkinshaw stiffened. 'That was the message I received. It should be here in a week.'

'Tell the truth, Edward.'

'What do you mean?'

'You know what I mean. I passed by the Broomielaw on my way here. There's no wharf booked on any likely due date. They say there was a date booked in your name, but you informed them the shipment was going to be managed by someone else.'

Walkinshaw sucked his cheeks in. Eventually, he looked into Kingan's eyes like a child caught snatching cakes from the table. 'I'm trying to sell the contract on to fund the purchase of another. I spotted an opportunity on a cotton shipment. Ramsay was selling low for quick money—'

'Ramsay? That villain!' Kingan felt a chill in his gut. 'You've already bought Ramsay's bill?'

The younger man looked down at the floor. 'Yes.'

'How could you!' hissed Kingan. He wanted to punch the dishonest fool but instead rose from his chair and paced to the window. Virginia Street was bustling but he took no notice of the crowd. He cursed himself for having taken his eyes off the business at such a critical juncture. He turned. 'Have you sold on the Riga bill?'

'Not yet.'

'Thank God. To whom did you try to sell it?'

'The Ship, the Royal, the Glasgow. The Bank of Scotland.'

'Aitken?' Kingan's face blanched. 'I thought I ordered you not to have dealings with him.'

'He gave me a fair hearing,' blurted Walkinshaw. 'He's considering the matter.'

Kingan stilled as he sensed the imminent danger. 'You've not tried Watson?'

'No!'

Kingan scanned Walkinshaw's face, wondering, 'Is he lying?' He concluded that he was desperate but not that stupid. He returned to his desk. 'We must keep the contract with the Riga merchants. We settle with the shipping agents and then sell the cargo as usual. I'll take charge of the matter.'

Walkinshaw's lips pressed tight. 'But I need to sell it on to pay for the Ramsay contract! The funds are due.'

'That's nothing to do with me. I played no part in that trade.'

Walkinshaw sat head bowed.

Kingan threw up his hands. 'You were going to keep the profits from this manoeuvre for yourself. To stop them from being included in the capital and income split on my retirement. How did you think you would get away with it?'

There was no reply. An icy silence intervened. It was broken by Kingan. 'Settle this matter or if not, I'll begin proceedings.'

Chapter 5
The First Is One Too Many

A week after the meeting with Walkinshaw, Kingan sat at his rosewood desk reviewing customs paperwork. The Riga trade was back on track. The study was stifling. He opened the window and looked down onto the slow-flowing river. A couple of carts stood in the shallows, the skinny, stooping horses drinking the brown water. Porters, burlap sacks on shoulders, swerved through white-bonneted maids on the riverside path. The afternoon air was sooty from the cotton mills down river and the bottle factory upriver. He thought of closing the window but decided that noise and smell were better than itchy skin.

He walked back across the red twill carpet to the occasional table where his maid had laid a tray. On it was a letter from his cousin in Largs, a couple of invoices from his tailors, three invitation cards and a note from Oswald. His cousin's letter informed him of the arrangements for his visit to take the waters.

The first invitation, to a ball, he decided to refuse as it clashed with Largs. The other two were for dinner parties. He accepted both, even though he disliked one of the hosts. Oswald's note said that he would be popping in this evening. His townhouse residence was four hundred yards away, beside his Ropeworks whose fibres Kingan often had to brush off his frock coat when out for his late afternoon stroll.

A couple of hours later, Kingan's drawing-room door swung open. Oswald strode in.

'James!' shouted Kingan heartily. 'How are you?'

'Fashed, John,' he groaned. 'Fashed.'

'The mill?'

Oswald was the proprietor of a cotton spinning mill at Barrowfield just outside Glasgow, whose workforce was forever troublesome.

Oswald flopped down into an armchair. 'No. It's these damned letters.'

Kingan's ears pricked at more scandal. But Oswald's obvious unease made him wary. 'Let's have a drink.'

He went to the crystal decanter and poured two large brandies. He watched as Oswald gulped down his, then poured him another.

'Nancy's received another?' asked Kingan.

Oswald swallowed. 'No, me.'

'Oh—'

Oswald retrieved a folded page from the pocket in his waistcoat. 'It came this morning. Read it.'

'Do I have to?'

'I'd welcome your thoughts.'

Arm outstretched, Oswald held the letter out between thumb and index finger. Kingan took it with care and unfolded the page.

Sir

You rather fancy that I had forgot you. Take no fear of the kind into your head, for that can never be. I am by far too much taken up with you ever to suppose that could happen. I shall proceed to tuck upon yourself.

What a dreadful tyrant you are with that durty wane. You will never marry the mother yourself nor suffer those who have long since come during the years of discretion, to indulge themselves of her. You have neither reason nor humanity.

Why don't you marry? There are many a young lady would be glad to get you. She should not be older than twenty-three or so. Depend on it, you will regrate it when you will be unable to mend it. I for my part think you would make an excellent husband if you would lay aside the results of some of your follys, specially the last.

You have no notion of a married life or you would never hang on so long like a thing of no use. You are a fool.

What would you have been without an estate? There would have been no living with you. I wish you would conduct yourself with a little more modesty for you breed yourself enemies when you could be suitable and well-licked if you chose. No person will submit to your airs and nonsense. Who can spend more money in the year than you?

So what is my motive for molesting you? Because I am angry with you. What can you say so that I am afraid you will think I am meddling with things I have nought to do with? You will I make, no doubt wonder who.

Kingan sighed as he passed it back. *Whoever's written it has certainly caught something of his character,* he thought. 'Illiterate twaddle,' he boomed then peered at his friend. 'Disregard it, James. It's meaningless.'

Oswald bristled. 'I don't find it so.'

'Surely, you can't attribute any substance to it.'

Oswald cleared his throat and said quietly, 'I have a child.'

'You've married?' gasped Kingan.

'No!'

Kingan scratched his brow. 'I take it that's what the "durty wane" refers to.'

Oswald nodded. 'She's four months old. The mother is Mary MacLean, the nursery nurse at Shieldhall. Do you remember her?'

Kingan shook his head.

'I have them living in Stirling.'

Kingan's eyes widened. 'You recognise the child!'

Oswald blushed. 'Mary confided in Nancy about her pregnancy. My blethering sister told my mother who insisted the baby be baptised an Episcopalian, like her. I called her Marie.'

'Your name's not on the church register?'

Oswald bowed his head.

For a minute, Kingan was speechless at his friend's stupid deviation from the norms of his rank. Then he snorted, 'Still sprightly, I see!'

The forty-four-year-old Oswald's face reddened. 'That damned craven deviant! Watson!'

Eyes wide, Kingan sat back. 'I thought you didn't believe your mother and sisters.'

'He's the author.' Oswald slammed the rest on the armchair. 'Definitely! I told you what he said to Nancy at his dinner.'

'You did,' said Kingan. 'At the Literary Society. But, I'm still not sure how that shows he wrote her letter. Why did she go to his dinner, anyway?'

'To get back at him.'

'That didn't work.'

Oswald reached into the pocket of his frock coat. 'Here's Nancy's letter. Read it.'

'No! She's a lady. What are you doing with it?'

'I'm collecting the letters. My mother insisted I hire an agent to investigate Watson after the last episode.' He paused. 'I'll read it.'

'Not all of it.'

Oswald shrugged. 'Here's the relevant section.' He read out in a strong voice, '*You know you need have no plan upon Mr Leishman for he is going away to Dublin with Miss G McCall so he cannot take you both. Some person told me you were dining with him on Monday of the Sacrament. You are no doubt doing all you could, so you cannot blame yourself thou' you should not make out.*'

He fixed his eyes on Kingan. 'He's taunting her. In the letter and then to her face at the dinner. She's much disturbed.'

'Oh,' sighed Kingan. He felt sympathy instead of irritation towards her and, to his surprise, a tinge of jealousy at her attention to the Minister.

'He can't do this to my family, John!' exclaimed Oswald, putting the letter back in his pocket. 'We're not going to be easy pickings for some jumped-up cashier!'

Kingan scraped his hand through his hair. 'What are you going to do?'

'I'm going to prove he's the author. Then punish him.'

'How?'

'What every gentleman should do to uphold his honour. Fight a duel.'

Kingan guffawed. 'A duel?'

Oswald's eyes blazed. 'Yes! And I'll win. Easily. You know I'm an excellent shot.' He fixed his bulging eyes on Kingan's then pointed. 'And you'll be my second.'

Kingan shrunk back in his chair, thinking, *My God, he's serious.*

'These days are over, James. Duelling's virtually illegal. Look at what happened to Stuart.'

'He got off!'

The trial of James Stuart had been a sensation. Stuart, a Whig, had shot Sir Alexander Boswell, a Tory, dead in a duel in Edinburgh which was called after he had slandered Boswell in an anonymous article. Stuart had been tried for murder. Contrary to all expectations, he had been found not guilty. The jury had accepted the argument that a man's reputation is like his property; he can take all steps, including mortal violence, to prevent its theft.

'How do you advise I protect my honour?' asked Oswald.

'Certainly not a duel.' Kingan stared at his friend. 'Be careful with honour, James. You know what they say. "When a man has a wound and knows not where, he looks to his honour and finds it there."'

'You're wrong! Honour, John, is the attribute which distinguishes us, Gentlemen, from the likes of Watson. I can't be seen not to uphold it.'

'Sue him in the courts then.'

'Too time-consuming and expensive.'

'Have him spend a day squirming on the repentance stool at Govan Kirk.'

Oswald's eyes glinted. 'That's not funny.'

'Thrash him!'

Oswald pressed his lips together. 'A thrashing wouldn't meet my ends,' he said after a minute. 'When the time is right, he must offer me directly in public an unrestricted apology. Only that will satisfy my honour.'

'That'll destroy him, his family and his bank.'

'So, be it.'

Kingan sat back, alarmed by Oswald's certainty. He sipped some brandy. 'James, I hardly know Watson. I certainly don't approve of how he makes his money. But I do know, he's a fighter. And from what I hear, a dirty one.'

Oswald reached for his glass and emptied it. He remained silent, chin down.

Kingan rose, brought over the decanter and filled their glasses to the top. He decided to have another go at dissuading his friend. 'If knowledge of the letter comes out, it'll put you in a difficult position, especially the news of your child. Think what it would do to your reputation. Your prospects of being a candidate.'

Two weeks before, at the annual Fox Club dinner, the Whig Darling Henry Brougham had addressed his adoring fellow believers, including Oswald and Kingan. He had told them they must be ready. Parliament was very unstable. There could be an election soon. Oswald had tried for the Clyde Burghs seat two years before. He intended to try again.

'I wouldn't do anything peremptory,' continued Kingan. 'It would look very bad if you spoke out before you have conclusive proof. That would make you the slanderer. Let it rest. The letters will pass.'

Oswald stared straight ahead, jaw clenched as tight as his fists.

Chapter 6
The Best for the Best Alone

The gaslight poked through the autumnal dampness. Under it, an assortment of street-life gaped at the queue of carriages. Last in line, Kingan surveyed the Quality as they went to Walker's Hotel: the Dennistouns, the Campbells, the Strilings, the Hamiltons. What he had gleaned from the invitation was correct: the gathering was about the best for the best.

At the front door, a footman led him to the cloakroom, where he handed in his top hat, cane and gloves. He went up to the double door of the assembly room where the considerable figure of "The Major", Archibald Douglas Monteath Esq, stood. A gap-toothed smile spread across the pockmarked, red-nosed face of the ex-officer of the East India Company's army. 'Good to see you, John,' he rasped.

They shook hands.

'And you, Major. An honour to be invited. Many coming?'

'Thirty—three in total.'

Kingan smiled. 'Very select. Any bankers?'

Monteath chuckled, 'Only, one, Mr Dennistoun of Golfhill.'

Kingan entered. At the long room's end was a table covered with a dark green baize cloth. Facing it in arcs, were two rows of chairs upholstered with blue silk. Some were occupied. Most of the attendees were milling around another table at the room's side of the room on which rested various decanters. A fire was blazing in a marble fireplace inset with porcelain plaques displaying Dutch rural life.

Someone tapped his shoulder. He turned. Oswald smiled.

Kingan repaid the warm welcome. He pointed to the top table. 'A stellar cast on stage tonight.'

'The Elephant Looter's done well,' he said alluding to the Major's other nickname based on the oft told, never denied tale that he had made his fortune by relieving a Maharajah of an elephant carrying a cargo of precious gems. 'Not so sure about the main player though.'

At the table's centre, Sir Archibald Campbell of Blythswood, Tory MP for the Clyde Burghs dressed in the old style with his trademark, embroidered white silken shirt with cambric ruffles, was receiving salutations from a queue of cronies, all from the city's West Indian interest.

'Don't worry, James. Old actors always retire.'

'The sooner, the better,' hissed the Whig.

'Let's get a drink,' said Kingan.

'I thought Cowan had prohibited it.'

Kingan hesitated. Cowan was his nephew and physician. The gout, which had been affecting him for years, had returned a couple of weeks ago. 'Just one will do no harm. I'll keep off the wine and brandy. The rum will look after me.'

As they sipped their drinks, the Major moved to the centre of the top table, on his left Sir Archibald, on his right, Provost Mungo Nutter Campbell. Oswald and Kingan took their seats at the end of the second row beside a bay window overlooking the still crowded Buchanan Street. As they did so, staff closed the curtains.

'Thank you, Gentlemen, for coming this evening,' began the Major. 'Provost Nutter Campbell will open the proceedings.'

Short of frame and handsome of face, the Provost rose. His dark blue eyes travelled along the rows of chairs. His lips usually tight and straight, curved into a smile.

'Welcome, my friends,' he intoned in his Kirk Elder voice. 'May I begin by offering you my unfeigned and most cordial thanks for your positive response to Major Monteath's invitation? Can I especially express my undying gratitude to our dear Member of Parliament for his presence among us and of course, for his stout and untiring labour on our behalf?'

A series of 'Hear! Hear!' met his remarks. Oswald's nose wrinkled as if a waft of sewage had blown in. Kingan steeled himself for more verbiage.

'We are here today to consider the establishment of a Gentlemen's Club, an amenity sadly absent in our great city. For many decades, the spirit of enterprise has reigned in this Dear Green Place, instilling in us an unquenchable thirst for trade. Our profits have endowed our city with fine thoroughfares, outstanding buildings, beautiful gardens and splendid churches. That thirst for progress has driven us forward into these new times, the age of manufacturing. But, still, we strive to match the quality of our city to that of our accomplishments.'

He paused to sip some water.

'He's not going to drawl on about this city for the dead idea,' Oswald whispered to Kingan.

'I hope not,' said Kingan. 'Who wants to stroll with cadavers?'

'What we lack,' continued the Provost, 'is a crucial amenity. An elegant setting which promotes among men of honour the easy conviviality which our labours merit. A Gentlemen's Club! Many of you will have visited Gentlemen's Clubs in London or Manchester—even in Edinburgh.'

He grinned at the hissing.

'Their commodious rooms facilitate social intercourse. Their fayre surpasses that of the best taverns in their cities. Their subscriptions are at a level which attracts the exceptional and deters the mediocre. Glasgow rightly celebrates its many clubs. But splendid as these may be, none brings together the full range of our city's Quality throughout the day, every day of the week. This Dear Green Place cries out for such a facility. Gentlemen, with the deepest sense of obligation, I urge you to support the founding of a Gentlemen's Club in Glasgow!'

He sat down to loud applause. On its quietening, the Major invited comments.

Oswald shot up his hand, but The Major overlooked him and chose another. The third occasion this happened, Kingan noticed Sir Archibald smirking. Eventually, Oswald received the nod.

'Many thanks, Lord Provost, for your excellent speech,' he began. 'And your most welcome proposal. I assure you that you have my strong support. A few weeks ago, I had the pleasure of visiting one of London's most salubrious clubs, the Travellers. I was struck by the deportment of the members, by the liberality of their expression. Men with opposing views challenge each other civilly without opprobrium, unafraid that their words might give rise to malicious rumours.'

'I propose that there be a clause in the club's constitution requiring members to respect each other's right to confidentiality. A single breach, especially if it leads to public innuendo, should lead to immediate expulsion.'

He sat down to confused silence apart from a lone "hear, hear" from the back of the room.

Again! thought Kingan. *'There's no escaping.'* Oswald's pursuit of Watson dispirited him. Letters and even more letters, so many he could open a library. He turned to him. 'Why didn't you just name Watson?'

Oswald glared at him. 'I should have!'

Speaker followed speaker, each trying to surpass the other with their expressions of support. Kingan waited, musing on how to add some sparkle to the event. When the Major announced, 'one last comment,' he shot up.

'Gentlemen, distinguished guests,' he began, his hands on his lapels, facing those seated. 'I too am enthralled by our Provost's proposal. You, who are acquainted with me, know that my yearning for enlightenment often conduces me to the most genial of our Dear Green Place's many taverns, inns and clubs.'

Happy with the chuckles, he put on a learned air.

'Most evenings, I leave such gatherings, uplifted. Occasionally, however, I find myself disappointed. Why? Was it the setting? The company? The conversation? No. None of these,' he paused. 'It was the wine!'

'Fine wine refreshes the palate and unlocks curiosity. Bad wine inflames the gut and dulls the intellect. It's death in a bottle.' He raised his half-empty glass. 'Gentlemen, our club's calling card should be the quality of its cellar, its motto, "Free from death in a bottle!".'

He sat down, enthused by the laughter. He spotted Nutter Campbell glaring at him though the Major and Sir Archibald were smiling. *You win some, you lose some,* he thought.

Sir Archibald provided the address to end the first part of the meeting. Despite his position, he was a plodding speaker. He finished by expressing the hope that the club would offer "poor travellers" like him, good quality overnight accommodation when they arrived weary in Glasgow.

The Major came back centre stage.

'Are there any dissenting voices?'

Silence reigned.

'Let's move on to how we establish the club.'

A full discussion ensued. Kingan kept quiet, pleased by the consensual gusto. The main topic was the club's exclusivity. Eventually, they agreed to limit membership to between one hundred and one hundred and fifty members, split equally between invitees and appointees. A priority was to invite the Duke of

Hamilton and the Earl of Glasgow. After the spaces for invitees were filled, those desiring appointment could apply. They would have to seek two invitees' nominations and would be subject to a members' ballot. The name of the club was to be the "Western".

Chapter 7
Attention to Detail

Watson sat in his oak-panelled office. He checked the spaces between the matched pairs on his mahogany desk: copper paperweights, gold-plated letter openers, inkwells with quills. Assured that they were equidistant from each other, he went to the only objects on the shelves to his right: matching table clocks with bases of blue and white Delft porcelain. The same. There was nothing on the walls but a solitary etching of a rhinoceros, black on gold. Why? To make his clients wonder why.

He had been fourteen and working in his father's bank when it had failed due to catastrophic losses from speculation. A Trust had taken over its running. The next year, his father's death had seen him ejected from the business. He and his older brother James had spent the next ten years buying and selling goods from Glasgow's many bankruptcy auctions. In tenement closes and the back rooms of taverns, they had begun dealing in bills of contract. He had befriended Adam Aitken, a friend of his brother-in-law, who had steered their way through some trades the Bank of Scotland wouldn't touch.

After a legal battle in his thirties, the brothers had retaken control of the bank. They had avoided taking deposits and concentrated on trading bills of contract. James Watson had died last year. After the funeral, Watson's other brother Gilbert, a Writer of the Signet, who had been struggling after the paralysis of his right hand, had accepted Robert's invitation to become a partner in the bank.

Content with his desk, Watson sat back and thought about Mr Edward Walkinshaw, who a teller had told him five minutes before, had arrived. As always, Watson had said, 'let him wait.'

He had never met the third son of a branch of an old merchant family who like all such, prohibited from inheriting their father's assets, had had to develop his own route through life. Of greater interest was his partner, Mr John Kingan.

His lips curled. Many times, he had listened to Aitken bitterly denouncing Kingan after having been made yet again a figure of fun. The merchant's badinage seemed relentless. Aitken's grievance was shared by many bankers. But, so far, Watson had avoided it.

It was odd Kingan's partner coming to him. Usually, the bank dealt with the lower, more desperate end of the merchants, those in need of rapid money or the inveterate risk takers.

He went over the note he had received from Aitken, who had turned down Walkinshaw's request for a bridging loan to cover the costs incurred in the purchase of a bill of cotton. He had advised Walkinshaw that Watson might purchase the bill for the cotton contract. All very convoluted.

Watson had made enquiries at the Exchange. He had learned that Kingan had taken over from his partner a Riga contract and was trying to wind up his partnership with Walkinshaw and retire. Retirement had often brought Watson an opportunity. But Kingan was a canny operator. What Walkinshaw was proposing didn't sound like his way of doing business.

Watson rose and chapped on the closed door. He waited in the centre of the room. A minute later, Walkinshaw entered. Watson proffered his hand, his mouth smiling but his owlish eyes probing. His hand lingered to assess the merchants. It was clammy and over-tight. Watson, happy that he had control, smiled and signalled his prospective client to take a seat.

'We haven't met before,' said Watson. 'I knew your father. A fine man.'

'I miss him greatly,' sighed the merchant.

'I received Mr Aitken's note. Most interesting.'

Walkinshaw looked at the desk. 'Do you still have it?'

'In my head. Paper clutters the mind.'

'Oh.'

'You're in business with Mr John Kingan. How do you find him?'

Walkinshaw shifted in his chair. 'I've known him since I was a boy. I was his apprentice before entering into partnership.'

Watson picked up on his evading a straight answer. 'You have his full approval for why you are here?'

Walkinshaw crossed his long legs and looked away. On turning back, he said, 'I don't need it. I am acting on my own behalf. Is that a problem?'

'For him, yes.' He stared at the other coldly. 'And for me.' On seeing his prey's mouth open, Watson softened his expression. 'But, not an insuperable one. It depends on the level of risk I will carry with purchasing your bill. That has just increased considerably.'

'Why?'

'You have no history as an independent trader. You're acting without your partner's knowledge on a bill of contract which you bought in both your names. Obviously, that will increase my discount rate on the purchase.'

'And if I obtain his agreement to our transaction?'

'You know he won't give it. As he'll have told you, he's not very complimentary about my establishment. Which is unfortunate—for you.'

Walkinshaw's eyes narrowed.

Watson, happy at the impact of his brazenness, put on a friendly smile. 'Only unfortunate. Not a reason for terminating any business. What happened to the contract on the Riga cargo?'

'Mr Kingan's dealing with it.'

'Why's he not dealing with the cotton?'

'We have an agreement.'

'All very complicated. Would you mind giving me the details?'

Walkinshaw rubbed his chin. 'Alright.'

Watson shouted, 'Jackson!'

Fifteen minutes later, the clerk left with the details in a leather ledger.

'Thank you, Mr Walkinshaw. Do you have anything more to add?' asked Watson.

Walkinshaw paused, 'We haven't discussed your terms for the purchase.'

'Soon. First, I must carry out some verification.'

'Verification? Do you think I'm making this up?'

'Of course not,' poopooed the banker. 'Verification is integral to our affairs. My bank takes risks that others do not. That's why you're here. I'm duty-bound to undertake some prudent aggregating of details about any proposed trade. Don't you agree?'

'I suppose so,' Walkinshaw muttered.

After he had left, Watson went over the interview. Walkinshaw had nothing behind him except Kingan whom he was deceiving but wasn't intelligent enough to outwit. He would fail. But profit often comes out of a fall. And if it involved Kingan, so much the better.

He rang his handbell. Jackson entered. 'Go find Bell. Tell him to come to the meeting room.'

Watson went to the adjoining office to collect Gilbert. He found him reading a book, which he promptly closed with his good hand. Younger, taller and with full black hair, he had a handsome dash. Many found it difficult to believe they were brothers.

'How did it go?' asked Gilbert.

'As we thought.'

Gilbert nodded.

'I've asked Bell to come.'

Five minutes later, Geordie Bell entered. In his early thirties in a black velveteen coat and a bright red handkerchief around his neck, he stood to attention in front of the brothers, clasping a brown felt hat. In a ruddy, broad face, between heavy-lidded eyes, perched a fleshy nose. His eyes were dark and watchful.

'We have a verification for you, Bell,' said Watson's eyes twinkling. He liked his porter. The Irishman's loyalty bordered on devotion. His trust in his servant had always been rewarded, in contrast to his dreamy brother.

'Thank you, Master.'

'We need something on a Mr Edward Walkinshaw. Jackson will give you the details.'

'The usual. Friends. Clubs. Taverns. Gambling. Family mishaps.'

'I know he goes to the Green Cloth,' interrupted Gilbert. 'And the What you please.'

'The Green Cloth's bad enough,' spat Watson. 'But that bunch of effete theatricals who cavort at the What you please—' He shook his head as Gilbert blushed. 'Walkinshaw's partner, Mr John Kingan, doesn't know about his visit. See if there's anything there.'

'When for, Master?' asked Bell.

'Next week. The usual price. Jackson'll issue you a purse.'

A week later, they reassembled in the meeting room. Bell told them what he had discovered in the market for information: clerks, carters, porters, waiters, barmaids, ladies of ill repute, household servants. The last was the priciest, some even refusing out of loyalty to or, more commonly, fear of their Masters. This time, the cab drivers had been the most helpful.

'He has certain nocturnal habits, Master,' reported the porter. 'They take him to a house in the Briggait. Selective for gentlemen of his class.'

Gilbert smirked but his brother's expression grew hard.

'I smelled the vice upon him,' snarled Watson. 'And his affairs with Kingan?'

'Kingan's people are very wary. All refused my offer of a dram and maybe more. I know the two have fallen out about the dissolution of their partnership but, more than that, I learned nothing.'

Watson's mouth turned down. There would be no business with Walkinshaw. He never rewarded whoring. He would have loved to have something on Kingan but, it wasn't to be. He turned to his servant. 'Thank you, Bell. That will be all. You can keep what's left in the purse.'

Bell bowed and left.

'Well, Robert,' began Gilbert. 'Do we take up Walkinshaw's offer?'

'No!'

'Why?'

'We could certainly secure a profit. He's malleable. He's desperate. But he won't keep his word. He's betraying Kingan. He's betraying his wife. He would betray us.'

Chapter 8
The Ball

Kingan groaned. This was so boring. He wiggled his toes on the crimson bolster. They ached but were free of the piercing pains. He knew, however, that once he stood up, they would return. He had been sprawled across his rose-patterned chaise longue in the drawing room, for most of the last week, laid low by the gout.

The ball to celebrate Mr John Miller's return from Jamaica would be starting. A week ago, the decorators had moved out from his new house on St Vincent Street. Kingan, soon to be a neighbour, longed to see the décor. More acute, however, was his craving for good company.

He decided to go.

He rang the bell. A moment later, the maid appeared.

'Yes, Master?'

'Tell Mrs Hunter to prepare a large draft of laudanum. Then bring it here.'

On its appearance, he gulped it down. He lay eyes on the ceiling until nausea passed and the glow came on. Then he lowered his feet gently and stood up. No pain. He walked slowly to the door. Then more quickly, he traversed the hall to the green carpeted stairs.

An hour later, clad in his best maroon velvet frock coat and gold silk waistcoat, he finished a large glass of brandy before the gig arrived.

Twenty minutes later, he arrived at Miller's. He stood as if paralysed at the foot of the main staircase captivated by the clumps of sugar canes in gold warp floating through the plush red Brussels carpet in which they were embedded. He tittered at the typical Sugar Baron gaudiness.

'You're late, Mr Kingan!' broke his trance.

He dragged his eyes away and looked up. Leaning over the balustrade was Miller, his almost square, creased face atop a stocky frame. They grinned at each other. On Kingan reaching the landing, they shook hands.

'Dinner's just over,' announced Miller. 'You missed a fine white soup.'

'Apoloshies,' replied Kingan.

Miller scanned his face. 'Your eyes are strange. Are you well?'

Kingan smirked. 'I took a little laudanum for the gout.'

Miller peered at him.

'And your good wife?' asked Kingan in a steadier voice.

'She's dancing.'

'I thought I felt a tremor,' chirped Kingan.

Miller's icy stare surprised him. Before he could apologise, the host had moved off.

Kingan went to the anteroom to the ballroom. He stood dithering when a deep-throated laugh jolted him. His eyes were pulled towards its source. He felt the warm embrace of her slow, subtle smile. He had no more taken his first step towards her when her eyes froze. It was then he saw at her side, Mr Thomas Hagart of Bantiskine. Her husband nodded to him, his eyes menacing. Kingan returned the gesture. He bowed to Mrs Elizabeth Hagart, each averting their eyes from the other.

He had courted Miss Elizabeth Stewart as she then was, ten years before. The attraction was mutual despite there having been a twenty years age gap. The news that her father had arranged her betrothal to Hagart had crushed him. Soon after, she left with her husband for the West Indies. He had heard that she had returned to Scotland but tonight was the first time he had encountered her.

The Hagarts turned and entered the ballroom. Kingan stood still, oblivious to the pats on his back. He replayed the tender welcome in her eyes and how quickly they had turned to a flashing fear. He winced in pity at her plight.

He sought out a waiter and pulled a glass of Glasgow Punch off the tray. He drank it quickly, savouring the chill of the iced water, the smooth taste of the rum, the cleansing of his palate by the lemon. He moved through the open doors into the ballroom.

The heat, noise and colour hit him. Under the gas lights, the glistening gold and ebony studs played up the contrast between the white shirts and the blacks and dark blues of the men's cravats, dress coats and trousers. The red or green uniforms of the yeomanry officers added vibrancy.

At the opposite wall sat the ladies in their muted blues and greens for the unmarried (modesty being a sign of purity), vivacious yellows and oranges for the married. Most had flowers protruding from their shaped, curled hair, some feathers. His eyes were drawn to the bare necks and shoulders above the décolleté gowns. Mulatto servants, the men in powdered wigs, golden waistcoats and breaches; the women in low-cut, high-waisted, bright yellow embroidered gowns carried glasses of negus or Glasgow Punch on silver trays.

He moved to the fluttering red satin curtains by the opened windows to catch some of the night breeze. He spotted Nancy at the other end of the room, her eyes already on him. Delight oozed through him. She smiled and beckoned him with her fan to come to her. Tentatively, he moved around the perimeter of the dance floor, stopping a couple of times to mop his brow and check she was still watching him. She was.

He bowed on arriving in front of her. At her side sat an attractive woman of similar age whom he didn't recognise, dressed in a pale blue plain gown. The simplicity of the other's dress heightened his appreciation of Nancy's gold lace ballgown trimmed with pearls. Two peacock feathers were pinned together in her hair.

'Miss Nancy,' he gushed. 'Such a beautiful gown!'

She beamed. 'Thank you very much, Mr Kingan.'

He bent over closer to speak into her ear. She raised her open fan to protect his words.

'Are you enjoying the ball?'

'Very much! And you?'

'I've just arrived. My gout delayed me.'

'Oh—I was going to ask you to mark my card.'

'My apologies.' He looked at her tenderly. 'You enjoy dancing?'

'I love dancing!' she enthused.

They laughed, their eyes remaining on one another. He felt uplifted by her radiant confidence. She looked away. His eyes fixed on her uncovered shoulders. Resisting the urge to stroke one, he flushed. He had not felt such desire for a woman of Quality since Elizabeth Stewart.

He heard clapping. Miller, standing on a small platform by the orchestra, announced a quadrille. The floor filled. Kingan noticed the Hagarts joining three other couples. He looked away and saw a handsome, athletic youth accompanying a beaming Mrs Miller, her body squeezed into a fine silver lace gown. Her husband, satisfied that no lady with an invitation card in her hand had sat through two dances in a row, waved to the orchestra leader. The music commenced.

As the spectacle became livelier, their attention, like most in the room, focused on the exuberant Mrs Miller.

'So, that's how they dance in Jamaica,' commented Nancy.

'Must be the heat,' replied a fascinated Kingan.

They tittered.

The quadrille ended, the ladies' chairs refilled. They chatted, comparing how the season had gone so far. Engrossed in her words, he didn't notice the young buck until he stood in front of her and bowed.

Her eyes danced at his fulsome request for her presence on the floor. She checked her card, took his outstretched hand, then smiled at Kingan as she rose. 'You must visit Shieldhall soon, Mr Kingan.'

'I will.'

He watched her for a few minutes. To his surprise, she danced well, gracefully moving from partner to partner. He wondered if he should stay but decorum said otherwise. He returned to the anteroom. A group had congregated around two people dressed in unusual fashions. He went over and found himself standing next to a tall, well-built, blonde-headed youth.

'Mr John Kingan,' he announced to him.

'Mr David Watson of Linthouse,' came the reply.

Kingan took a step back.

Watson's older son showed no reaction to Kingan's name. 'Let me introduce you to my friends. They're French. I spent some weeks with them two months ago in Lyon. My father reciprocated their hospitality. Do you know my father?'

Kingan nodded.

The others surrounding the couple were bombarding them with questions about life in France.

At a suitable interval, David Watson said in excellent French, 'Permettez moi de vous presenter a Monsieur Kingan.'

Kingan shook the hand of the rather staid husband then bowed to his vivacious wife, who responded before her husband could, 'C'est notre plaisir, Monsieur—Gin can.'

Kingan enunciated the two syllables separately, 'King an.'

'Gin—gam,' stumbled the wife, who then giggled.

Kingan joined in the sport, enunciating singsong couplets of the syllables. The bystanders laughed.

His pleasure was cut short by a stabbing pain in his foot. He excused himself and looked for a waiter. Finding one, he consumed two glasses of Glasgow Punch but within a minute, the pain returned. He decided to leave. He hobbled to the ballroom to give his goodbyes. Nancy was not there. Miller's son was on the platform.

At the top of the staircase, he saw Miller engaged in conversation with a tall mulatta, his forehead almost touching hers. Kingan discerned their Caribbean patois, not understanding a word. Miller turned and, on seeing Kingan, switched quickly to a loud English. Kingan signalled he was leaving but Miller gave him the cold shoulder.

He spent the next two days exhausted on the chaise longue. The next morning, he received a letter. He recognised the handwriting of the address. It started with "Mr Gingham". Wide-eyed, he opened it:

Well, to the point. Your attentions in a certain quarter were extreme and disagreeable to me as a friend of the lady. She received your attentions so well before as she was ignorant of your character and opinions in regard to women. Now she would be more upon her guard.

What the hell did you have to do with that woman anyway, you pumpkin of a thing. Don't blame me if you get into trouble. A good servant lass will taste as sweet in a corner as she did and you will run no risk there, you that think stolen water as sweet and bread eaten in private as pleasant.

You can draw from this you are a good deal talked about. I always thought you a cursed impudent puppy but never before thought you a damned unprincipled villain. You have good teeth but everybody is tired with having them always stuck in their face. Be grave and more lick your time of life.

He resisted the impulse to crush the page and reread it. It was obvious that David Watson had told his father. *It had to come,* he thought. He cursed Watson. Then Mrs Oswald's words came back to him. 'It's not what the letter says, it's what the writer knows.'

Chapter 9
Vinegar

The gout lasted two weeks, much of which he passed brooding on the letter. He tried downplaying it as he had with that of the previous year. But it touched a nerve. He had no doubt about its writer, Watson. Initially, his rage focused on his gall but it waned, replaced by scorn at his cowardice. Ashamed of its contents, especially the reference to Elizabeth Stewart, he told no one about the letter. He found succour in his bond with the Oswalds. James was in London. He would wait to tell him face to face.

As the pain subsided, he resumed his afternoon strolls, walking slowly and with a stick. On returning one late afternoon, a card was waiting from Kirkman Finlay inviting him to join him and some old friends from Grammar School in a kippered salmon lunch at the Buchanan Arms at the Govan waterside. His spirits surged at the opportunity for the company and good food. He was sick of boiled chicken, lime juice and gooseberry preserve.

He woke Saturday morning ache-free and remained so for the next few hours. Relieved and refreshed, he dressed for the lunch.

Once at the tavern, the excellence of the fare reinforced his feeling of good health. His resistance to his friends' blandishments to join them in the claret crumbled. Soon, to his delight, he was the centre of attention, the anecdotes and quips flowing.

The meal ended, he baulked at returning to Clyde Street. He remembered Nancy's invitation to the ball. Shieldhall was nearby. Why not? Her mother would be taking her nap. Margaret could act as a chaperone. He made his goodbyes and told the coachman to take him to Shieldhall.

On arriving, the day being warm and his spirits high; he decided that he would walk back to Glasgow. He dismissed the gig.

'How are you, sir?' asked Williamson, the butler, on him reaching the front door.

'I'm very well, thank you. I was visiting the area and thought it appropriate to pay my respects to Mrs Oswald.'

'I'm sure that she would welcome that but, unfortunately, she's sleeping.'

Good, thought Kingan.

'Miss Nancy is visiting Miss Hutton. Miss Margaret is here.'

Kingan hid his dismay with a smile.

Williamson showed him to the conservatory, where the clan of spaniels rested in the sun's heat, amplified by the glass panes. He bowed to a surprised Miss Margaret.

They exchanged pleasantries. He turned down her invitation to tea. The conversation turned to her nephews and nieces. She gave a lengthy account of the educational progress of each of the four. By the time she had reached Mabel's near-perfect recital of some psalm, his eyelids were drooping.

His eyes snapped open when the door creaked open. Nancy in a full light brown pleated skirt, black jacket and riding boots, tossed her white hat with a muslin veil onto a chair. He grinned broadly as his eyes caught hers.

'Mr Kingan!' she exclaimed. 'Such a pleasure!'

He rose and kissed her proffered gloved hand. 'All mine. Did you enjoy your ride?'

'Yes.' She sat down beside her sister on the couch opposite Kingan. 'I was over at Holmfauldhead, visiting Miss Catherine.'

'How is she?' asked Margaret.

'Much better,' replied Nancy. 'The tearfulness has passed.' She turned to Kingan. 'Poor Catherine remains much affected by the loss of little Catherine, her niece.'

'A year ago, now,' whispered Margaret.

'I didn't know,' said Kingan.

There was a moment's silence broken by Nancy. 'How have you been? Your gout went?'

'It returned worse.'

'Oh, how awful!'

'Today's the first day I've felt really well.' He described his lunch.

Margaret's face hardened. 'Are you sure you should have been drinking with your condition?'

Her tone disquieted him.

Nancy intervened. 'Mr Kingan's a man of strong constitution,' she paused. 'Would you care for a refreshment?'

'I've already offered,' declared Margaret.

He hesitated. The Oswalds kept an excellent madeira. But Margaret was a strict abstainer. 'Some iced water would be most welcome.'

Nancy rang a bell. A maid came.

Kingan changed the subject, 'I hope to attend the Theatre Royal on Thursday to see *Guy Mannering*.'

'Oh, I just loved the novel,' cooed Nancy. 'Scott really is the Master.'

'The Wizard of the North!'

'But the production wasn't well received in Edinburgh.'

'That's of little import. Scott himself regards the play highly.'

Over iced water, they chatted about Scott's poetry. Nancy was lukewarm towards it, preferring the newer romantics, especially Byron. Kingan opined that his celebrity was based more on his adventures than his literary worth. They challenged each other, chortling at each other's views.

Margaret sat silently during their conversation. After ten minutes, she excused herself. The spaniels needed walking.

As the door shut, he looked at Nancy. Her eyes were warmly on his. Encouraged, he asked, 'Did you enjoy Mr Miller's ball? I missed you on my exit.'

'Greatly! After my last dance, I looked for you but was told you'd gone.'

He smiled broadly, moved by her attentiveness to his presence. 'My gout returned.'

She studied his features. 'I must make life difficult at times.'

'It does,' he dithered.

'Is it bothering you now?' she asked, eyes tender.

'No.' An urge to disclose his true burden took over. 'After the ball, I received one of those letters.'

She put her hands to her cheeks and groaned, 'Oh, no!'

'It's of little import,' he lied. 'Compared to my last a year ago, it's watered wine.'

'If you don't mind me asking, what does it say?'

'It referred to certain events at the ball. It erased all the pleasure I had. Slander. Trash.'

She waited.

'It refers to my tendency to humour,' he continued, voice quavering. 'It makes scurrilous allegations about my friendships.'

'With whom?'

He blushed.

'With women?'

He nodded.

She hesitated, then said gently, 'I saw Mrs Elizabeth Hagart at the ball.'

He averted his eyes.

'Oh, John—' she sighed.

He flushed at her use of his Christian name.

'I know how that affects one,' she sighed. 'My letter had the same allusions.'

He stared at her. 'I'm certain Robert Watson wrote the letter.'

He told her his grounds.

'Of course,' she snarled. 'He's like his father, David. The Nips!' She looked around then edged forwards in her seat. 'Miss Catherine told me that Mr Rowan also received one last week. Being a rather stoic gentleman, he's not much upset. He showed it to her. It contained the usual tittle-tattle about him and Widow Nanny Campbell. The strange thing was it was signed "Vinegar". James has never told us that any carried a signature. Did yours?'

He shook his head.

She sat back. 'Vinegar?'

'Mr Nip must be in a pickle.'

They laughed.

'Miss Catherine told me that in the letter, Watson claims to have written five hundred,' said Nancy.

'Five hundred! You would have thought he would have enough to do running a bank.'

They tittered, then sat quietly for a minute.

'Are you afraid, John?'

'About what?'

'About the slanders becoming public.'

He was but didn't want to admit it.

'I am,' she declared, sniffling. She dabbed her nose with a handkerchief.

His eyes moistened at her vulnerability.

'Tell me about your garden, Miss Nancy,' he said cheerily, to lift the mood.

Twenty minutes later, the carafe of iced water finished, the conversation returned to the theatre. His eyebrows rose when she expressed an avid wish to see a new play she had read about, *Presumption or The Fate of Frankenstein*. He inquired if she had read the novel on which it was based.

'Of course!' she replied.

He agreed to escort her to the theatre should the play arrive in Glasgow.

He heard the dogs yelping in the hall. Margaret was back. Conscious of arriving in Glasgow before dark, he indicated he had to leave. She offered him a carriage but he insisted he would walk.

Ten minutes later, Kingan went with her to the front door. He bowed, took her hand and kissed it. On rising, their eyes drank in each other's regard.

'A bientôt, Mademoiselle.'

'A la prochaine.'

On reaching Clyde Street, wishing to keep alight the happiness of the day, he dashed off a note, in a style he hoped she would find suitably theatrical.

*You must know, Miss Nancy, that I met my friend yesterday on my way home and we had a short **DIALOGUE**:*

K—Servant—Sir.

Vinegar—I think all your symptoms of the gout are gone.

K—Yes, pretty well.

Vinegar—Will you return and dine with us?

K—Cannot. You seem to be hoarse.

Vinegar—I have got a bad cold someway.

K—You should use Vinegar.

Vinegar—Vinegar!

K—Yes, for the mouth and throat, it is excellent when it agrees with the constitution.

I'll have a printed garment down in time for the festivity. Yours—K.

Two days later, about six in the morning, Mr George Rowan went with a farmhand to his barn. On the doors opening, he noticed a slate sticking into the ground. He extracted it. String criss-crossed the flat surface, holding a folded page.

'How did this get here?' he asked the farmhand.

'Somebody must have thrown it through the slit in the wall during the night.'

Rowan frowned. He untied the string. He recognised the handwriting. He read the letter. Its first lines were:

So, I find you have been showing my letter!
What can be thought of a fellow that would do a thing of the kind. I thought you had even a smidgen of a gentleman or I should never have troubled you with any letters.

It was signed "Vinegar".

Chapter 10
Don't Tell

A few months after his visit to Shieldhall, Kingan was leaving the Ship Bank where he had deposited the funds from the sale of the Riga shipment. His mood light, he walked up Argyll Street, his advance slowed by the stiff wind and the crush of hawkers, criers and beggars. He kept an observant eye for ne'er do-wells. He stopped by a haberdashery window as an obvious dipper came near. He let him pass and was about to set off when he spotted Mr Adam Aitken.

He gulped on realising that the Agent of the Bank of Scotland had also seen him. Hatless, clad in a black, double-breasted jacket, his antagonist strode towards him.

On arrival, Kingan met his adversary's cold blue eyes. 'Mr Aitken.'

'Mr Kingan.' His narrow face stern, Aitken towered over Kingan. 'I was just thinking of you.'

'Oh—'

'I've just come from the Infirmary,' continued the banker. 'I have a poorly aunt there. I bumped into Dr Richard Wilson in the corridor. He told me about an incredulous tale your crony, Mr James Oswald, is putting about. About these letters in Govan. Claiming Mr Robert Watson is their author!' He moved closer. 'And you are abetting him!'

Kingan took a step back. *What the hell is Oswald doing?* he thought.

'What do you have to say about that?' thundered Aitken.

'Abetting James in slandering Robert Watson? I've done nothing of the sort.'

'Wilson told me you are!'

'How?'

'Concocting some crazy story about vinegar!'

Kingan narrowed his eyes. *'Vinegar? What's he talking about, my story?'* Then it struck him. *'My note to Nancy.'* Aitken's eyes bore into him. *'What to say? I can't divulge Oswald's belief in Watson's guilt without his approval.'* He looked at Aitken and blurted, 'There is a damned scoundrel whom we suspect as the author, but I can't say who it is.'

Aitken's nostrils flared. 'Take care, Sir, if your blasphemy refers to Mr Watson! Him writing these letters—' He pointed up the street. 'You might as well accuse the statue of King Billy!' He settled a moment, then affirmed, 'I'm going to inform him of your mischief.'

Kingan couldn't help himself. 'King Billy?'

Aitken clenched his fists, as he shouted a frustrated 'blah!' He turned to march off, but Kingan interposed himself.

'I strongly advise you to speak with Mr Oswald first.'

'Why?'

'Because he holds certain information which will be of interest to you. Let's go to Ropeworks Lane now.'

Aitken pulled a pocket-watch from his waistcoat. 'I can't. I have an appointment.'

'Can you come this evening?'

Aitken pressed his lips together. After a moment, he responded. 'Alright. Arrange it with Oswald.'

'I will.'

'Can't you ever hold yourself back from these couthy capers, Kingan?' sneered Aitken.

Kingan gritted his teeth.

He watched as the banker marched up the street, waving away a beggar. He went directly to Oswald's offices. His friend wasn't there. He left a note about his encounter. That afternoon, he received the reply. Oswald had responded to the banker directly. They were meeting at Oswald's apartment at nine; Kingan had to come at eight. He thought of refusing but judged it was better to mount his own defence.

He couldn't eat dinner. Watson's denouement was happening before Oswald had proof of his guilt. And he was central to it. The note to Nancy, how had that come about?

He arrived at Ropeworks Lane at eight. He struggled up the tenement stairs. He was sweating as the butler showed him to the drawing room where his Oswald waited. After brushing off enquiries about his health, he agreed to the offer of a cognac.

'Why did you tell Wilson about Watson's guilt?' asked Kingan. 'I thought we had agreed that you would wait until you have conclusive proof.'

'I have it. All the vinegars.'

'Eh?'

'The signatures on the letters. Your note to Nancy.'

'How did you see my note?'

'Nancy gave it to me to make sense of Rowan's letter in the barn.'

Kingan's eyes clouded. 'Letter in the barn?'

'The day after your encounter with Watson, Rowan retrieved a letter from his barn. It started with *So I find you have been showing my letter*". It was signed Vinegar. Watson knew that his previous letter to Rowan signed "Vinegar" had been shown to others because you confronted him with the word in your meeting.'

'Because I confronted him with the word "vinegar"?'

'In your meeting by the Clyde. How else would you explain his strange response to your mentioning "vinegar"? You set it out so well in your Vinegar Note. Don't you see how it all comes together?'

Kingan felt his stomach churn. 'Come together?'

'The proof I've been waiting for.'

Kingan felt his chest tighten. *'Where is this going?'* he asked himself. *'I'll put a stop to it.'*

'Have you told anyone else about the note?'

'Smith.'

'Smith!'

His expression sheepish, Oswald nodded.

'He blabs like a widow!' Kingan rubbed his forehead and pondered his options. Let it go or ask Oswald to withdraw his vinegar tale. Half of Glasgow would probably already know of it. Most of them would be further convinced of its veracity if Kingan tried to have it retracted. Anyway, Oswald would never agree. 'What's happening this evening with Aitken?'

'He's asked to see some of the letters. I agreed. He's offered the help of one of his tellers who investigates their forgeries to examine the handwriting. What do you think?'

Kingan's heart sank at the thought of Aitken becoming involved. *'What was Oswald thinking?'*

'I don't trust Aitken. He's close to Watson. We shouldn't let him see any letters. Turn down the offer of the teller.'

'But if the teller were to say the letters are in Watson's handwriting, we have the final piece of evidence. We can move on him then.'

'Aitken's hardly likely to cooperate in us humiliating his friend.'

Oswald thought for a moment. 'Alright. But it's too late. He knows about the letters. To convince him of Watson's guilt, I must show him some. I've already set three aside. They're on that table.'

He pointed to an occasional table by the window.

'He'll tell Watson.'

'So be it.'

Kingan fixed Oswald with a disapproving stare. 'Think of the consequences, James. What are you going to do once Watson knows?'

'Not this again, John! We've been through it before.'

'But James, it's premature! I've already said, without proof, you become the slanderer, not him. We need to convince Aitken not to tell.'

'How?'

'I've no idea.'

Oswald stood up and paced to the window. He returned after a few minutes. 'Alright, I'll hold off until I have decided on a suitable punishment.'

At nine sharp, the butler showed Aitken into the drawing room. Kingan gave the banker a stiff greeting, then took the armchair opposite the fireplace. The two friends sat on either side of him, facing each other.

Oswald came straight to the point. 'I have three letters set aside for you, Mr Aitken. I warn you that their content is improper, especially about matters concerning the ladies. As for the offer of a teller, I think at this time that would be a step too far.' Aitken simply grunted.

He retrieved the letters from the table and passed them to the banker. Neither of them was Oswald's.

'I'd appreciate being able to study these on my own,' said the banker.

Oswald rang a bell. A footman appeared and showed Aitken to the study.

After he left, Kingan rose and went to the window. He wished he had eaten earlier. His stomach burned. He kept his eyes off Oswald, who sat reading the Herald.

After twenty minutes, the footman led Aitken back. Kingan sat back down but Aitken remained standing in front of Oswald. 'I see nothing linking these to Mr Watson,' he stated, handing back the letters.

Kingan immediately thought, *he's lying.*

Oswald placed the pages on the occasional table at his side and said softly, 'Please sit down, Mr Aitken.'

Once Aitken took his seat, Oswald asked, 'Are you sure of your opinion?'

'I am. I've had extensive correspondence with Mr Watson. I'm very well acquainted with his handwriting. That on these letters is not his.'

'Are you sure?' asked Kingan. 'You seem to have taken an extraordinarily long time to come to what you suggest was an easy decision.'

'Of course, I'm sure,' snarled Aitken. 'Why are you so sure? Are you a handwriting expert?'

Kingan was about to return his scorn when Oswald intervened. 'We have other evidence, Mr Aitken.'

Aitken sat back. 'Let's hear it then.'

Oswald went through the saga of Nancy's printed gown, Watson's comments to her at his dinner and to Kingan's acute discomfort, the Gingham letter. He then turned to Kingan. 'Tell Mr Aitken about the Vinegar Note.'

Aitken turned to Kingan. 'Yes, let's hear about this Vinegar Note,' he sneered.

Kingan cursed Oswald silently. He swallowed as Aitken's eyes bored into him. 'It started with Mr George Rowan of Holmfauldhead receiving a letter signed, Vinegar.'

'How did you know?' barked Aitken.

Kingan hesitated but he had no choice. 'Miss Agnes Oswald told me. Miss Hutton, Mr Rowan's sister-in-law, told her.'

'I have copies of the letters,' intervened Oswald.

Aitken shook his head and tutted.

Kingan went on. 'After she told me, I met Mr Watson on the Clyde pathway near Govan on Saturday evening. We engaged in conversation.'

'Was Archibald Lawson there?' interrupted Aitken. 'He's been staying at Linthouse this past fortnight. He and his cousin Watson have been field preaching on the open ground by the village. They've been travelling out from Glasgow together.'

'Yes. He was there.'

Aitken scowled.

Kingan began on the interchange with Watson. Without thinking, he started mimicking the banker's stentorian voice, exaggerating his surprised expression on first having heard "Vinegar" and his confusion thereafter. Aitken's face reddened, his eyes blazing. Kingan ended with the tale of the letter in Rowan's barn, imitating the old man with a half-sung, 'I see you have been showing my letters.'

He recomposed himself during the minute's silence, pleased at his bravado in front of the laced-up Aitken.

Aitken remained still, clenched hands folded on his lap.

Oswald then said, 'Don't you see, Mr Aitken, how your friend's response to John about the word "Vinegar" was abnormal? How it betrayed that "Vinegar" was his signature? Why else would he have responded so? His further letter to Mr Rowan confirms this. 'I see you have been showing my letter.' How does he know that Rowan had shown the letter to others? From the conversation by the riverside. 'Mr Aitken, we do have conclusive evidence as to Mr Watson's guilt.'

Kingan felt a cold sweat at the word "conclusive". *'That's not what we agreed.'*

Aitken leaned toward Oswald. 'You call your friend's performance evidence?' he snarled. 'I've known Robert Watson for many a year. He may have many faults, but he's no scandalmonger. In no way does anything I've heard here change my opinion.'

'I beg to differ,' responded Oswald.

'That's your prerogative, Mr Oswald,' said Aitken, his eyes feverish. 'But I ask you to consider this. What you've told me is of great import to Mr Watson. His bank. You must give me permission to inform him of your suspicions so he can defend his reputation. He's already been libelled "a damned scoundrel"!'

Kingan flushed.

'But Mr Aitken,' said Oswald. 'Think of the damage to the city's bankers' reputation if it becomes known that one of their numbers is writing these letters.'

'Are you going to put your so-called evidence in writing?'

Kingan glanced at Oswald. To his relief, he heard him say, 'Only when it's irrefutable. Until then, I'm asking you to desist from letting Mr Watson know about my proof.'

'I repeat. Mr Robert Watson has a right to know of your accusations. I'm willing to act as a broker.'

'And if I, as a man of honour, give you an assurance that I will personally confront Mr Watson with a written record of my evidence when I gather even more telling findings.'

Kingan nodded his agreement.

Aitken looked down at the floor.

'I don't think the Head Office of the Bank of Scotland would be best pleased with you being seen to stand by a slanderer,' said Oswald harshly. 'Proven or not.'

Aitken continued staring at the floor. After a minute, he raised his eyes and said quietly, 'I accept your assurance.'

Chapter 11
George

Kingan passed the next weeks waiting. But the confrontation with Watson didn't come. Aitken had kept his word. He met Oswald a few times, at the Hodge Podge, the Literary Society, the Western Club. Hiding his resentment at his embroilment in what was now referred to as the Vinegar Letters, tired him. Despite adding even more letters to his collection, Oswald was no further forward in obtaining the "irrefutable proof".

To his dismay, he didn't manage to settle with Walkinshaw. They hadn't met but he knew from his old clerks that the young man's woes continued. The impasse heightened his yearning to exit the partnership and finally retire.

He saw Nancy once at Perry's ball. In a corner, she apologised for having shown her brother the note. He accepted it graciously. After that, between her dances, they passed the evening pleasurably. Their time together passed in an instant. He parted with a promise to visit her the coming week.

One afternoon in late November, the sun low in the sky, Kingan went to view the boats at the Broomielaw. As he slithered over the slimy wharves, he felt a cramping pain in his feet. He decided to return home. As he was ascending the steps to his front door, the muscles in his jaw spasmed. Despite cold compresses, the pains continued through the evening. He took some laudanum and managed to sleep. He woke midmorning, unable to raise his head from the pillow. The light streaming through the slit between the curtains burned his eyes. Eventually, his low moans brought in Mrs Copperthwaite, his temporary housekeeper. She called Dr Cowan, who started his uncle on a range of treatments.

Mrs Copperthwaite had worked for him for five years until she had married two years ago. Still childless, she had agreed to return to his service when his cook, Mrs Hunter, who had carried out many of the housekeeping duties, had left. A tall, red-haired woman in her late 20s, she had agreed to stay until he moved house.

Over that day, Kingan's vision blurred. In the evening, a darkness descended as his sight left him. Cowan attended again. He wished to admit Kingan to the Infirmary, but the latter refused due to his fear of contagion.

For two weeks, Kingan lay in his room, day after day, blind, a throbbing pain behind his eyes. Fear suffused his thoughts. He began to compose himself for a world without light. He imagined himself as one of those "symptoms bores", looked upon as failures by their peers.

Then, the pain diminished but his vision did not return. He began to eat porridge to supplement his clear broths. Mrs Copperthwaite hired a nurse.

Finlay, Hunter, Dunlop Donald visited but not Oswald. He heard about him at Nancy's visits. She spoke about the letters, which now seemed ephemeral. Her readings of poetry brought relief to the pain. He even began to appreciate Byron. The lingering smell of her patchouli perfume lightened his heart. He passed a lonely Christmas. Its highlight had been pastries from the Neapolitan bakery sent over by Nancy.

#

On the evening of a cold Boxing Day, he was woken up from a snooze by Nancy's voice. His spirits leapt. He heard clearly her, then her sister Margaret pleading with Mrs Copperthwaite for a short time with him. Eventually, the housekeeper relented; she would wake him. They promised to retire as soon as possible.

A minute later, they were by his bed, loosening their tartan lambswool shawls and undoing the straps on their white starched bonnets as Mrs Copperthwaite and the nurse propped him up on the pillows.

'How are you, Miss Nancy? Miss Margaret?' he rasped. He sensed Margaret's disquiet, pictured her gaping at him, then heard her whisper, 'We should leave.'

He heard the rustle of their dresses as they rose. He put his hand out. 'Please, stay. I can't put into words how welcome is your presence. I may not see you, but I can hear you well enough and—' Sensing an awkwardness between the two, he asked, 'Something's pressing upon you?'

They were silent for a moment. Then he heard them sitting down. Nancy began. 'We've just been to Ropeworks Lane. We had hoped to catch James before he left for the Dennistouns to pass Hogmanay. Unfortunately, he'd already departed.'

'What was the reason for your urgency?'

'I've received a Vinegar letter, Mr Kingan,' sniffled Margaret.

'Oh—' He slumped back into the pillows at the sound of the "V" word.

'My mother's most distressed,' said Nancy. 'She wanted us to share it with James before he caught the steamer. I know you've misgivings about helping him with the letters. But your opinion on whether we should hire a rider to take it to him now or delay it until his return would be most welcome.'

'Why is the letter so concerning?'

'It's about George.'

'Your nephew?'

'Yes,' whimpered Margaret.

Kingan had often heard about George from Oswald. Like his own father, Oswald, was an acolyte of useful learning, the application of science to commerce. Dissatisfied with Glasgow's schools, he himself supervised his nephews' education in the same bare room by the stables where he had been taught.

George was a lackadaisical twelve-year-old, academically well behind his brother Alexander, who was ready for University. Frequent upbraids by Oswald, scolds by his grandmother and whippings by his tutor had made no difference to his performance. Margaret acted as a surrogate mother since his real mother had left. She fawned over him. Nancy took a middle pathway.

'Did the letter smear you as well?' Kingan asked Margaret gently.

'A little. According to Mr Vinegar, I'm "by no means offensive though very plain looking" which, although it pains me, is not a bad description of my appearance.'

'It is not!' bristled Nancy.

'It's what it said about George,' continued Margaret. 'It says he requires regular whippings to counteract his "stupid learning".'

Nancy took up the tale. 'The letter was most offensive about his tutor, Mr McKenzie. According to Mr Vinegar, he's a "merciless flogger" who was fired from his last post for intimacy with one of the daughters in the house.' Her voice tightened. 'He says Margaret also punishes George regularly. And that her beatings have made him "an even greater liar".'

'That's terrible,' said Kingan.

'I've never so much as laid a finger on dear George,' protested Margaret tearfully.

'There—there,' said Kingan, patting the bedclothes at his side.

'I'm sorry to have put this onto you, Mr Kingan,' continued Margaret, wringing her hands. 'With you being in this state 'n' all.'

He was about to offer more words of comfort when Nancy intervened. 'There's more, John. We have proof that Mr Vinegar wrote the letter.'

'Oh—'

'We had a talk with George. We asked if anyone outside his family had ever spoken to him about what goes on in his classes. At first, he said, "no." But on prodding, he told us that after the Sabbath service a few weeks ago, he and Alexander had been playing with the Rowan boys when Mr Vinegar who had been conversing with Miss Catherine, called him over.'

'He asked him if he was a good scholar to which George answered, "I would be if they didn't punish me so often." Vinegar said, "But, you must deserve it." George shouted, "I do not deserve it!" After our interview with George, I rode over to see Miss Catherine. She confirmed every word.'

'And that's when we decided to look for James,' said Margaret, her expression now resolute.

'Do you think we should send the letter on to James now?' asked Nancy.

Kingan thought for a moment. He recalled Oswald's devastating grief over the death of his brother Richard, George's father, to whom he had vowed that he would protect his children. By calling George a "liar", Watson was throwing down a gauntlet. Oswald would erupt. Playing out the letter's consequences, however, over the inebriation that was Hogmanay was a bad idea. 'No. It can wait. A few days aren't going to matter.'

'What do you think's going to happen?'

'I don't know.'

A silence passed over the room. It was broken by Nancy. 'I must thank you, John, for the time you've given us. We were so upset. We feel better now.'

His lips parted at her use of his first name. A moment later, he was taken aback, as was her sister, when she lifted his hand and lightly kissed it. She placed it at his side where it lay as if paralysed. It lay still but his heart rushed.

There was a light knock at the door. Their time was up.

Chapter 12
Blackball

In his hand, a glass of cognac; on his thighs, the Edinburgh Gazette; Oswald sat in the reading room at the Western Club. On his mind was Margaret's letter. He went through its contents for the umpteenth time since he had returned from the Dennistoun's Colgrain Estate.

He sipped more brandy. The affair had to stop. Watson had aimed low before, but his nephew was a target beyond contempt. He couldn't face another evening like yesterday, berated by his mother and sisters. After a few minutes, his head drooped. Cheering from the billiard room woke him with a jolt. He rubbed his stiff neck, downed the last of his glass, then rose to leave.

He walked past the mostly empty desks. To the left-hand side of the door was a noticeboard on which were pinned pages with news from the club's committees. He shuffled over. The top contained a list of new applicants for membership. The ballot would take place tomorrow. He looked at the four names. The last was Robert Watson Esq of Linthouse.

He took a couple of steps back, moved forward again and refocused his eyes. The text hadn't changed. The proposers were Adam Aitken Esq. and another banker, Robert Scott Esq.

'It can't be so,' he whispered to himself. 'Watson here? This special place for gentlemen? After all, he's done—'

He tottered into the hall. A footman in the club's gold and blue livery approached and enquired if he was all right. Oswald asked him to call a carriage.

As he was returning to Ropeworks Lane, his mind raced. Gradually, the flood of indignation began to recede. It dawned on him. This was the opportunity. He grinned. The banker himself had shed a light onto his route to retribution. Oswald decided to blackball Watson. And he would make sure that the whole Western Club knew the reasons why.

#

He woke the next morning, the evening's ballot, his first thought.

Later that morning, he went to a meeting at the Tontine Rooms over the development of a new street on the edge of Glasgow Green. Attending was Monteath, The Major, President of the Western Club Committee. Oswald asked him to stay after the meeting. The two were alone when Oswald, in a light-hearted voice, made his announcement. 'This evening, I'm going to blackball Mr Robert Watson.'

Eyes blank, the question, 'Why?' stumbled from the Major's mouth.

'Because he's a scoundrel who has wounded deeply my family.'

'What?'

'We've been the object of some of these obscene letters which have been circulating in Govan Parish. Watson's their author.'

The Major had no words, his face expressed his incredulity.

Oswald set out dispassionately the reasons for his opinion. He then excused himself as the Major started his protests.

#

Oswald took his time preparing for the club. He changed his clothes four times before settling on his most recent purchase, a navy blue, merino wool, double-breasted frock coat with black satin lapels. After arriving, he saluted a group in the hall which included Kirkman Finlay, Mungo Nutter Campbell and The Major. Their eyes, filled with foreboding, turned towards him. Finlay signalled for him to join them, but Oswald smiled and marched directly to the billiards room where he pretended to interest himself in a match.

The club was full for the elections. Those who had been invited to apply were forbidden from attending. Oswald joined the queue of members waiting to vote.

On each of the reading room's right and left walls stood four tables arranged in two pairs, one pair for each applicant. On the first table in each pair sat a white porcelain dish covered by a black cloth under which were small white and black balls. Beside it was a white card with the applicant's name. On the second table rested a polished mahogany ballot box. The club steward stood by the fireplace, supervising the voting.

When Oswald's turn came, he strode directly to the table with Watson's name. Raising the cover well above the dish, he selected a black ball. He looked up at the steward, whose stern face stared straight ahead. Holding the black ball between his thumb and index finger, so it was visible to all, he dropped it through the hole in Watson's ballot box. Glee lit up his face. Head upright, he marched out of the reading room.

He decided not to call for a carriage but to walk home. He descended the stairs at a trot. As he crossed the entrance hall, he became aware of the Major staring at him. Oswald waved at the lugubrious ex-soldier. He recovered his top hat and gloves and stepped out to the gaslit pavement.

#

Later that evening, as members and their guests were leaving, the steward supervised four servants, each carrying a ballot box and a porcelain dish with the respective applicant's card placed on top, to the secretary's office. Waiting in the office were the Major and the secretary. The servants placed the boxes and dishes on a long rosewood table and laid the card beside the box they had brought in. They and the steward then departed.

The two club officers decided to leave Watson's box till last. With relief, they found that none of the three other boxes contained black balls. The Major then unlocked Watson's box. He sighed as he saw not one but four black balls.

Chapter 13
The Bankers' Tryst

Watson woke with the sunrise, eyes instantly alert. Today would be his, his ratification as a peer of Glasgow's realm. It was arriving mid-morning, confirmation of his membership at the Western Club.

He dressed carefully in his newest black frock coat, white starched collar and shirt and dark blue cravat. After a hurried light breakfast, he retreated to his study to calm the expectation with the Bible. He chose the most appropriate passage, the Parable of the Wheat and the Weeds.

Two hours later, he was waiting at his favourite spot, the study's bay window looking across Linthouse's rolling greenery and the brown river to the grey mansion of Stobcross. He recalled the rainy morning when the bailiffs had come to eject his family from there, his first home. Only he hadn't wept. When he had commissioned Linthouse's refurbishment, he had made sure that this window offered an unobstructed view of the past, which today he would totally eclipse.

A carriage drawing up on the gravel courtyard disturbed his meditation. He smiled. 'Cometh the good seed.'

After a minute, he heard Aitken's voice in the hall. He descended to greet his friend who was saluting Iris, bedecked in her Sabbath best for the occasion.

Watson strode over, hand out. 'Adam!' he shouted. 'You needn't have! The mail would have been fine.'

A look of trepidation crossed Aitken's visage before it returned to its normal sobriety.

Watson looked at Iris, her eyes bright with expectation. 'Is the drawing room ready?'

'The footman just swept the armchairs.'

He turned to Aitken. 'Please come.'

The two men sat down. Watson raised his eyes to the window at the sound of another carriage arriving. He noticed that Aitken looked down.

A moment later, Gilbert strode into the room. 'Robert,' he said breathlessly. He turned to Aitken. 'I received your note, Adam.'

The hairs on Watson's neck prickled. A dread he hadn't had for years reappeared.

Iris came over to stand behind him.

'You better leave, Iris,' he said, a quiver in his voice. 'I fear this is going to be gentlemen's business.'

After she had exited, Aitken swallowed and then began, 'Robert, as your main proposer for membership of the Western Club, it's my duty to inform you of the result. Major Monteath told me it first thing this morning. After hearing him, I sent a note to Gilbert.' He hesitated, 'I'm afraid your application's been turned down.'

'Eh?' gasped Watson.

'You were blackballed.'

The life went out of Watson's eyes. 'Oh God—' he groaned. He began coughing, bending over. It seemed for a moment that he was going to fall.

Gilbert steadied him, waited until the coughing had died down, then went to the door. He shouted for a glass of water.

No one spoke until Gilbert, having barred Iris, who had been hovering at the door, from entering, returned with a full glass. After taking a few sips, Watson returned the glass to his brother, who said, 'tell us what happened, Adam.'

'There were four black balls.'

'Four!' shouted Watson.

'One was James Oswald's. Monteath told me that beforehand he had adverted his reasons for blackballing you.' Aitken hesitated. 'He alleges that you are the author of these letters which have been circulating in Govan Parish.'

'What?' gulped Watson. 'That trash?' He looked over at Gilbert, whose eyes looked like they were diving out of their sockets.

'Say that again,' said Gilbert.

'Oswald's been gossiping about you and these letters for months,' said Aitken. 'They say they have proof that you wrote them.'

'They?' asked Gilbert.

'Oswald is working with Mr John Kingan,' spat Aitken.

Watson let loose a strangulated cry like a wounded animal. *Kingan! That scoundrel!* For a moment, he thought that given the enmity between the two, Aitken was making it up. But no. Kingan was a satirist and a prankster. Bankers had been the butt of his humour for years. This would be the type of thing he enjoyed.

He felt acid surging to his mouth and reached out, hand shaking and lifted the glass of water to his lips. Once finished, Gilbert took it off him. He looked at Aitken, who seemed on the point of tears. He thought carefully of his words, 'They say they have proof. When did you learn about all this, Adam?'

Aitken looked like a rabbit in a snare. 'About three months ago,' he murmured.

'Three months ago!' cried Gilbert.

Watson's wounded eyes glinted at the man he had thought his friend. 'You didn't tell us?'

'I couldn't tell you,' said Aitken, his voice ragged. 'Oswald swore me to secrecy.'

'Secrecy about what?' barked Gilbert.

'About their proof.'

'Which is?'

Aitken related his meeting at Oswald's apartment: the printed gown, the Gingham letter, the Vinegar letters and Note. He made no mention of Oswald's threat about what would happen if he had informed Watson then.

Watson sat slack-jawed, unable to comprehend the saga.

'What a tissue of piffle!' exclaimed Gilbert. 'Nancy Oswald. What has she got against you, Robert?'

'I've no idea,' mumbled Watson. He looked at Aitken, his eyes imploring. 'This encounter on the Clyde pathway?'

'Oswald puts great store on it,' replied Aitken. 'He considers Kingan's note conclusive of your guilt. You should have seen the joker's performance relating to what happened, full of venomous artifice.'

'But I've never met Kingan by the Clyde!' sobbed Watson, shaking his head.

'Damned villain!' screeched Gilbert.

Watson's eyes turned black and feverish, his neck corded. If Kingan had been in front of him, he would have throttled him. But that death was too quick. He tried to scream out his hatred but began coughing.

When he calmed after the fit, Aitken fixed his eyes on his. 'You know, since I saw Kingan performing that evening, I've had a gut feeling that he's behind all this. The juicy anecdotes in the letters are so much his style. The story of this invented encounter is so typical of his japes. Now, I'm sure he duped Oswald into blackballing you, Robert. He insinuated into Oswald's reasoning that you're the author. The blackball has one aim, to divert attention from Kingan's guilt.'

The words sliced into Watson, draining the little colour remaining on his face. After a minute, he whispered, 'You should have told me about your meeting, Adam.'

'I'm sorry, Robert,' whimpered Aitken, eyes watering, voice cracking. 'I'm so sorry. There's nothing in my life, I regret more. Nothing!'

The room chilled.

Gilbert broke the awkwardness. 'It certainly reeks of Kingan. Oswald's a popinjay. He couldn't have thought this up.'

'And that ludicrous sister of his—' spat Watson. He slumped into his chair. 'The bank? Who in Glasgow will trust a slanderer? All this.' He waved his hand over the room. 'My standing in the Kirk.' He shivered. 'What am I to do?'

'What you've done for years, Robert,' remonstrated Aitken, eyes black through his tears. 'Fight! Fight! I'll be with you. And Our Maker. I swear that I will not rest dormant until I've made good my heinous concealment.'

Watson averted his eyes. Aitken's evident remorse helped him hold back his own. He remembered the words, 'Like a muddied spring is the righteous man who gives way before the wicked.' I am not thus.

'What will we do?' asked Gilbert. 'Go after Oswald who has slandered you or Kingan who tricked him or both.'

A weariness came over Watson. Options. Attention to detail. Decision. But his mind, too clouded, couldn't engage his usual clear thinking.

'My advice,' said Aitken, 'is to deal with the perpetrator of the crime, then its cause. We make Oswald apologise for the blackball but while we do so, we build the platform for Kingan's hanging.'

Watson liked the metaphor. He nodded.

'Monteath thought the other three blackballers believed in Oswald's smears,' continued Aitken. 'He suggested we write to Oswald seeking an apology.'

'Won't the Western?' asked Gilbert.

'Monteath doesn't want the club involved in what happens next. He fears it could further damage the club's reputation.'

Tears came to Watson's eyes. 'The disgrace,' he sobbed.

'You need to rest, Robert,' said Gilbert tenderly. 'This has greatly affected you.' He fixed his eyes on Aitken. 'We need to move expeditiously. The more the delay, the more Oswald and Kingan's smears will stick.'

Aitken nodded. 'I think Oswald will refuse to apologise. We need to threaten him with the consequences of that. Damages through the Courts.'

'I think we should avoid that in the first instance,' said Gilbert firmly. 'Better seek local arbitration on whether he has grounds for his blackballing. If found to have not, Oswald should apologise publicly. What do you think, Robert?'

Head drooping, Watson mumbled, 'Alright.'

'Adam and I will draw up a letter to Oswald seeking his apology so you can approve it now.'

'I'll take it directly to Oswald,' said Aitken. 'Then return to Linthouse to let you know his response.'

On the point of exhaustion, Watson whispered, 'Good idea.'

Chapter 14
Vinegar's in His Bottle

Late afternoon after the blackball, Kingan was enjoying the gentle breeze coming through his drawing room's opened windows. Sitting in an armchair, a blanket covering his legs, dressed in a padded woollen dressing gown, a gauze bandage protecting his eyes.

A few hours before, Mrs Copperthwaite had read out Oswald's note:

John
Mr Vinegar is back in his bottle! How so? I'll tell you this afternoon.
James

Where is he? thought Kingan. He cursed his blindness. He had wanted to go straight to Ropeworks Lane after receiving the note but couldn't. His health had improved. He could make out shapes. The light no longer hurt his eyes. Cowan, his physician, though, had insisted on him continuing to wear a bandage.

He was snoozing when a carriage stopping in front of his front door awoke him. On recognising Oswald's footsteps on the staircase, his heart beat faster. A minute later, his head turned to where he smelled Oswald's smell of brine, leather and citrus.

'You look like Rameses, John,' bellowed Oswald. He strode across the room and knelt down in front of his friend. He clasped his hand. 'Great to see you up and sitting! You got my note?'

'Of course! A better remedy than a dozen of Cowan's potions. Well done!' They laughed. 'Yesterday must have been exquisite for you?'

'The opportunity we'd searched for months. Out of the blue. A Godsend!'

Oswald rose and pulled forwards an armchair. He related yesterday's events. Kingan listened intently without comment. The bandages started to irritate his eyelids. He went to rub them but pulled back his hand. 'What next?' he asked on Oswald finishing. A silence intervened.

'I've just met Adam Aitken.'

Kingan's forehead wrinkled. 'Why's he involved?'

'He was Watson's main sponsor. He came a couple of hours ago on behalf of Watson, demanding an apology.'

'An apology?'

'Yes. From me! The temerity!'

'What did you say?'

'I refused point blank! I tried to set him on his way. But he refused to leave. Never seen him so adamant. Harping on about Watson's reputation, his family, the bank. I told him he deserved it, trying to pass himself off as a gentleman after that dastardly letter to Margaret. He wouldn't have any of it.'

Kingan felt the air go out of his lungs as news of his antagonist's involvement took away his earlier sense of exhilaration. 'Aitken'll be hurting about acceding to your pressure not to tell Watson about us knowing he's the author.'

'He was! Kept going on about that meeting. Suggested there's an Iago in the affair. Utter rubbish! Then, he threatened me with legal damages. I told him where to go.' A look of satisfaction spread over his face.

'How did you end it with him?'

'In the end, he proposed arbitration. I agreed. I've nothing to lose. It's sure to find in my favour. It's the ideal way, John, to obtain what we've discussed long and hard, Watson's public apology.'

'But Watson will only seek arbitration if he's convinced that he'll win?'

Oswald didn't respond. It struck Kingan that it was the first time he had considered such an eventuality.

'I presume he's stalling,' said Oswald after a minute. 'Hoping for some salvation.' He moved closer and said smugly, 'Aitken told me that Watson almost collapsed at the news of the blackballing.'

Kingan stared at his friend. 'Take care, James. Watson's ruthless. He has Aitken by his side who's much the same.'

'You're too wary, John. I have their measure.'

Kingan grimaced.

Oswald patted his knee. 'It'll soon be over, John. Aitken's drawing up the arbitration's terms of reference as we speak.'

Chapter 15
The Most Difficult Fight in the City of Life

After Aitken and Gilbert had left, unable to sleep, Watson resisted his wife's pleas and rose from his bed. He went to the study and opened his volume of the works of Reverend Hugh Binning, the Covenanter philosopher. He sought the texts addressing his main concern: would his just expectation of peace eternal be damned by the whirling onslaught upon him? Would it destroy the ground and foundation of his confidence for present and future times: that strong city of the self within which hope and love were reposed, its walls his defence against the injuries and calamities?

Two hours of study later, he arrived at his conclusion: damnation would come only if he doubted his faith, his only true defence in this, his most difficult fight in the city of life. That he would never do. Face pallid but his mind steady, he went to the drawing room to wait for Aitken's return from Oswald.

#

Twenty minutes later. Aitken arrived soon joined by Gilbert. They sat across from him in front of the blazing fire. Aitken recounted his meeting.

Oswald had been as arrogant as ever, but he had agreed to arbitration to avoid the Courts. So cocksure was the merchant; he had accepted Aitken's offer to draw up the terms of reference. Both sides were to appoint their own referee to determine whether Watson had written the anonymous letters and caused them to be sent and judge whether Oswald had such grounds as to warrant him believing that.

The merchant had agreed to apologise if the arbiters found the contrary but in return, he had insisted Watson should do the same if the opposite occurred. Oswald had agreed to submit copies of the anonymous letters to a handwriting expert if Watson submitted copies of letters that he had written himself. Aitken had agreed.

Watson pondered the result. He concluded that it was a good sign. A first reward for his resistance, for his faith. 'Thank you, Adam.'

'Doesn't he suspect Kingan?' asked Gilbert.

'I suggested there's an Iago. He totally rebuffed the idea. He has no insight.'

'We can use his blindness to Kingan,' said Gilbert.

'How?' asked Watson.

'One step would be obtaining from him examples of Kingan's handwriting for the handwriting expert to show they're by the same hand as the Govan letters.'

Aitken grinned. 'The Vinegar Note. I put it to him that given the importance he placed upon it at our meeting, the arbiters should have sight of it. He demurred, then agreed. I'll find a way for the expert to examine it.'

'And who's to give the opinion on the handwriting?' asked Gilbert.

'The arbiters will choose an expert. I have someone I'll put to them.'

'But you usually need more than one letter to identify an author,' said Gilbert. 'A single allows room for doubt about authorship. We'll need more than the Vinegar Note. I don't think our bank holds any from Kingan. Does yours?'

'We've mainly dealt with his partner, Walkinshaw.'

A glow came across all their faces.

'Walkinshaw,' cooed Gilbert.

'Do you think he'll give us some of Kingan's letters?' asked Aitken.

'He'll need some encouragement,' said Watson.

'I'll send Bell,' said Gilbert.

'Not that type of encouragement. At least not yet.'

Gilbert studied his brother, who nested his fingers under his chin.

'Up to two thousand,' intoned Watson after a moment.

Gilbert inhaled. 'We can find that.' He paused, then declared. 'I'll visit Walkinshaw this evening. I'll keep Bell waiting outside in case he's needed.'

Watson nodded. A plan was emerging, incomplete but still a plan. His faith in His Maker was sustaining him. 'The terms of reference should cover the arbiters considering if anyone apart from me has written the letters.'

'Agreed,' replied Aitken.

'What happens when the arbiters uncover Kingan's guilt?'

'I'll add another paragraph,' suggested Aitken. 'About you having the right to take any measures you might think fit against any person from whom the arbiters indicate the letters originated.'

'Will Oswald agree to that?' asked Gilbert.

'He's so full of himself, he'd sign his mother's death warrant. He wants this over. Quickly.'

'And our referee?' asked Watson.

'How about Robert Davidson?' said Gilbert. 'We've used him as a writer in the past. He's a Professor at the college. He has considerable standing.'

'Oswald will object. He doesn't want any lawyers or bankers involved. Is there someone else?'

The two brothers looked at each other. 'No one springs to my mind,' muttered Watson.

Aitken thought for a moment. 'I have a suggestion. Before setting out for Linthouse, I had an unavoidable appointment with Mr Charles MacIntosh.'

The brothers' eyebrows rose.

'A Fellow of the Royal Society,' said Gilbert. 'Our most eminent scientist. Who could be more reputable?'

Watson stroked his chin. 'Indeed. But isn't he a friend of Oswald?'

'He is,' said Aitken. 'But I have reason to think he may favour us. When I told MacIntosh that I had to curtail our meeting to come here, his ears pricked up. He asked if it was about the blackballing. I told him yes, then rebutted his understanding that you were the letters' author. He asked why I was so certain. I replied that I had very strong grounds to believe that the author is Mr John Kingan. He almost fell to the ground.

Then he thought about it. "It could well be," he answered with some bitterness. "He is the most awful joker." His son had been most distressed after having been the subject of one of Kingan's anecdotes at a dinner party.'

Watson clasped his hands under his chin. Something which had disappeared this morning began to reappear. Hope.

'His appointment is immediately after Oswald's tomorrow,' continued Aitken. 'About an investment in a new type of textile to keep out the rain. I can stage an impromptu meeting between them at the bank and put to him being an arbiter. That way, Oswald will see his nomination as impartial.'

Watson's eyes moistened in gratitude.

Aitken peered at Watson. 'Robert, you're tiring. Are you happy with Gilbert and me drawing up the terms of reference?'

'Of course.'

Chapter 16
Arbitration

If the blackballing tickled the Quality's curiosity about the Vinegar Letters, the arbitration made it into the number one topic of conversation. Only a murder would have been more scandalous but far less titillating. The players' prestige could only have been improved by the inclusion of an aristocrat.

Oswald wallowed in the attention. Many praised his public service in outing the slanderer. He approved the terms of reference without a quibble. Aitken's staged chance encounter with MacIntosh worked. Under pressure, the scientist agreed to be an arbiter, reassured that Oswald's referee was Mr Charles Stirling of Cadder, a long-standing magistrate and scion of a distinguished merchant clan. MacIntosh had forthcoming business to attend to in London. Oswald set his mind at rest. The process would be over in a couple of days. Subsequently, the arbiters accepted Aitken's offer of his meeting room at the Bank of Scotland for their deliberations.

#

At their pre-meeting, Aitken had little difficulty persuading the two to agree to his proposed handwriting expert, Mr William Home Lizars, Scotland's foremost engraver, designer of banknotes for the Bank of Scotland and most importantly, key expert witness at the trial of James Stuart. His commission was to compare samples of letters from each party in the dispute to see if the handwriting was the same. He was kept in the dark about the circumstances and putative writers so no bias could enter his deliberations. Aitken drew up his contract.

After having read the documents submitted by the two parties, Stirling and MacIntosh decided to expedite the arbitration. The first morning, they would interview Oswald to assess if his charges were substantiated. In the afternoon, Lizars would give his expert opinion. They would then write their report.

#

At 10 o'clock, Oswald arrived for his interview to be greeted by a bank clerk who showed him to the meeting room. He had expected Aitken but there was no sign of him. He handed over his brown cape, top hat and white kid gloves and went to the meeting room. He strode in, head high. Seated behind a long dark brown table matching the panelled walls, sat Stirling and MacIntosh, each with a notebook in front of them, to Stirling's side the submissions for examination.

Little light penetrated the long thin window with iron bars. They rose. Oswald offered his hand to each of his friends in turn. Eyes glowing, he searched into theirs. Stirling was as if he were on the bench, dispassionate pale eyes under a high forehead and over a bulging, vein filled nose. Rotund in the torso and face, MacIntosh's expression was almost surly. Even his most notable feature, the shock of white curls, seemed formal.

Oswald sat down at the opposite end of the table. Then it started, the constant background to the next hour, the sound of his bouncing knee brushing the bottom of the table.

The questions started immediately; the arbiters acting as a team. One asked a question and the other noted the answer, then vice versa, their expressions unchanging. On two occasions, Oswald discomfited by their lack of response, asked, 'Was that clear?' They nodded in unison.

Oswald calmly told his story, punctuating each episode with expressions of outrage. At its end, MacIntosh reached for the Vinegar Note. He raised it. 'Tell us again, James, why you put such great import on this?'

'As I explained, it was written in the days following Mr Rowan's letter, the first signed "Vinegar". Mr Kingan wrote it after an encounter with Mr Watson who reacted strangely to the use of the word "Vinegar". The next day came a second letter to Mr Rowan, again signed "Vinegar", with the text "I see you've been showing my letter."'

He paused after his coup de grâce. There was no reaction from the arbiters. Irked, he raised his voice. 'Sir, the linkage of the three clearly indicates Mr Watson's guilt. His reaction to Mr Kingan's use of the word "Vinegar" was most unusual. It can only be explained by his prior knowledge of its use as a signature in Rowan's first letter. In the second letter, he expressed his knowledge that the first had been shown to others. How did he know that? It can only be from Mr Kingan's use of the word "Vinegar" during their encounter.' Chin jutting, he crossed his arms.

For a moment, MacIntosh's eyes sparked before resuming their impassive stare. 'The note is written in a comedic format rather than the more expository which I would have expected.'

'That's John,' chuckled Oswald.

MacIntosh's lips curled. He put the note, lying on the table, back in its original place. 'I think that's our last question, Charles.'

Stirling nodded. 'The sequence of events is complex, James. It would be useful for you to submit a report so that we don't misinterpret their significance.'

'Are you asking for one from Mr Watson?'

'We might,' replied Stirling. 'Depending on what we make of yours.'

Oswald scowled. 'When do you want it?'

'By the end of the week.'

'I'll see what I can do.'

'Good,' said MacIntosh. 'We won't finalise our report until we've received yours.'

Stirling nodded. 'Do you have anything to add, James?'

Oswald replied in the negative. Brow furrowed, he rose slowly. He shook the hand of each, reminding them of the need to expedite matters, then left the room.

#

An hour later, a tall, elegant man, dressed in a purple frock coat and matching cravat knotted in a bow, entered the bank. Despite the strong wind outside, not one of his long, silvery hairs was out of place. The waiting Aitken greeted Mr William Home Lizars, then led him to the meeting room where he introduced 'the world-famous engraver' to the arbiters.

Over tea and sandwiches, the arbiters quizzed Lizars about his methods. He explained that he started with a document's overall style, then the format of individual letters. Then, he discerned if there were signs of concealment by the author.

Stirling then asked, 'How long will you take?'

'Two hours, Sir.'

'We've set aside an office for you. It belongs to Mr Aitken. I'll call him.'

Two minutes later, Aitken entered. 'Are we ready?'

Lizars smiling, nodded as did the other two more gravely.

Aitken went to the table and separated the submitted documents into two piles, Oswald's and Watson's. He surreptitiously checked that the Vinegar Note was in the first, under the three anonymous letters, then lifted both and accompanied Lizars to his office which was lit by additional candelabras.

After two hours, the engraver returned alone to the meeting room carrying the documents. MacIntosh was reading *The Herald,* Stirling some correspondence.

'Have you reached a view?' asked Stirling.

'I have, Sir.'

Lizars set down the two piles on the table. He pointed grandly at Watson's letters in the pile on his left. 'These letters have all been written by the same person. There is no match, however, between them and the letters and note in this pile,' He pointed to the other pile, hand palm up like a magician. 'Which are all written by the same hand.'

MacIntosh's eyes widened. 'Are you sure?'

'That's my firm opinion.'

Stirling shook his head, muttering, 'Much as I feared. A damned fine mess!' It took a moment for Lizars' words, about the similarity of the Vinegar Note to the anonymous letters, to leave their import. 'Does that implicate—' He drew back from mentioning Kingan's name, aware that they couldn't inform Lizars of the details of the parties involved.

'That's what it looks like,' said MacIntosh. 'You're sure about the note?'

'It certainly looks that way,' replied Lizars. 'If you want more certainty, I'd need to examine more samples.' A silence came over them, the air replete with misgivings.

'What do you think we should do, Charles?' asked MacIntosh.

Stirling frowned. 'Our remit is to determine if the letters submitted by one party were written by the same hand as those submitted by the other. Mr Lizars says they weren't. The implication of his opinion is that there is a third party involved in the anonymous letters whom I know well. And I know it's impossible for him to have written these letters.'

'But it's also in our terms of reference that we report on any findings which may point to another person being the author.'

Stirling's lips curled. Lizars kept silent, observing the interchange.

'Perhaps Mr Aitken can help?' said MacIntosh.

'Perhaps,' grumbled Stirling.

'I'll get him.'

On the banker's entry, Lizars repeated his findings with the same theatricality. Aitken slumped into a chair, his eyes closing to hide his tears.

'Are you alright?' asked Stirling gruffly.

Aitken pulled himself together. 'I am. My apologies.'

Mr Lizars needs to carry out a further assessment,' said MacIntosh, turning to Aitken.

Lizars harrumphed, then said, 'My commission was to examine documents submitted by two different parties. I am now being asked to confirm that the note is written by the same hand as the letters, both submitted by the same party. The letters' contents are libellous. The note appears to be some form of private joke. Any finding on them could have implications for my reputation. If you want a firm opinion on their authorship, I need more examples of the handwriting of the person implicated. I need a firm steer from you, Gentlemen.'

MacIntosh and Stirling looked at each other. It was MacIntosh who spoke. 'We have a duty to exclude if there is a third party involved in this affair.'

Stirling hesitated, then muttered, 'Alright.'

'Good!' said Lizars. 'But I need more material.'

'I have some letters from the note's author,' said Aitken.

MacIntosh's eyes widened but he kept silent. Stirling looked to the ground.

'They're in my office,' announced Aitken. 'You can examine them there.'

The banker scurried off, followed by the engraver, the anonymous letters and note in his hands. In his office, he extricated from a safe, the letters obtained from Walkinshaw by Gilbert Watson earlier that week. He left Lizars at his desk and went back to the arbiters.

The three sat at the table, each keeping their eyes off the others. After a few minutes, Stirling rose from his chair and began pacing back and forth before growling, 'I didn't sign up for this!'

The others shrank back in their seats.

He turned to Aitken. 'What the hell are these new letters!'

'By coincidence, I had some business letters written by Mr Kingan. We have been doing business with him, through his partner Mr Walkinshaw.'

'But they're in dispute.'

MacIntosh intervened. 'What bothers you, Charles?'

'I agreed the examination of that damned note could be included as part of our remit and, as I understand it, of Lizars' contract. But not these new letters! Any opinion on them is ultra vires. We can't, therefore, make any reference to them in our report.'

Aitken tried to speak but MacIntosh went first. 'I agree with you, Charles. Lizars' expert opinion should be confined to his contract.'

'Good!' barked Stirling.

'But, you cannot ignore the findings concerning these new letters,' blurted Aitken.

Stirling glared at him. 'It may be in our reference or the arbitration, but I repeat, it is not in Mr Lizars' contract. His opinion on any similarity among the anonymous letters, the Vinegar Note and the other letters, is irrelevant!'

Aitken fell silent.

Just then, Lizars entered without knocking. 'Gentlemen,' he began, almost breathlessly. 'The handwriting in the letters, which you have just given me, is indistinguishable from that in the anonymous letters and the card. There are remarkable similarities in the shape of the long letters, "y", "g" and "j", the use of a single "l" instead of the double "ll"' and the recurrence of phrases such as "honest man", "eternally yours", "I see that".'

Stirling slumped in a chair. MacIntosh glanced at Aitken, whose eyes gleamed.

After a minute, Stirling lifted his head. 'Given the repercussions of the latest findings on the two original sets of submissions, I move that we commission further expert opinion on them.'

MacIntosh pondered the proposal. 'That would be useful.'

'I have a colleague in Edinburgh, Mr Thomas Clerk,' said Lizars. 'I can show him the documents tomorrow and obtain an opinion.'

MacIntosh looked at Stirling, who nodded then added. 'Until then, the matters we've discussed are held between us and us alone.'

The tension in the room lowered. After a few minutes, Lizars said, 'It's my custom to write my opinion while the memory of my findings is still fresh. Are you happy with that?'

MacIntosh nodded as Stirling grunted assent.

'I must go,' apologised Stirling. He shook Lizars' hand, then the other two.

After a few minutes, MacIntosh excused himself and thanked Lizars. Aitken would organise the handling of Lizars' report.

Chapter 17
Word Is Out

Three days later, Mrs Ishbel Copperthwaite walked along Clyde Street. Pinning her dark green tartan shawl to her chest, she turned away from the river, her destination Sweenie's Italian Warehouse where several boxes of oranges had been due to arrive this morning. Her Master loved them. Tall, thin, redheaded with a pale complexion, she sped on, her spirits rising. There was sure to be an opportunity for a chat in her native tongue.

She joined the queue at the fruit baskets in the spacious, brightly lit emporium, its high-shelved walls packed with packets and jars. An aproned attendant kept guard. She looked over the row of bonnets but didn't spot an acquaintance. Then she recognised the soft lilting Gaelic of her land. She turned. Senga MacDonald, the housekeeper at Mr Spiers' town residence, waved. Ishbel purchased the permitted five oranges and then stopped by her friend. They agreed to meet by the dry provisions.

Standing apart from the bustle, they greeted each other warmly. Then, Senga moved closer, her green eyes bright.

'I heard something this morning which caused me great consternation.'

'Oh!'

'I was supervising breakfast when my Master said to my Mistress that he had been in company at the Saracen's Head with Mr Gilbert Watson the evening before. You know, they say his brother, Robert, is the writer of these letters?'

'My Master is certain he is.'

'Well, it appears Mr Watson has been cleared by some august jury.'

Ishbel's eyebrows rose. 'Yes?'

'There's worse.' She looked around then whispered, 'My Master said it turns out your Master wrote these smutty letters.'

'What?'

She dropped her voice lower. 'Mr Gilbert Watson let Mr Spiers see a report from the world's greatest expert on writing letters. It proves after the most thorough examination, that the letters' handwriting was Mr Kingan's. Well! You should've heard my Mistress. Shocked to the marrow! My Master said he had been on first seeing the report. But not now. Sending anonymous letters was just the type of prank Mr Kingan was famous for.'

Ishbel flinched. 'That's malicious gossip put about by the Watsons. I'm surprised at Mr Spiers!'

They agreed to disagree and went their separate ways.

#

She hurried back to Clyde Street. Kingan was dozing in the drawing room. He could see clearly now but the lassitude remained. She decided to leave her news till later.

After an hour, she heard the bell. She went to him and asked if she could sit next to him by the raging fire.

'Of course,' he replied smiling, stretched out on the chaise longue.

'I have some news, Master.'

He tilted his head towards her, in the expectation of a juicy servant's tale. 'Tell me.'

She swallowed and then recounted her conversation with Senga.

On her finishing, he grimaced. 'What a load of rubbish! Don't you think your friend is making it up?'

'I don't think so, Master. She's not like that.'

He ran his hands through his hair. 'A report by an expert?' Doubt set in. Yesterday, he had sent Oswald a card asking him what was happening with the arbitration. There had been no reply.

'Did she give you this expert's name?'

'Just that he's the world's greatest.'

He exhaled. 'I need to find out what's going on,' he told himself. 'Organise a porter to take a card to Mr Oswald.'

'Do you want me to write it?' She had been taking his dictation since the illness began.

'If you could. If he's not at Ropeworks Lane, get the porter to find out where and go there immediately.'

#

After she had left, he contemplated what he had just heard. *Me writing the letters! Farcical. A feint by Watson to divert attention from his guilt.* But a foreboding grew. *Why the silence about the arbitration?* He lay for the next few hours, turning these thoughts in his head, becoming more and more exasperated.

#

He had begun to despair of his arrival when he heard Oswald's heavy tread in the hall. He left the chaise longue for the armchair.

'John, how are you?' barked Oswald in his usual bonhomie on entering. 'Your eyes. No bandages.'

'Better,' responded Kingan icily.

'Oh—' Oswald sat down opposite Kingan. His foot's nervous tapping began. 'Your note said you wished to talk about the arbitration.'

Kingan glared at him. 'I heard this morning about some report Gilbert Watson's sharing in the taverns. It says I'm the author of the anonymous letters.'

Oswald stiffened. 'There's no official report yet. Stirling and MacIntosh haven't written it. Lizars' opinion will be included in that.'

'Stirling and MacIntosh? Lizars?'

'Charles MacIntosh is Watson's arbiter. Charles Stirling's mine. They interviewed me but hardly took any notice of what I presented. Stirling's been most disappointing.'

Kingan shrugged.

'William Home Lizars is their handwriting expert.'

'The engraver. What does he know about handwriting?'

'He was a witness in the Stuart trial.'

'And?'

Oswald paused. 'The arbitration's been difficult.'

Kingan's face reddened. 'Why did you ever agree to it?'

'Wheesht, John. You'll do yourself damage.'

'Just tell me about the handwriting.'

The tapping became a drumbeat. 'Lizars' opinion was that the handwriting in the anonymous letters wasn't Watson's.'

'So, the arbiters are going to say Watson's not the author?'

'Probably,' muttered Oswald. 'They're seeking further opinion on the handwriting.'

Kingan felt his gut flutter. He collected his thoughts. 'That doesn't explain this report saying I'm the author.'

'I've not seen any such report but, I did hear a rumour about one. I asked MacIntosh yesterday before he left for London. He hasn't seen it.' Oswald hesitated. 'He told me that Lizars examined the Vinegar Note. His opinion was that its handwriting was the same as the anonymous letters. MacIntosh said that's what is in this other report.'

Kingan swooned, then put out a hand to repel Oswald, who was moving towards him. 'Oh no,' he moaned. He whispered all he could think to say, 'Nobody asked me about my note being examined.'

'Aitken asked that it be submitted. He already knew about it from that meeting we had. I agreed. I thought it would help our case.'

'Our case?'

'Alright, my case. Somehow, it got shown to Lizars. Probably Aitken.'

Kingan felt like punching him. His hand tightened on the armchair rest. 'How the hell did you let him take charge?'

Oswald's face reddened. 'He's not in charge.'

'Well, you certainly aren't!'

'I've objected, John. Most strenuously! I've pointed out that Lizars is not independent. He's done work for the Bank of Scotland, engraving notes.'

Eyes wide, Kingan sat back. Each fact seemed more outlandish than the previous. 'What's happening now?'

'They've asked me to compile a report of my evidence, which I've started. Their report will await MacIntosh returning from his business in London. That's where they're seeking further expert opinion on the handwriting.'

'Did he take my note to Nancy?'

'Yes.'

'Without my permission. Never!'

Oswald went quiet. After a moment, he announced, 'Lizars didn't just base his opinion on your note. He examined more examples of your handwriting. Somehow, some letters by you were found.'

'How?'

'I heard from my clerk, Walkinshaw gave them.'

'Walkinshaw!' He looked wildly over the room. 'Oh God, can it get any worse!'

Oswald hesitated. 'I can only presume that Aitken reached an agreement with him.'

He glared at Oswald and spat, 'Watson and Aitken have outwitted you, haven't they?' He paused on the verge of tears as self-pity surged through him. 'What a malodorous charade! I'm the chump. The diversion. Now, no-one believes that Watson wrote these letters. You have to give it to the scoundrels. They know how to manipulate the truth. A bloody shame for me.'

Oswald hung his head. 'It's not over yet, John.'

'Tell MacIntosh he doesn't have permission to show any of my damned letters to any damned expert. Just get them back!'

'But it could help.'

'No!' yelled Kingan, his hands slamming the armchair rests.

'I'll speak with Stirling.'

Kingan clenched and unclenched his hands. 'Why didn't you tell me all this sooner?'

'I was worried it would damage your health.'

Kingan snorted at his dissembling. He turned his head away. 'You can go now.'

Chapter 18
The Moral Burning

For the next week, Kingan stayed in his apartment stewing. Racked with an intense resentment at the deranged Watson, the treacherous Walkinshaw, the evil Aitken and the incompetent Oswald, his heart split with hatred.

His bitterness dispelled his lassitude. He went for a walk by the river for the first time in weeks, cane in hand, accompanied by a footman. He spotted Allston, a fellow Hodge Podger coming towards him and stopped, a welcoming smile on his face. The merchant, however, sneer on his thin face, eyes averted, hurried past him. Shaken, Kingan returned home.

The following days, anxiety for his future replaced bitterness. He brooded on his reputation. Would it ever recover? Could he live without attention? The clubs, the dinners, the balls, the theatre, the races. Conviviality was fickle. Good company abhorred deceit. Was that his fate?

He had no choice but to defend himself. Oswald was no help. Finlay, Hunter, Dunlop Donald. None of them had been in touch since this false report had started circulating. Nancy was the only person who had visited. But she was a woman.

#

Oswald sent a note. The London handwriting experts had been inconclusive. That hadn't stopped Watson, who appeared to have recovered from his distress. He learned from Nancy that the banker was spreading the word among the Govan gentry about his proof of Kingan's "corrupt and sinful calumny".

#

He decided to confront Walkinshaw. A rainy evening, he went to the traitor's house without warning. Startled, the young man showed him into his dining room, the dishes of his meal still on the cup-marked table. Kingan looked around. The floor was littered, the windows grimy. From the adjoining room came the sounds of an infant crying and an irate woman scolding.

There were no pleasantries. 'Why did you give Aitken my letters?'

'I didn't.'

'Don't lie!'

Walkinshaw breathed in. 'I gave them to Gilbert Watson.'

Kingan's eyes filled with loathing.

The other's head dropped. When he looked up, he said, on the verge of tears, 'He told me he had come, under the direction of Mr Stirling and Mr MacIntosh, with Mr Oswald's approval. They wanted a few letters for the arbitration. He pledged that they would only be viewed by the arbiters and returned directly to me.'

'And you didn't think of asking my permission?'

'Gilbert Watson insisted that I conceal the matter from you. I refused. But he threatened to take me to the magistrate.'

'With what?'

'Their verification,' he mumbled.

'What have they found out?'

'I can't say. Only, it would prejudice my financial situation. I was afraid. I relented.' He stared doe-eyed at Kingan. 'I'm sorry, Mr Kingan. Please forgive me.'

Kingan knew there was more to his story but pressing him for it would be unsuccessful. He looked around. Walkinshaw was clearly desperate. He had obtained what he wanted. 'Where are the letters now?'

'They haven't returned them.'

Next door, the crying had become wailing, the scolding, screeching. *It's useless seeking more*, he thought. He left.

#

Two days later, he sent this letter to the arbiters.

Gentlemen

I have delayed till the return of Mr Mackintosh to represent to you the nature and extent of a very grievous and cruel injury that has arisen to me, as I am informed, from your proceedings as arbiters in the reference between Mr Oswald and Mr Watson.

Having been confined to the house by severe indisposition, it was only lately that I learned that letters of mine had been obtained from my late partner Mr Walkinshaw which you had subjected to the opinion of an Edinburgh engraver who had reported that it was in the same handwriting as the anonymous letters which formed the subject of your reference. This opinion has now been published everywhere by Mr Watson as that of the arbiters and was received by the public as proof that I was the writer of these letters and Mr Watson was not.

On questioning Mr Walkinshaw how he came to give up a partnership letter for such a purpose without my consent, he made the following statement: Mr Gilbert Watson came to him, threatening him with a legal process to compel delivery of my writing adding that, no use whatever would be made of it beyond inspection by you, by whose authority, he had come to demand it. On which, Mr Walkinshaw so strongly beset and afraid of offending his bankers, gave up the letter in question.

The situation in which I am placed is one of great cruelty and singular novelty. Being no party to the appointment of you as judges, you are as to me without jurisdiction. Yet, you have put me on trial but without citation. Evidence is procured from one at the expense on his part of a breach of confidence. Your ex parte report comes forth to the world claiming the conviction and sentence. Execution follows, of course: a moral burning and branding of my good name and character.

It is a humiliation to have to defend one's self against such a charge but no alternative is left me. I beg leave to say that most humbly, I shall submit to your inquiry fully. May whatever disgrace and infamy my worst enemy may desire to inflict, come to me if I ever saw or heard of one of those letters till they came to the persons to whom they are addressed.

#

He waited a week for the arbiters' reply. They denied; *decidedly and unequivocally that you have to blame us for the injury which you say you have sustained and we trust we shall be able to prove that to every unbiased individual.* They claimed no knowledge of how the letters were procured from Walkinshaw nor of how the alleged report had appeared.

Raging, he wrote an urgent card to Oswald demanding he intervene and instruct them to offer him the opportunity to defend himself.

Within two hours, he had a reply from Oswald. He had just written to Stirling and MacIntosh. He would refuse to submit his report to the arbiters and impede the finalisation of the arbitration unless Kingan was interviewed.

That evening, Kingan received a note. The arbiters would visit him tomorrow afternoon.

#

Late afternoon, the two referees were shown to the drawing room. A fire raged in the white marble fireplace. Kingan knew Stirling well, MacIntosh less so, the scientist being an infrequent attender at social gatherings.

As the maid was serving tea, Stirling began, 'We don't want this to be a formal interview, John, more of a conversation. I hope with all my heart, we can reach a position suitable for us all. Believe me, this has not been an easy business. Can I just repeat what was in our letter? We regret deeply the injury that has been caused to you.'

MacIntosh nodded, his eyes, to Kingan, sincere.

'I appreciate that,' said Kingan.

'Tell us what irks you, John. Let's start with the anonymous letters. James told us you share his views about Watson's authorship.'

'I do,' replied Kingan.

'You received one yourself,' commented MacIntosh.

Kingan told them about the Gingham letter and his grounds for believing Watson had written it.

Stirling and MacIntosh listened intently.

'Do you mind telling us about your meeting with Mr Watson on the path by the Clyde?' asked MacIntosh on his finishing.

Kingan stiffened. This meeting was supposed to be about Walkinshaw giving his letters to the Watsons. He relented. 'Alright.'

He related his tale, avoiding the theatricality which had so angered Aitken. On finishing, he scrutinised their expressions. Stirling retained his sang-froid but

MacIntosh's lips were tight. He focused on the scientist, 'Does that meet your needs?'

'It does. Thank you.'

'As I said in my letter, my main qualm with you is with the documents obtained from my partner which were submitted to Mr Lizars, without my consent.'

'We assumed your consent had been obtained, John,' said Stirling. 'If we'd known that you hadn't agreed, we would never have considered them.'

'Nobody told us not to use them,' intervened MacIntosh.

Kingan grimaced. He didn't believe him but had no evidence with which to challenge him.

'John, we give you our word,' said Stirling. 'That our report will make no reference to your partnership letters with Mr Walkinshaw. Or for that matter, to what is called the Vinegar Note.'

Kingan glared at him. 'Will you put that in writing?'

'Of course.'

Kingan shifted in his chair. This wasn't enough. 'And this other report by Lizars.'

'We have nothing to do with that. It formed no part of our proceedings.'

'Can you not point out it's a falsehood?'

'We haven't seen it,' said MacIntosh. 'And it would be beyond our terms of reference to allude to it.'

Kingan wanted to shout out 'liar!' but restrained himself. Puce faced, his voice raised, he spat, 'You can't possibly believe that I'm the writer. If I'm guilty of that, I deserve to be hanged as high as Hammam!'

'We can only do what's in our terms of reference, John,' said Stirling firmly. 'It's not an open-ended legal investigation.' He paused. 'I recognise that this is most unpleasant to you. But we can't accede to your request.'

Chapter 19
Apology

In front of the open bible on the lectern, face reddened by the blazing fire, eyes half closed, palms upturned, Watson sang out in his strong baritone, 'O come, let us sing unto the Lord. Let us make a joyful noise to the rock of our salvation—' Flanking him, his enraptured wife and sons followed in plainsong harmony.

At the psalm's end, he paused, then intoned, 'These last days, Oh Lord, have threatened our lives. During the darkest of nights, I delved deep and long into why You, Master, had rebuked me. I uncovered the extent of my sinning. My wrath at my wickedness drove me into the trough of despond. But my faith is deep. Its power lifted me upwards towards Your light. And, today, I will receive my absolution. Thank You, My Lord. Thank You.'

'Thanks to the Lord,' came the enthusiastic chorus.

Watson smiled broadly at his family, who each, in turn, kissed him gently on the cheek. He wiped the tears of happiness from his eyes. In his core, he had recovered the certitude given by faith. He was ready.

#

Three hours later, eyes still bright, he sat with Gilbert in their bank's meeting room awaiting James Oswald. Between them on the table lay the arbiters' report, which had arrived the evening before. Oswald had capitulated and provided his own report two days before. Now, his hour of surrender was nigh. Watson reread his absolution:

With regard as to whether Mr Robert Watson had written or caused to be written or sent or caused to be sent, the anonymous letters referred to by Mr James Oswald, we have after most anxious and deliberate investigation come to the opinion that Mr Robert Watson did not write or send or cause to be written or sent, the anonymous letters alluded to.

With regard as to whether Mr James Oswald had such grounds as to warrant him believing that Mr Robert Watson was the author, we have come to the view that Mr Oswald had no such grounds.

On finishing, he turned to Gilbert, who returned his smile, saying softly, as he squeezed his hand. 'Victory comes to the just.'

'But the campaign continues.'

'It does. "The wages of the righteous is life, the income of the wicked, punishment."'

'And Kingan will earn his in full.' Watson's expression hardened. 'The money?'

'I've arranged it. Walkinshaw will receive the funds tomorrow.'

'You did well, driving him down.'

'Fifteen hundred is fair.'

It had been Watson's idea to have Oswald sign his letter of apology in front of the arbiters (because of Kingan's grumbles, Aitken was judiciously absenting himself). The ritual was to be the first "eye for an eye". The merchant had prevaricated then grudgingly agreed. Soon, the arbiters would arrive: Oswald would be bringing his letter, which Watson intended to use in his pursuit of Kingan.

#

MacIntosh arrived first, ebulliently shaking the brothers' hands. Then, Stirling, stern and reserved. They chatted while sipping tea, served in the white crockery embossed with "J&RW" in royal blue.

At the appointed time to the minute, Oswald entered, head high, chest out, alone. He proffered his faux bonhomie on the arbiters as if he had come upon them at the Tontine. He bowed to his erstwhile antagonist and on rising, extended his hand. Watson couldn't help but release a sigh of rapture. His face beaming, he flung his hand to take the others. He maintained his palm in his foe's waiting for the other to let go first. After a minute, Oswald did then perfunctorily shook Gilbert's hand. He straightened and pulled from the inside pocket of his emerald green frock coat, a folded page. Watson's face flushed.

'I have here my written apology, sir,' he announced to Watson, his eyes flat, his voice firm. 'If you would kindly attest to your acceptance of it as a fit document for our purpose. If accepted, I'll sign it.' He handed it to Watson.

Watson took it, then read it slowly. From yesterday, came one of Binning's sayings. *Believe and then you have overcome before you overcome and this will help you to overcome in your own person. Then consider the strong Helper you have, The Spirit.* His Faith had taken him to this moment. On finishing, he announced, 'I accept your gracious apology, Mr Oswald. I hope that from this day on, our families will resume the friendship we've enjoyed over many years.'

Oswald stood with a fixed smile. 'I hope so, Mr Watson,' he replied, his voice rasping. He went to the table where a quill and ink bottle was waiting and signed the letter. He rose, took a step back. 'I'm afraid I have some pressing business, Mr Watson. If you could excuse me?'

'Of course.'

Their eyes locked on each other. Watson searched for signs of his defeated foe's usual brazenness. Instead, he saw defiance, a defiance easily overcome.

Oswald shook his hand then each of the others and left.

As soon as the door closed, MacIntosh growled, 'Well done, sir!' He raised his teacup. Gilbert slapped Watson's back. Except for Stirling, they all laughed.

Five minutes later, the arbiters gave their apologies. As he exited, Stirling leaned over to Watson. 'I bumped into the Major yesterday. He asked me to tell you that he's waiting for a letter from you applying for membership in the Western. You need no proposers. You'll be approved at the next meeting.'

Struck speechless, Watson wiped the tears trickling down his cheeks. Stirling hurried out.

#

The room once again quiet, Watson ordered more tea. A footman came with coal and rekindled the fire. Once their underling had left, they remained still for some minutes, wallowing in their satisfaction.

'I was surprised by Oswald's meekness,' began Gilbert.

'It's skin deep.'

'He's desperate for it to be over.'

Watson's lips curled. 'For him.' He stared at Gilbert. 'We must start now on the next.'

'Next what?'

'Punishment. The Major told me my membership of the Western is in the bag. Once it's accepted, we can move to do to Kingan what he tricked Oswald into doing to me. Have him banned from the club and let the four corners of the earth know why.'

Gilbert frowned, then nodded his assent.

'We must build a watertight condemnation. We still have Oswald's arbitration letters, the Vinegar note. Lizars report.'

'And Miller's letter.'

Having seen Lizars report to the Watsons, Miller had handed over to Gilbert a letter his wife had received after his ball last year. She was still recuperating from its venomous comments about her dancing (*'you spoiled the whole concern with your hobbling and sweating. One gentleman said he could not get the smell of you out of his nose for two or three days'*), her husband's predilection for mulattas (*'The truth is honest John is more at home with the Black Woman.'*) and worst, her trying to live above her proper station (*'You have no idea of modesty. You were with people who were all above you in rank and education, yet you pretended you were on the line with them.'*).

Miller had concluded that the author had been Kingan and had given licence for the Watsons to use the letter against him.

'And MacIntosh.'

The scientist had written to them earlier. After the arbiters' interview with Kingan, they had spoken with Watson's cousin, Archibald Lawson, who had denied in the most strident terms, ever having met Kingan by the Clyde. If pushed, MacIntosh would confirm that he was of the opinion Kingan was a liar and probably wrote the letters.

'What about Stirling?'

'He wants nothing more to do with the affair.'

'We need more though,' declared Watson. 'Preferably, an eyewitness who saw Kingan writing the anonymous letters.'

'Bell can start fishing tomorrow.'

'The sooner, the better. Also, we need to hire a Writer to get everything down in formal statements.'

'I'll see to it. And Adam Aitken?'

Watson hesitated. 'We have much to thank him for. Commissioning the second report from Lizars was a masterstroke. But, let's keep this in the family from now on. I'll speak to him.'

Chapter 20
Lily Patrick

The bleach fumes hung in the air, trapped by the low-hanging grey clouds, streaked red by the timid sunrise. Well used to the stench, Lily still couldn't avoid her daily bout of coughing as the vapours tickled her throat. Once finished, she straightened and, with a full pail in each hand, staggered from the pump towards the light from the open back door. She cursed that she had forgotten her mittens. Inside, she dumped the pails on the kitchen floor with a grunt, taking care that only a few drops of water spilled over the brim. She shook off her muddy clogs at the back wall and plonked down on a three-legged stool.

Looking up, she glowered. Sitting opposite was the daily spectator, Jock the Coachman, waiting for his treat: the sight of her stockinged calves as she laced up her boots. At times, for her and Cook's merriment, she prolonged the act, smirking as the spit drooled down his pock-marked chin. Today, however, she wasn't in the mood. She tied them up as quickly as possible and took the pails over to the kitchen stove where Cook was stirring the porridge.

The two women smiled at each other. As Lily warmed herself, she cocked her head towards Jock but addressed Cook, 'Isobel's no' givin' him enuff agin.'

'Must be the new bairn.'

'Ah'm fed up fillin' in fir her,' sighed Lily, wiping her forehead with the back of her hand.

'The Master says he'll get a new maid in if she disnae show up tomorrow,' Cook shouted so that Jock could hear her menace.

He moved off. The door shut.

Lily squatted down by a pail. Hand-cupped, she drew some water and then sipped it like a cat. She looked dreamily out of the window at the courtyard, which Jock was crossing to the stables.

'Ye bidin' here for a minute?' asked Cook, wiping her brow.

'Naw,' replied Lily rising. 'I need tae sweep the stairs afore they get up. An' that man's comin' tae see me this efternoon.'

'Dinnae tire yersel' oot then,' chortled Cook. 'No, that ye normally dae!'

Thursday was a hard cleaning day: making beds, stacking clothes, changing towels, sweeping floors, airing the bedrooms, changing and washing the bedclothing and shining all the fittings and ornaments in the seven-roomed house.

In the hall, she retrieved the heavy broom from under the stairs. As she swept, her mind went over the events of five days before when she had visited home for the first time since she had started with Mr Cairnie, Manager of the Denny bleachfields, last year.

#

A card had come from her brother to her Master, saying her mother had been ill and requesting that Lily be permitted to visit. She had rushed to Govan. On reaching her parent's house, she had found her mother no more sick than she usually claimed. Her cobbler father hadn't taken long to come to the real reason for her visit.

He had met a Geordie Bell, whom she didn't know, once a coachman at Linthouse, now a porter at the Watsons' Bank. She knew Robert Watson from the Govan Kirk, having taken care as a child to avoid his austere countenance and reproachful eyes. Bell had had a proposal for the family. He had invited her father for a whisky in the backroom of the Buchanan Inn to discuss it. Excited at the chance of a sup at the village's best tavern, her mother had insisted on coming too.

Bell's proposal had been simple. Fifty pounds would be coming his daughter's way if she shared some information about her old master, Mr Kingan and his connection with certain letters he had written.

On her visit, seated at the table in the bare, dirt-floored room littered with his cobbling tools, her father had leaned over. 'It's fir ye talkin' aboot thae wicked letters the Quality hae been havin'. Mr Kingan's wrote them.'

Lily's eyes had glinted. 'Whit!' She had looked at her mother. 'Like the wan ye tauld me. Aboot the Auld Laird Rowan an' Widow Nanny Campbell.'

'Wheesht!' had scolded her mother.

'Aye, these,' had said her father.

Frowning, Lily had thought it over. '*Master Kingan writing these letters? Well, he likes a joke.* How much is he offerin'?'

'Fifty!' she had screeched having heard her father's response. On recovering her wits, she had said. 'I'll see whit this Geordie says.'

Her father had insisted she do the necessary, come what may. His eyesight was failing. Cobbling, always hard, had become even more so.

She'd just finished lifting the clothes off the floor in the second son's bedroom when she heard Jock. 'That's the man fae Glasgae t' see ye, Lily. He's waitin' in the kitchen.'

She cursed. She still had to air the mattress to finish the room. She went to the Master's bedroom and studied her pasty face with its light blue, round eyes, in the mirror on the Mistress's dresser. She shut her thin lips tight to hide the gap between her front teeth. She was sixteen but retained a childlike air. She pushed her mouse-brown hair under her bonnet, then straightened the white linen collar and the pleats in her black percale full-length dress. which drooped on her small, thin frame.

She thought of her old Master. She still felt bitter at having been sacked by him instead of Jeannie Hunter, who had deserved it more. She had overheard her current Master crowing at the dinner table that "Longman Kingan" was in trouble with Mr Watson, "an" may he suffer in hell for it!' He didn't deserve that. But fifty pounds! That could see her well for the rest of her life.

#

On entering the kitchen, her eyes narrowed when she saw a man in his late twenties, in a black velveteen coat and with a bright red handkerchief around his neck, seated at the kitchen table. A crumpled brown hat lay on the table. A grin spread across his high-cheeked face but his heavy-lidded eyes gleamed threat.

Nae bad, she thought. *'But be careful.'* She met his stare. 'Hello, Mr Bell.'

'Hello, Lily.'

She liked his Ulster accent. 'I prefer Miss Patrick,' she stated, putting on a Quality voice. 'But as a favour, you have my permission to use Lily.' She smirked before her expression hardened. 'Ma faither telt me ye were comin'.'

'He told you why?'

'Aye.' She looked over his head. The clatter of pots and pans in the basin accompanied Cook's cusses at Isobel's absence. Lily leaned over till her face was six inches in front of Geordie's. 'Ye're gaun tae gie me fifty pounds fir tellin' tales aboot Master Kingan.'

Bell's eyes widened. 'Fifty Pounds?'

'That's whit ye said to ma faither.'

'I did not.'

'Well, Ah'm nae doin' nuthin' fir less.'

He hesitated. Cook moved to the far end of the kitchen to retrieve a pan. 'Can we not go somewhere else to have this discussion?'

'I have my reputation to think of,' she retorted, eyes coquettish.

Bell grimaced. 'I'll speak with my employer about the reward. It depends on what you tell me about your old Master.'

'Afore Ah speak, Ah need tae know whit ye're gaunnae dae wi' whit Ah tell ye.'

Bell's face was etched with irritation. 'My employer is seeking justice regarding claims Mr Kingan made that he had written the letters among the Govan Quality?'

'Ah heard Mr Watson's daein' the same.'

He paused. 'That's why I'm here. I met with your old colleague, Mrs Hunter.'

'That auld bitch! How much are ye payin' her?'

'She says you used to carry letters for Mr Kingan.'

'Aye, Ah did.' She paused as her dander rose 'Whit mair's she been tellin' ye? She no give ye what ye want?'

'I've just spent three hours in a coach getting my arse bruised deep black,' he hissed. 'D'you think I'd be here if she told me what I want!' He calmed. 'Just answer my questions. Did you see Mr Kingan writing letters in the two years before you left his employ?'

'Aye.'

'Did you carry any that he wrote to the addresses on the letters or give any to a porter or take any to the post office?'

'Aye.'

'Which of them?'

'Ah'm definitely gaunnae get money fir this?'

'You are,' he sighed. 'I promise you as I promised your father.'

'An' Jeannie Hunter n'aw, if Ah ken her.' She hesitated, then stated, 'Ah didnae take any direct. He didnae like me wanderin' aboot the streets. But Ah did tak some tae the porters at the stance awn the corner ae Clyde Street an' ithers tae the post office.'

'I'm going to read a list of names. I want you to tell me if you carried any letters addressed to them. Alright?'

She nodded.

He took out a notebook and pencil stub from his coat pocket. 'Mr Colin Dunlop Donald?'

'Aye. Af'en.'

He made a tick. 'Mr Kirkman Finlay?'

'Aye.'

'Miss Agnes Oswald.'

'Ooh la! The delightful Nancy! No.'

He went through a list of forty persons, most of whom he and Watson's writer's agents had identified as recipients of anonymous letters. In the end, he said, 'You've told me you carried letters addressed to twenty persons. Are you definite that your master wrote them?'

'Aye, Ah am.'

He smiled. 'That's excellent, Lily. I'll let my employers know of your co-operation.'

'When am Ah gettin' ma money?'

'You'll have to go to the offices of a Writer in Glasgow to get it. A Mr Renny. I've got the money for your passage here and a wee bit extra for your trouble today. Take the mail coach tomorrow. I'll meet you at the final stop.'

'It'll tak' me a whole day tae get to Glasgae 'n' back,' she whinged. 'Ah cannae go. Isobel's aff sick. There's only me an' Cook.'

'You need to go if you want your money,' said Bell, eyes hard. 'And you'll need to give a statement about the letters. Mr Renny will ask you some questions about them.'

Her brow furrowed. 'An' that'll be aw there is tae it?'

'That's all.'

Chapter 21
The Avalanche of Grudges

The late spring sun barely warmed the drawing room. Kingan stared blankly at the white flowered trees with blue parakeets on grey branches against a lime green background. The Chinese wallpaper had arrived from Finlay's warehouse that morning. A roll had been set out over two occasional tables. His eyes took in nothing. He had lapsed back into "why me?" mode. The avalanche of grudges had submerged him again.

#

Oswald's cowardly apology rankled less than his refusal to backtrack on exculpating Watson for the letters. Kingan had written to him a month ago requesting this in writing, "The reply had been more" redolent more of a politician than a friend. Moreover, Oswald had declared himself now neutral in the matter. This had wounded Kingan deeply. That his best friend had pushed him into this hell was bad, but even worse, was his washing his hands of him. *God curse him!* thought Kingan on receiving the reply. They hadn't spoken since.

His mood curdled further as he imagined Watson's demented glee at his latest lying smear. He and his brother were putting it about that Kingan's episode of blindness had been caused by a thrashing. After learning of Kingan's lustful advances on his wife, Hagart had beaten him up after Miller's ball. Watson also held some letter purportedly written by Kingan about Miller's wife, so filthy that he couldn't let others see it apart from a few tasty snippets.

Only the odd invitation came, mainly from friends since the Grammar School. For a time, he had gone to the Western Club every couple of days. Excellent premises had been rented on the edge of the Blythswood Estate.

Demand for membership had surpassed expectations. For the Quality, it was the place to see and be seen. Having to catch an acquaintance's attention, however, then their excuses for cutting short conversations had dispelled any pleasure. He had given up going.

Two good Samaritans stopped him from falling more deeply into despond, Nancy and most strangely, Walkinshaw.

Walkinshaw had settled his arrears. The partnership had been dissolved. Kingan had thought of pursuing the young man. The money had obviously come from Watsons' payoff for his treachery. But he didn't want to kindle further interest in his affairs while the denigration was ongoing. Surely, it would pass. Anyway, the sum would pay for decorating his Blythswood house. At last, he could move from Clyde Street.

He had spent hours oohing and aahing with Nancy, sprawled over catalogues of wallpapers, furniture and fitting, their eyes moving from page to page, then to each other, checking for excitement or indifference. Her warm approval of his tastes had comforted him.

The thought that soon he would be in her sparky presence broke through his ennui. His focus returned. He studied his purchase more closely, then smiled wanly. It would look good in the new drawing room.

#

Mrs Copperhwaite knocked and entered.

'Are you receiving Miss Oswald here, Master,' she asked. 'Or the new house?'

'Here, Ishbel.'

She looked at his padding dressing gown.

'I'll dress,' he said, embarrassed by his appearance of lassitude.

In his dressing room, he flicked through his wardrobe and then tried on various permutations of frock coats, trousers, cravats and waistcoats. He was unable to choose. Eventually, he put on a vaguely remembered combination. He studied himself in the mirror and then shivered. It was the same attire as for Miller's ball. He changed into a crimson velvet frock coat with a matching waistcoat, trousers and cravat. Relieved, he went to the drawing room. Its pink walls reflected the newly brightened afternoon sun.

A few minutes late, Nancy entered. He admired her copper-coloured, chine silk gown with patterned red and white rose bouquets. Her patchouli scent made his skin tingle. He inhaled deeply as she loosened her starched bonnet, which she handed to the maid, letting her ringlets hang loose. He took her hand and kissed it. The warmth in their eyes flowed as they waited for the maid to depart.

'Sans turban aujourd'hui?'

'Mais oui, Monsieur!' She looked him over, her expression one of tender concern. 'You look thin, John.'

As always, with her use of his Christian name, he flushed. 'You know what it's like, Nancy.'

'Poor you.' She took his hand and squeezed it. He led her to the wallpaper. 'It's perfect!' she exclaimed, clapping her hands.

He chuckled, her spark cheering him.

'It will go well with the new sofas.'

They discussed their plans for the room's décor, then moved on to the contrasting style of the dining room, engrossed in the detail of cornices and inlays, vases and carpets. Exhausted, they went to sit side by side on the sofa.

He faced her. Her expression turned stern. He wondered what was coming.

'I have some news, John.'

'Yes?'

'About Watson.' She hesitated. 'I met Miss Catherine at the Kirk's last Sabbath. She told me he and his cousin, Archibald Lawson, had visited George Rowan the previous Wednesday, ostensibly to discuss some open-air gospel readings the two are planning with Reverend Matthew. But that was a cover. The true reason for their visit was to bad mouth you.'

His lips curled. 'What's new?'

'Archibald Lawson was the more forthright of the two. He declared repeatedly that he had never ever met you on the riverside pathway. He called your note, "a total farrago".'

His head drooped. It had come. 'That note,' he moaned. Then, turning on the object of his most severe recrimination, himself, he yelled, 'Fool that I am!'

She shrank back. 'That's a bit dramatic, John!' She peered into his eyes. 'Why does the note perturb you so?'

He remained silent, his eyes away from hers, turned to the floor.

'You didn't meet Watson that evening,' she said more quietly. 'Did you?'

Flushing, he shook his head. 'It was a joke,' he said, voice trembling. 'For you. I thought you understood to be so.' Then, with a bitterness, he added, 'It wouldn't have mattered if your brother hadn't blabbed about it. Without my permission.'

'Oh, John!' she sighed. She went to his side and lightly kissed his forehead. He bowed his head and wept. She gently rubbed his back. 'You meant no harm.'

Her caress stilled his impulse to flee. After a minute, he drew back from her.

'Do you want a brandy?' she asked.

'No,' he said, not wanting a servant to see him in this state.

She waited a minute. 'There's more, John.'

He looked at her, moist eyes wide.

'Watson claimed to have a witness who saw you writing the letters and then took them for delivery to known recipients of the Govan letters.'

His mouth fell open.

'Miss Catherine told me that he's not saying who's the witness,' she continued. 'Presumably, it's a servant.'

It took him a minute before words came. 'I've had many servants over the years. Maids, housekeepers, cooks, coachmen, footmen.'

'You told us at Shieldhall that there was a maid who might have been involved in your first letter, the one you suspected came from Gilbert Watson.'

'Oh, her. Lily.' He searched his mind. 'Paterson or something like that. She left on bad terms. She was a good worker but she and the cook, Mrs Hunter, argued all the time. Their shouting got too much. Chastisement made no difference. One of them had to go. It hadn't been difficult. Mrs Hunter had worked at the barracks. She made the most delicious curry. I gave the servant girl a good reference.'

Her pale features and cocky attitude came back to him. 'She had some spirit, but I don't think she would become involved in something like this, though.'

'My mother says all servants have their price. And there's no better operator in the market than Watson.' She fixed her eyes on his. 'You need to match his skulduggery, John or you're frit.'

'It'll blow over, Nancy. These things always do.'

'It won't. Watson's insatiable for your downfall.'

The firmness in her tone made him stare at her.

'You need a lawyer, John. No one's helping you get out of this.'

'Least of all, your brother.'

Nancy's eyebrows rose. She paced to the middle of the room. 'My mother is most displeased with him. You know about Mary MacLean?'

He hesitated, conscious of his having sworn confidentiality to Oswald. That accord, however, was now null. 'He told me about her and his daughter. Watson knows of them. It was in James' letter.'

'She's pregnant again.'

Kingan grinned ruefully.

'There's more. Barrowfield Mill is oozing losses. He's agreed on a loan with a group of banks to bail him out. The mill is its surety.'

'With Watson?'

'No, but Aitken's in the mix.'

He shook his head, thinking, *Could it get any worse.* 'Your brother's as useless at business as he is at keeping his trousers up,' he hissed.

She laughed throatily.

'You find it amusing?' he challenged.

'The way you said it.'

He took in her smiling face. A feeling of warmth swept him up. He rose and took her hands. Surprised, she laughed again. They stood thus for a minute, each one's glowing eyes on the other. After what seemed an hour, they separated.

An uncertainty fell on him. 'You won't tell anyone about the note?'

'Of course not!' She winked. 'It's our secret. The first of many.'

Chapter 22
The Financial World

Watson sat at his favourite table at the Western, beside the window overlooking the corner of St Vincent Street and Buchanan Street. He came to the club at least twice a week now: to lunch and, more importantly, to be invited. Oswald's apology had erased the blackballing's effect on his reputation. Sympathy for his plight had made him approachable.

He surveyed the street below. Suddenly, the throng pulled back. A bag had fallen and splashed. A young woman screeched. She got to her knees to capture the trout writhing on the ground. A redheaded urchin darted from the door of Munsie's hut with its panoramas of Waterloo, scooped the prize and sprinted up Mitchell Lane. The white-bonneted maid chased him. After a moment, she returned, shoulders heaving. 'Keep a tight grasp on what you have,' he whispered to himself.

He lifted his head. A smiling Aitken strode across the room. Watson rose, wiped his hands on a napkin and shook hands.

They usually met a couple of times a month to go over the financial world. He looked upon their business relationship as an alliance, the wise walking the wise.

'How are you, Robert?' asked Aitken, eyes gleaming, as he took his seat.

'Well and you, Adam?'

'Hale and hearty!'

Usually, at this juncture of their encounters, they would share the recent gossip about Glasgow commerce. Today, however, Watson's mind was on other matters.

'I have some good news about Kingan,' he announced.

Aitken's eyes widened. 'From that maid?'

Watson grinned. 'We found her. She's been most helpful. Gave a statement to Renny that she saw Kingan writing letters, which she took for delivery during the dates we provided. Renny and Bell had identified thirty recipients of the anonymous letters. Bell read her a list of forty names to her, the thirty and another ten Quality with no links to the letters.'

Watson sat back. 'She identified twenty who we knew had received anonymous letters. Three of them had told us that they had never ever received a letter or card signed by Kingan. She had taken letters or cards addressed to all three either to the post office or to a porter. Not one of the ten we threw in was identified by her. Renny repeated the same exercise with the same result.'

Aitken clapped his hands. 'Well done, Robert!'

'Bell did well.'

'He's a good servant to you.'

Watson smiled. 'He's a very good servant.'

'Keep him close. His type is essential.'

'He has attention to detail. I noticed it when I first started him as a groom at Linthouse. The way he relaxed the horses before brushing, the preparation of the combs and picks, the thoroughness of the wash. I sent him to the Kirk school for a couple of years, then made him a coachman. Now, he's my eyes and ears on the street.'

'Do you still intend to use the maid's statement to have Kingan expelled from the Western?'

Watson nodded. 'Until the wrongdoer pays back for the wrongs he has done, there can be no partiality. Her statement will clinch it. The Joker will be swallowing vinegar until his last days on earth.'

'Good for the gout!'

They laughed. The waiter arrived to take their orders.

After he had gone, Aitken asked, 'Are you sure you don't need my help?'

'Very sure, Adam. You've done enough. What happens next must be perceived as being purely between myself and Kingan. We've taken care of Oswald.'

Aitken nodded. 'He won't intervene. Especially now. After the loan.'

They moved on to the financial situation. Aitken shared details of a meeting he had attended with the Bank of Scotland directors. The number of bank bankruptcies was shooting up. What had been a downturn was turning into a crisis, sparked by Gregor McGregor, a disgraced army officer. He had invented a South American country and had issued worthless bills and bonds, all avidly bought up. The scam had come crashing down. Now, the Treasury was being forced to curtail banks issuing promissory notes.

'Because of that fool,' hissed Aitken. 'We'll all have to tighten up.'

Watson sat quietly. The decrease in the availability of loans had shrunk the level of trade in general and in bills of contract in particular. Merchants were more wary and argumentative. His margins had tightened these last months, forcing him to safeguard his savings.

'Perhaps it's a good thing, Adam,' he wondered out loud. 'Thrift and sobriety have been lacking in our world for some time.'

'You're right. Look at Kingan and his new house.'

Watson's nose wrinkled at the mention of his foe. 'Modesty is his life-long enemy.'

'He'll pay soon.'

'With all this turmoil in our world, the quicker the better.' Watson lowered his voice. 'He's become close to Miss Agnes Oswald.'

Aitken's eyebrows rose. 'Her latest?'

'They've been seen together at Finlay's warehouse. Without a chaperone. Splashing money on Chinese porcelain and the like.' He stilled, eyes flinty. 'He has no shame.'

'Do you think she knows that he wrote that letter to her? The one about the printed gown.'

'If she does, she's hiding it.'

'Maybe it makes no difference to her.'

'I wouldn't put her past that. I've always had my suspicions. All that adoration of everything French.'

Chapter 23
The Clawman

Ishbel Copperthwaite didn't like the fleshers, especially at six in the morning, with the dripping carcasses being brought in after slaughter in the back shop. But Dr Cowan had insisted and she was keeping to his instructions; liver, preferably lamb, at least once a week. Keeps the blood thin and the skin bright, he had said. Vitality in every pound.

And she couldn't trust the new maid, Morag, now by her side, after the grey, off-smelling, irremediable lump brought back last week. She would do the ordering and let Morag hold the bag with the liver at arms-length to keep the blood from staining her gown. Ishbel would beat off the dogs.

She had pointed out her choice and was waiting for it to be cut when she felt a tug on her gown. She turned.

'You're the women who's looking for tales?' asked in Gaelic a thin, red-haired lass.

A half hour later, on returning to the half-empty apartment at Clyde Street, the flitting to Blythswood having begun, she waited until her Master's breakfast dishes had been cleared. She fidgeted with the top of her apron. 'As you asked, Master, I put the word around bout Lily Patrick. This morning, a Senga McLeod, not long arrived from Skye, came to me at the flesher's. She had some news.'

'Oh,' said Kingan, putting the Herald down.

'She's a waitress at the George Hotel. Last week, she served a man with a claw.'

'A claw?'

'That's what she calls a withered hand.'

Kingan's ears pricked. It must be Gilbert Watson. 'Go on.'

'He was with an old man who always takes tea at ten, at the George. They call him the Major.'

'Monteath.'

'Senga said there was a strange force coming out of the claw, which was resting on the table. She stood off, getting up the courage to take the Clawman's order. The Clawman mentioned something about Lily to the Major, then your name came up. Senga's English's not the best. She heard "committee" a few times. She had no idea what that was. But from the way they talked, she worked out it must be some form of gang or coven.'

'Must be the Western Club Committee.'

Mrs Copperthwaite's lips curled. 'What does it all mean, Master?'

'Nothing good.'

After she had left, he went to his office and rummaged in his desk drawer. He found the monthly communication from the Western. The next committee was in three days.

#

Ten minutes later, a gig was taking him to the offices of Wright and MacDowell Writers, his newly hired lawyers.

A clerk showed him to Wright's office. Light streamed through the iron-barred window, painting the long room in different shades of brown. The lawyer was sitting behind a battered table. At two corners rested unsteady piles of documents. In front of the lawyer were two fat, leather-bound books, both open. Behind him was an open glass-doored bookcase stuffed with ledgers. More paperwork was deposited on top of it and on the floor.

Wright, a tall stooping man with grey hair, rose and shook Kingan's hand, then motioned him to sit. He moved some papers from the ash chair in front of the table onto the desk.

'What a coincidence! I was just composing a card. We've found her.'

'Where?'

'In Denny. At a Mr Cairnie's. The proprietor of the bleachfields.'

Kingan cringed.

'You know him?'

'From my days in the muslin trade. He's an oaf.'

He fixed Wright with a steady stare. 'I too have some news. I believe Watson is on the point of having me expelled from the Western Club.'

Wright pursed his lips. 'What makes you think that?'

Kingan explained what he had heard this morning.

'Interesting,' reflected Wright.

'I think that we need to get to the maid urgently. I believe he's going to use her words at the Committee which meets on Friday.'

'That soon.'

'Yes. He probably has a statement from her claiming I wrote anonymous letters. We need to find out what she's said to whom? Then, contradict her at the club.'

Wright thought over his words for a minute. 'She's biddable?'

'Maybe, if we handle her correctly. Get her to rescind her words or, failing that, reveal enough to cast doubt on what she's said to Watson's people.'

Wright nodded. 'We need a statement from her. I'll go myself to Denny tomorrow. I'll send a card now to this Cairnie demanding he make her available or face redress.'

#

Late morning the next day, Thursday, Kingan received a note from Wright saying he had been tied up in court. He cursed the lawyer and rushed round to his office. He was shown to Wright's partner, MacDowell. Flustered, Kingan explained his predicament and pleaded with MacDowell to interview Lily that afternoon. MacDowell, a short man with a sturdy torso and florid face enclosed in grey, mutton-chop sideburns, took pity and agreed. As time was pressing, he asked Kingan to accompany him to Denny and brief him on the case during the journey.

In the gig, MacDowell had so many questions about Lily, the letters, the arbitration that Kingan became even more anxious. His answers became terse. Eventually, exasperated, he blurted, 'If it would help, I could speak to Lily directly.'

'That wouldn't be helpful. It could prejudice the legal standing of her statement.'

'But she trusts me.'

'You sure? You dispatched her.'

'I can't just go all the distance to Denny and sit in the coach! This needs to be settled today.'

MacDowell frowned. 'Alright. Here's what we'll do. I'll take the statement alone. I'll pass it on to you. If there's anything I've missed. I'll question her further.'

Kingan sighed, 'Alright.'

The mood between them had soured with the exchange. To lighten it, Kingan decided to tell MacDowell a joke.

'You know Cairnie can't hold his drink.'

MacDowell shook his head.

'When fu', he's a total boor. One night, after a long quaffing, he came home at a questionable hour. Along with manifold scuffs and bruises, he had a bloody gash on his forehead.'

'How did ye get that?' asked his grump of a wife.

'I bit mysel',' said Cairnie.

'How could you bite yourself on your forehead?'

'Ah shtood on a chair.'

MacDowell's tilted his head back in laughter. Relieved, Kingan joined in, camaraderie established.

#

Thirty minutes later, they removed the handkerchiefs from their lower faces as they presented themselves at the bleachfield offices. A clerk told them to wait. A minute later, a tall and well-built man in his thirties arrived. He didn't extend his hand and said in a Yorkshire accent, 'I'm Mr Hall, Mr Cairnie's foreman.' He looked them over. 'The note said there would be one person, a Mr Wright.'

'We're neither,' responded McDowall his feet wide apart. 'I'm Mr McDowall, Mr Wright's partner.' He turned. 'And this is Mr Kingan. He's—'

Hall cut across. 'The letter writer? Why's he here?'

'My client accompanied me on the journey to brief me. Otherwise, we would have missed the appointment.'

Hall glared at Kingan, who returned his stare.

'Alright,' said the foreman after a moment.

He escorted Kingan to a storeroom, then took MacDowell to the meeting room where Lily was waiting. Hall went to sit with the maid, but the lawyer objected. A heated exchange ensued, the foreman making it clear he was following Cairnie's instructions. It ended with the lawyer threatening legal action. Hall left.

Kingan sat frozen in the damp and ill-lit room, rising occasionally to pace from wall to wall for warmth. He was near the end of his tether when McDowall entered. 'How did it go?'

'Well. She's coy. Not a bad witness. Frightened about what Cairnie might do to her with you being here.'

'She told you what Watson wanted?'

'As we expected. About her carrying letters written by you. A Glasgow Writer took a statement. She didn't tell me who. I asked her about the names she'd given. At first, she was steadfast in her refusal to tell me.'

Kingan grimaced.

'After pushing, she did give me some names off her own bat. Here's the list.' He handed over his notebook.

Kingan studied it, then smiled. 'Good!' He paused, remembering the few times he had handed over letters to her. She had simply taken them and gone. 'I don't ever recall her reading.'

'I'll ask her about her learning. Any more questions?'

'No.'

As MacDowell opened the door, Kingan heard the rapid clacking of nailed boots on the stone floor.

'Oi!' shouted MacDowell. 'Come here!'

Kingan went into the hall but she was gone. 'Get Hall,' he ordered.

Just then, the front door opened and in strode the foreman with a flushed, fiery-eyed maid in a vice-like grip. He led her up to Kingan, who had joined MacDowell halfway down the dim passage. Hall let her go.

She shook herself, smoothed her white apron and straightened her bonnet. Head high, eyes clear, she stared at Kingan, then lowered her eyes and curtsied. 'Mr Kingan.'

She's lost none of her obduracy, thought Kingan. 'Hello, Lily,' he said cheerily as she rose.

She fixed her eyes on a point above his head, stood straight like an infantryman.

'Why are you doing this, Lily? Were you not treated well?'

A flicker of a smirk crossed her face, but she remained silent.

He glared at her, his mind revolting at the thought of being at the mercy of a servant girl. Her eyes glinted fearlessly. Angered, he went to reproach her but conscious of Hall's threatening presence, he said nothing. He turned to MacDowell. 'I don't think we have any more questions for Miss Patrick. Do we?'

'Not for now.'

Chapter 24
Facedown

The Western Club Committee met at eight. Around the table sat a selection of the city's gentlemen of honour with their tailored frock coats, well-cut hair and manicured fingers. The Major sat on the President's chair, his blue velvet sleeves on its gilded armrest. Behind him, the woven crest of the club, its initials embossed in gold thread against Glasgow's fish, tree and silver bell. He called the meeting to order.

For an hour, the meeting proceeded smoothly, paced by the Major's commanding manner. At the end of the last item on the agenda, Kirkman Finlay, his bald head shining in the chandelier light, put his hand up. 'Mr President, I wonder if I may make a point?'

'Of course.'

'I've heard, Mr President, that you're going to make a communication to this meeting on behalf of Mr Robert Watson.'

A stillness settled over the room. The once MP for the Clyde Burghs always commanded attention.

The Major cleared his throat. 'No. You're mistaken.'

Finlay stiffened and sucked in his cheeks. His composure recovered, he said firmly, 'I have reliable information that you met with Mr Gilbert Watson last week and agreed with him a statement to put to this Committee. It alleges that Mr John Kingan wrote these accursed letters in Govan and should therefore be expelled from this club.'

Gasps filled the room.

'Can you appraise us of the statement?' asked Finlay.

Instead of his usual gruff tone, a squeaky "It's been withdrawn" came from the Major's mouth.

'When will it come?'

'I don't know.'

'Mr President, I request that if Mr Watson is to be given the opportunity to present such a case to the Committee, then Mr Kingan should be accorded the right to defend himself in person.'

'This is not a court of law, Mr Finlay,' growled the Major. 'But I assure you if Mr Watson submits such a case, Mr Kingan will be asked to defend himself.'

'Given that we've just heard that Mr Gilbert Watson has already insinuated Mr Kingan's guilt to you, the President of our club, I move that Mr Kingan be given the opportunity now.'

The Major pressed his lips together and looked round the table. 'Any objections?'

The arm of Watson's second cousin, Allston, shot up. 'Mr Robert Watson is due to meet me here in an hour. I move that he be given the chance to present as well.'

Several members called, 'Aye.' But more groaned. After much grumbling, a "no" rang out.

Sir John Maxwell of Pollok spoke up. 'Mr President, this Committee was not established to resolve disputes about matters which have taken place outside the club. I move that neither member should be asked to present and that the matter should be considered closed.'

'Hear, hear' sounded from the majority around the table. Allston and a few others sat glumly.

Finlay, who had sat through the exchanges with a bitter smile, declared, 'I withdraw the proposal.'

Five minutes later, the Committee broke up.

#

Finlay found Kingan sitting alone at the back of the reading room.

Kingan looked up warily at his school friend's approach. 'What happened?' he blurted.

Finlay flopped down into a chair. 'We won and we lost. Watson's not got you expelled. In fact, he didn't even try, although Monteath cackhandedly revealed there had been a plot. Cairnie obviously told Watson about your visit to the servant girl. They pulled their case.'

Kingan pursed his lips then croaked, 'And the loss?'

'The overall mood in there was antagonistic. Most of the Committee still resent that Oswald brought dishonour to the club so soon after its opening. Some believe in Watson's fantasy that you put him up to it. To me, the problem now, however, is with the waverers. Because Watson pulled his petition, it looked to them that you were dragging the Western back into the cesspit.'

'But it was Watson who started it!'

'We're not in the playground, John. You need to keep your calm.'

Finlay took out from his inner coat pocket the two pages Kingan had given him earlier. The first was Lily Patrick's statement to MacDowell, the second from her old enemy:

Mrs Hunter, the deponent, stated that when Lily Patrick first came to work at Mr Kingan's household, she was very deficient in reading and writing. When she was sent with letters or cards, she applied to the Deponent to read the addresses for her. The Deponent told her the places to which the letters should be delivered, putting those uppermost which were nearest and so on with the others.

Kingan took them, then head drooped, stared blankly at the floor. Watson had swerved past his trap. Worse, the whole manoeuvre had rebounded. Now, he was even more the villain. After a moment, he asked, 'what do you think I should do?'

'The matter is in the court of public opinion, John.' Finlay's eyes narrowed. 'Many feel sympathy towards Watson, who's been seen to have suffered greatly. Many attribute that to you rather than Oswald. His distancing from you backs them up. You need to find a way to win back the favour of a key proportion of the gentry so they doubt Watson's calumnies. Then sit it out.'

Kingan brooded over his friend's words. He found it incredible that good company empathised more with a stuffed shirt like Watson than him. Then he remembered. He lifted his head, eyes sparkling. 'I've just received an invitation to a Turtle Dinner here, sponsored by the Earl of Glasgow. My stock can't be that low.'

Finlay smiled. 'You're still a popular man, John. As I said your good nature will win over the crowd. Just keep being seen.'

Kingan chuckled. 'Let's see if we can be at the same table.'

They chatted in a more upbeat manner for a few more minutes before Kingan excused himself.

The following week, he received a letter from the Secretary of the Western Club. Several members had objected to his presence at the Turtle Dinner. As such and unfortunately, the club had no choice but to withdraw his invitation.

Chapter 25
Housewarming

Kingan watched her nudging the Wedgewood vases on the heavy dark brown pedestals in the drawing room so that their matching gold and blue floral patterns were exactly parallel. The great double bay window was open, the bright sun giving the pink heavy velvet drapes an iridescent hue. The air was warm and fresh; the street noise sporadic and low.

'Perfect!' he cooed.

She turned and smiled in appreciation. 'Almost ready.'

'Happy?'

She pressed her lips together. 'The urns in the dining room corners are starker than these.'

'I thought that's what you wanted. The contrast in styles between the two principal rooms. Gothic versus Rococo.'

'But the Gothic should have some flourishes, like in Scott's new house.'

He knew to what she was referring. She and Margaret had visited Abbotsford. Margaret had taken copious sketches. But searching for replicas had taken weeks. 'These'll do for the moment. We can look for the necessary after the housewarming dinner.'

Her eyes took on the coquettish sparkle, which delighted him so much. 'Promise?'

He laughed. 'I do.'

She had virtually taken over supervising the move to Blythswood Place. At times, their discussions had taken on an edge. Her insistence on the incorporation of Wedgewood plaques in the reception room fireplace had driven him to distraction. But he had acceded.

Her irrepressibility had brought him some lightness after the facedown at the Western and the withdrawal of the invitation to the Turtle Dinner. The Quality's ongoing shunning smothered his spirit. He had almost lost the will to fight Watson. She had urged him to resist, agreeing fulsomely with Finlay's advice about keeping up appearances to eventually regain favour.

To her, however, the dinner party had been more about sending than responding to invitations, which anyway had now dried up. 'Take the whip hand! What could be better than a gathering of your friends? Here. Where they'll see you've never stopped being at the acme of taste and generosity.'

He had baulked at the very idea. Eventually, he wearily gave up resisting her and agreed to a housewarming dinner party. As the day approached, however, trepidation re-established its reign.

#

The day of the dinner, he was in the dining room, standing by a table that two footmen were polishing when he jerked to attention. The dull morning matched his mood. He heard her in the hall. He frowned and turned on his heels.

'I thought we agreed not to meet before the ball?' he said brusquely, on her arrival from downstairs.

Eyes wide, she stared at him.

He took her over to the window, looking down over his still-to-be-planted garden. 'We mustn't be seen as host and hostess. Watson'll make hay of it.'

'He already is, John,' she breathed.

He clenched his jaw. 'We don't need to give him more opportunities.'

She sighed. 'Alright. I know what you're saying. I'm sorry. But since I'm here, I'll check on a few things. The kitchen?'

'The housekeeper is perfectly capable.'

She drew back. 'What's troubling you?'

His eyes dulled. 'There are more.'

'Oh—' She tried unsuccessfully to fix her eyes on his. 'How many?'

'Eight. It's now twenty-eight out of forty invited.' They had selected the invitees because of their presumed loyalty to him. 'I'll cancel,' he moaned.

'You mustn't,' she said firmly. 'The damage would be worse,' she paused, then put on a smile. 'Twelve is such a manageable number for fun!'

'Fun?' he blurted. 'And this?' He pointed to the long mahogany table from which the footmen were withdrawing the extensions.

'The evening's going to be a success. We'll make it so!'

He grimaced. 'Let's go with it. But you mustn't stay long just now.'

'I'm just off to the kitchen.'

As she left, he felt a stabbing pain in his right foot. 'Oh, Blessed God, no!' he said to himself. 'The wine!' He had been drinking at least a bottle a night these last days. He went to lie down in his bedroom.

After finishing downstairs and being told he was sleeping, Nancy left.

#

Two hours later, he woke and went to dress. An ache remained. He rang for a servant to bring a draft of laudanum and, after some soul searching, a carafe of brandy.

At seven, in his deep red velvet frock coat and bright purple cravat, he gingerly descended the main staircase, with its new Axminster carpet with woven crimson, yellow, white and lilac dahlias, chosen by Nancy to mirror those in Shieldhall, spilling over the green chevrons. He took up a welcoming position facing the door in the reception room.

Finlay and his wife arrived first, then the Dunlop Donalds, the Kippens from Busby and, to his relief, a stiff Oswald. He felt light, giving out breezy welcomes, returning the invitees' responses with his old gusto.

After four more couples, Nancy arrived with her mother and Margaret. Their carriage had been delayed by mud on the toll road from the heavy afternoon rain. He looked on with pleasure as she smoothed the silver silk gown with gold stripes she had bought for the occasion. She and he loved the new style of flounces, belts and trimmings, especially the conch shell ornamentation at the bottom. To his delight, she had on a matching turban.

He welcomed them with his old brio. Nancy waited until Margaret had led her mother to the drawing room, where a preordained armchair lay by the black golden veined marble fireplace, before asking, 'Your gout is bothering you?'

'A little,' he chuckled. 'How do you know?'

'Your eyes,' she scolded. 'No matter.'

'James is here,' he said breathlessly.

'On time, for a change. You've spoken to him?'

'A little.' He shrugged his shoulders. 'Times are hard for him just now. The problems with the loans. I thank Our Maker, I'm out of it.'

'You didn't comfort him, did you?'

He looked down.

She rolled her eyes.

Her rebuke chaffed him. 'Remember, we've agreed not to be seen too much together,' he said curtly.

She turned sharply and moved off.

Despite the excellence of the fayre and the frequent refilling of glasses, the mood around the table was subdued, resembling more a Minister's gathering than a John Kingan party. He sat at the top of the table, Finlay (flanked by Mrs Oswald) and Nancy opposite. Kippen to his left and Dunlop Donald to his right.

He hardly touched the food. After the fish course, he felt her eyes on him and slowed down the rate as he was refilling his glass. By dessert, the table grew merrier. He listened to the reminiscences. He appreciated that some were serving him entrees to an anecdote. He couldn't respond, however. The laudanum had slowed him too much. By the last of the seven courses, he was seriously flagging. He looked up searchingly and caught Nancy's eye. To his relief, she smiled. He noticed that her mother was looking at them. He looked away and redoubled his efforts to get through the evening.

The meal ended, the party rose, the men passing to the drawing room, the women staying at the table.

Kingan waited for the drink to be served and the cigars to be lighted. He sat in the armchair previously occupied by Mrs Oswald. Around him, on other armchairs and on the two velvet-covered sofas, were individuals six months ago he would have called "friends", now "supporters".

Finlay opened the conversation. 'You look weary, John.'

'My gout troubles me.'

'That's not all, John. Be honest.'

'I am being truthful.'

'Well, I'll tell you what bothers me about you. This business with Watson.'

Kingan heard a mumbling of assent. He looked at Oswald, who turned his head. *Judas*, he thought. He hesitated, wishing Nancy was with him. 'You're right, Kirkman. That business at the Western—'

'He won't stop, John,' intervened Dunlop Donald, his long face showing rare signs of animation. 'He'll find other opportunities.'

'You've become a figure of fun, John,' said his old partner, Kippen. 'You've even replaced the bankers.'

Heads turned to Oswald, who remained silent. Finlay picked up the baton. 'I spoke to Gilbert Watson last week. He's more—How can I put it? Less biblical in his censure. But he was strident. Their end game is your humiliation, a public confession of authorship of these letters and of your plot to divert the blame onto Robert Watson.'

Kingan's face reddened. 'It's Watson who should apologise.' He looked around at their faces. All were stony. 'You know that, James,' he implored.

Oswald shifted in his armchair. 'I know you didn't write these letters. But neither did Robert Watson.'

'He did!'

Oswald shook his head. 'To my cost, I know he didn't.'

Kingan's eyes blazed as resentment at betrayal returned.

Finlay intervened, 'John, I've no idea who wrote these letters. I know it wasn't you. Maybe it was Watson. But, unless you take him on directly with a well, thought-out case, you will never recover your reputation. You'll become a hermit—and that'll kill you.'

'But you told me to ride it out. I have been. I haven't said a word about Watson being the author since the affair at the Western.'

'And what good's it doing to you?' Finlay hesitated. 'My advice was ill-founded. I apologise.'

'You must fight, John!' shouted Dunlop Donald in exasperation.

The others nodded.

'How?' cried Kingan in a querulous voice.

'In the Courts. Nothing else will work.'

All except Oswald grunted their assent.

He shuddered. The Courts would mean the public having a field day, feasting on his humiliation.

He lifted his eyes and looked at the cameo of his Minister father above the fireplace. A kind father who could never have imagined that his son would end up with their good name in the stocks. Branded a lying scoundrel by Watson, a scabrous evil-doer who had carried out the very heinous acts for which the name Kingan was being tarred. His eyes turned feverish in their hatred.

Chapter 26
Mr Jeffrey

Kingan looked over the waiting room, its opulence gratifying his expectations: the silk-covered upholstery, rosewood occasional tables, marble fireplace and German hunting scenes on the walls. Soon he would meet its owner, Mr Francis Jeffrey, leader of the Whigs in Scotland, Defender of Radicals, Editor of the Edinburgh Review and most importantly the celebrated advocate who had secured the acquittal of James Stuart who had owned up to killing another in a duel. The choice had been easy if expensive.

A gangly youth entered, bowed and introduced himself as Mr Jeffrey's clerk. He led Kingan up a sun-filled corridor to a well-polished door, which he knocked on and opened slightly. A baritone voice commanded, 'Come in.'

Jeffrey moved to the front of his desk, his smile welcoming, his dark blue eyes piercing. His black, speckled grey hair was swept back revealing a high forehead, his sideboards encasing a thin, handsome face with an air of amused interest. He wore a white cravat around his neck, between the high collar of a dark blue velvet frock coat. He extended his hand.

'Welcome, Mr Kingan,' he said, firmly grasping the other's hand. 'The witty, keen-sighted and right-hearted Mr Kingan.'

Kingan chuckled. Jeffrey must have read Reverend Samuel Parr's memoir of his journey to Scotland. Kingan had earned the epithet after an evening with the "Whig Johnson" at the Buck Inn ten years before. 'Sir, the pleasure is all mine,' he gushed.

'Your journey was comfortable, I trust.'

It hadn't been. The toll road had been rutted and bumpy.

'Comfortable enough, sir,' he lied, then regretted. Jeffrey's eyes seemed to see into him.

'Please, sit down, Mr Kingan. My clerk will be taking notes. You've had tea?'

'I have, thanks.'

The clerk sat down at the side of the desk, clearing a space among the papers. Kingan and Jeffrey sat facing each other, the former's hands fidgety, the latter's resting on his thighs.

'I've read the papers from Mr McDowell,' began Jeffrey. 'And as you know, I've met him here. So, I'm acquainted with the subject of the letters. What I wish to explore with you are two questions. Do you believe that Mr Watson wrote the anonymous letters? And why are you so aggrieved about his behaviour since the arbitration?'

Kingan hesitated. He had thought the meeting was to decide on the nature of the charges against Watson and the sum to be sought in damages. 'Regarding the first, initially I had reservations when I first heard about the letters, I doubted his guilt. But since my own letter, I've believed him to be the author.'

Expecting a follow-up question, Kingan paused. Jeffrey remained impassive. Kingan shifted in his chair. The silence grew into a minute. Kingan broke it. 'Don't you think Mr Watson is the author?'

'No, sir. I do not.'

Kingan's eyebrows rose. 'Why not?'

'The evidence against him is circumstantial. It didn't hold up at the arbitration. The expert opinion you commissioned contradicts Lizars. It disproves the handwriting is yours but doesn't prove it's his. You'll never convince a jury of his guilt. But most importantly—' He fixed Kingan with a penetrating stare. 'The letters were written by a woman.'

Kingan squirmed in his seat. *Preposterous*! he thought.

Jeffrey waited for him to settle. 'By dint of my practice, I've seen many libellous letters, Mr Kingan. These are among the most silly, venomous twaddle ever penned. No male intellect is capable of such utter and complete prostration. My conviction is that they're the composition of one of that wretched class of females whose hearts, full of disappointment and neglect, have soured their every good principle and benevolence.'

'A woman!' declared Kingan. 'They have neither the predilection nor the capability to mount and orchestrate a campaign of this volume and intensity.' He paused, discomfited by Jeffrey's amused expression. 'I've known many men throughout my years who've taken vicarious pleasure in outraging every generous feeling in their fellows. Poisoning the happiness of all within their reach. I have multiple reasons to believe Mr Watson is of that ilk.'

Jeffrey shook his head. 'Your enemy may be adept at producing malignity to blacken reputations. But, from what I've heard, he does so to secure a commercial advantage. Would that be his motive in writing these letters? To put at risk his bank?' He cleared his throat. 'As a man of letters, I tell you, the language displayed in these letters is feminine.'

Kingan blushed. *Why am I being challenged by my own advocate?* he thought. 'I beg to differ.'

For a moment, Jeffrey studied his face then said, 'Let's move on to my second question, your grievances?'

'They are many,' said Kingan, relieved at the change of topic. 'He has viciously wounded my standing to an extent that leads me to dread for my future,' his voice quivered. He sought further words, but they didn't come.

Jeffrey glanced at the clerk who sat, quill hovering above the paper. 'I can see, hear and feel the suffering he has wreaked upon you,' he said softly. 'Let's leave it for now.'

Kingan breathed in, surprised at his loss of composure. After a moment, he faced Jeffrey and nodded.

'My firm objective is to win this case for you, Mr Kingan,' continued Jeffrey. 'With that end, I'm informing you that, in my opinion, we have no chance of convincing a jury that Mr Watson has written these letters. The core of our case should be proving Mr Watson's motive and demonstrating his actions to wound you deeply by isolating you from good society. His motive was misplaced revenge. His actions were falsely accusing you of writing the letters. Both entail proving to the jury that you did not write these letters.'

'But he did write the letters! Can't we pursue his guilt?'

'Not if you want to win.'

Frowning, Kingan looked away. *Give up on proving Watson's guilt?* He asked himself. *No!* He would get another advocate. Then he remembered Finlay's words. No one is more skilled in front of a jury. Shaming Watson publicly by being awarded damages was what mattered most. That was the path to retaking his place in good company. He could demonstrate Watson's authorship later. He fixed his eyes on the lawyer. 'Let's proceed on that basis.'

Jeffrey raised his hand. The clerk began writing.

'Tell me with details of time and place, how Mr Watson has damaged your reputation.'

Kingan drew a breath. For the next hour, he related in a controlled tirade, Watson's slanders. The clerk scribbled furiously.

'Why do you think Mr Watson bears so much enmity towards you?' asked Jeffrey on Kingan finishing.

'I think his friend, Mr Adam Aitken of the Bank of Scotland, convinced him I'm the author.'

'Why did Aitken do that?'

'I told you about Oswald and my meeting with him. I think he feels remorse for not telling Watson about our interest then.'

'But why you rather than Oswald? You hinted in your account that there might have been some enmity between you from before that meeting.'

'I can't stand him. He epitomises bankers, cloaking his greed in self-righteous probity.'

Jeffrey peered at him. 'And what does he think of you?'

Kingan swallowed. 'I think he hates me.'

'Why?'

'I've a tendency to wit. Among the Glasgow merchants, bankers are much disliked. They're easy objects for satire.'

'And Aitken is your prime target?'

'Yes. After the blackballing, his resentment at that and his remorse over not stopping Oswald at the meeting led him to convince Watson that I put Oswald against him as part of some convoluted jape. Watson leapt on the chance to obfuscate his own writing of these letters.'

'You know my thoughts about the authorship, Mr Kingan.' Jeffrey sat thinking, then said. 'It sounds somewhat extreme. What grounds do they give for believing it was a jape?'

'They make great play about the note I made to Miss Nancy Oswald about my dialogue with Watson by the river.'

'Did you intend it as a joke?'

'Yes.'

Jeffrey scrutinised Kingan, who was wiping beads of sweat from his forehead. 'Have you ever written anonymous letters as a joke?'

'No!' *How could he say that?* Kingan asked himself. *Surely, he can't be taking Watson's side.*

'Don't worry, Mr Kingan,' reassured Jeffrey. 'It's obvious you didn't write these letters. I need, however, to be assured that your story is plausible and will stand up to attack. Your penchant for humour is a weakness which I've no doubt Mr Watson's defence will seek to exploit as a justification for his conduct. This Vinegar Note will be key in that.'

'We have many defences against that line of attack: your record in business, your place in a respectable society, the support of your friends, especially the Oswald family. Our victory, however, will also depend on offence. We need statements from those to whom Watson has libelled you. I've already discussed with Mr McDowell the gathering of these.'

'And the maid, Lily Patrick?'

Jeffrey's eyes narrowed. 'She must be annulled.'

Chapter 27
The Summons

Watson raised his eyes from the page on the desk in his study at Linthouse. He fought against his rising bile and reread the penultimate paragraph.

Therefore, the said ROBERT WATSON, defender, OUGHT and should be DECREED and ordained by decree of the Lords of our Council and Session, to make a payment to the pursuer of the SUM OF £10,000 STERLING, in name of damages for the gross injury he has sustained or is yet to sustain.

He sat back and wiped saliva off his underlip with the back of his hand. He looked again at the measured clauses: how he had "conceived a groundless malice and ill will" against Kingan then sought to "banish him altogether from respectable society" by accusing him of being the disseminator of letters which contained, "even such as were addressed to ladies' gross and obscene allusions and abominable insinuations".

'How come I didn't have an inkling of this?' he whispered. 'We knew something was happening but this? Ten thousand pounds? With what's going on with the banks, that'll finish me.' He slammed his fist down on the thick, stiff paper, then shouted, 'Damn him!'

From the larder where she was supervising the stocking of the week's provisions, Mrs Watson heard him yell. She immediately rushed upstairs. 'What is it?' she asked on entering the study, pulling at her green cotton gown.

'A court summons from Kingan,' he barked, eyes glaring as if she were to blame. 'He's suing me!'

'Oh—' She moved towards the desk to pick up the paper, but he blocked her. She backed off. 'What will you do?'

'I don't know yet!' he roared. 'It's only just arrived!'

She reddened, then bowed. 'Wigmore is waiting below. What shall I tell him?'

He'd forgotten. He was to tour the orchard with his head gardener to discuss this year's crop of Anjou pears.

'Send him away,' he said flatly. 'And Iris, make sure I'm not disturbed.'

She scurried out.

He moved to the bay window to gaze on Stobcross House across the brown river. The clouds scudded across the watery blue sky, moving as fast as the puffers and lighters on the river. He stood still until the pulse pounding in his head ebbed.

He went over to the desk to look at the list of those to whom he'd slandered Kingan. *They've only got a few*, he thought. 'He deserved the bad-mouthing. It was nothing compared to mine after the blackball.'

He pondered the charges further. There's no claim that I wrote the letters, he noted, only that I spoke about Kingan to others. I can easily justify that. He wrote them! He stamped his foot. 'Why am I the criminal?' he bellowed.

To calm himself, he went over to the bookcase and took out the leather-bound volume of Binning. He sat down by the empty fireplace and opened the book, looking for the text which had just come into his mind. He perused twenty pages before he found it. Its ending struck him.

Do not so much look on seeking victory over corruption as a duty, though we be infinitely bound to it, but rather as a privilege conferred upon us by Christ.

He contemplated its import. 'Vanquishing Kingan is more than just my duty, it's my privilege. An advantage has been given to me by God because of my righteousness, my integrity, my faith. My victory over him must be absolute. No more will his lust for calumny and deceit trample my dignity. The trial will be his ultimate censure, his final disbarment from trust.'

His mind turned to the fight. 'I have Aitken, Lizars, the servant girl, Hagart, Miller. I have the sinner's inadvertent confession of his felony, the Vinegar Note.'

Listing his armaments brought relief. He should get to the bank before closing. He called a footman, then told him to tell the stables to ready his horse.

#

An hour later, sweating, he strode through the wood-panelled atrium to the counter. A startled, spotty-faced teller lifted the corner flap.

'Is the meeting room clear?'

'Mr Gilbert's there, Master,' stammered the youth.

'Mr Gilbert?' retorted Watson sharply.

'Mr Gilbert Watson, Master,' he replied, eyes downcast.

'Is Bell here?'

'I'm not sure, Master. I'll look for him.'

'Tell him to come to the meeting room. And bring some water.'

Watson stopped at the meeting room door, thought about knocking but decided not to. He entered and saw his brother at the far end of the polished mahogany table, a candelabra lighting an opened book.

Gilbert jerked his head up. 'Robert!' he blurted, closing the volume with his good hand.

Watson stared at the leather-bound cover, his lips curling as he read its gold embossed title, *Gertrude of Wyoming*. 'Rather small for a ledger, Gilbert,' he sneered.

Gilbert blushed. 'I've just finished a lengthy meeting with Muir. I was taking the opportunity to rest awhile before signing off today's business. I thought you had an important matter at Linthouse.'

Watson reached into his frock coat's inner pocket and pulled out the summons. He pushed it down the table to his brother. 'Read this.' He pointed to the book. 'You'll find it twice as entertaining as that versifying.'

Gilbert picked up the document.

Two minutes later, a knock on the door sounded.

'Come in,' ordered Watson, not moving his eyes off his brother.

Bell, as ever red white-spotted kerchief around his neck, entered.

Watson followed his servant's progress to the top of the table, noting with approval his erect stance, hands behind back, eyes fixed on the cameo of the Watson's father on the dark wood panelled wall behind Gilbert. 'Bell, welcome.'

'Mr Watson, Sir!'

'Did you bring your notebook?'

'Yes, sir.'

Watson motioned to a chair. Bell, dabbing his forehead with a handkerchief, sat down.

Gilbert finished reading the summons and passed the document back to Watson. He nodded to Bell, who responded with, 'Mr Watson, Sir!'

Watson pointed to the pages on the desk. 'I've just received a summons—you know what that is?'

'I do, Master.'

'Mr John Kingan is suing me for spreading what he calls "gross and obscene allusions".' He took in Bell's pained expression with satisfaction. 'I'm going to fight him every inch of the way. From now. Today. Do you know what that means for you?'

'It means that from now, your fight is my number one priority, Master.'

'Exactly.' He turned to Gilbert. 'What's your opinion on the summons?'

'He has a cheek—'

'I know that. In law?'

Gilbert breathed in. 'It's a well-constructed document—'

'Meaning?'

'It's cogent about the grievance, assures that they have sufficient evidence to pursue redress.' He raised his eyebrows. 'Although I must say ten thousand ponds does appear excessive.'

'Ten thousand!' gasped Bell.

Watson disregarded the outburst. 'Can Kingan win?'

Gilbert scratched his damaged forearm, which was resting on the table. 'He has a good chance. Much depends on how we fight back.'

'My thoughts exactly.' He fanned his reddened face with his hand, then restarted. 'We'll mount a campaign on two fronts. The first, defence. I'm going toe to toe with him on his charges. I'll show that smear for smear, he has done worse to me than I to him.'

He peered at each in turn. Both nodded, Bell more vigorously.

'The second, offence. I'm bringing my own case for damages against Kingan for writing these letters and plotting to falsely blame me for having done so in order to obscure his guilt.'

Gilbert's eyes widened. 'Are you sure?'

'Of course, I'm sure!'

'You'll need an advocate. A good one. Jeffrey is nigh unbeatable.'

'Cockburn has a great record. He got Burke's wife off.'

Burke and Hare, aided by their wives, had committed sixteen murders in Edinburgh. They had sold the corpses to an anatomist. Hare had turned King's evidence. Burke had been hanged. His wife, who had aided in the murders and sold on the victims' clothes, had been found not guilty.

'Cockburn'll be expensive.'

'I'll also be seeking ten thousand pounds.'

Gilbert bit his lip.

'You doubt me, Gilbert,' proclaimed Watson in the voice he usually reserved for the Psalms. 'Don't! Cleansing this city of Kingan isn't just my obligation. Nor even my duty. It's my privilege! Given to me by Our Maker!' Eyes black with menace, he stared down at the others' quizzical looks.

'And Oswald?' inquired Gilbert after a minute.

'They say he and Kingan haven't met for months.'

Bell nodded.

'Kingan only has his attention for the sister,' continued Watson.

Gilbert chuckled. 'Her latest!'

'And oldest!' Watson turned his eyes to Bell. 'What do you think?'

'Your cause is indeed righteous, Master. And, if you don't mind an old member of the Downshire Yeomanry giving his view, you're right to match defence with offence. But Kingan's a clever foe. Look what happened when we tried to get him at the Western.'

'We moved too soon,' said Watson. 'We didn't tie things down. This time will be different. That's why you're here.' He turned to his brother. 'What do you think, Gilbert?'

'We certainly need to make our case watertight. In court, detail always decides.'

'As always, attention to detail.' He turned to Geordie. 'This is what I want you to do.' He went through the list he had prepared in his head on the ride over. As Bell noted each point with the stub of a pencil, Watson occasionally asked Gilbert for his opinion, nodded and told Bell to move on. In the end, Watson sat back. 'Summary!'

Bell flicked through the back to the start of his list. In his booming Ulster tones, he read out, 'Assure Lily Patrick's evidence and prevent her from going over to Kingan. Find others who've witnessed Kingan writing or sending anonymous letters. Keep a close eye on Mr Oswald and his sister. Obtain more names of those who have received anonymous letters and, wherever possible, copies. Pass all evidence collected to you then, Mr Renny. Lastly, support Mr Renny obtaining formal statements.'

Watson's eyes glowed.

Chapter 28
Oswald's Betrayal

Kingan looked out of the coach at Shieldhall, its wet whitewashed walls burnished by the sun burning brightly after the recent showers. The scene lifted the resentment he'd felt since his session with Jeffrey yesterday about Watson's summons. His eyes twinkled. He would see her soon.

As always, Williamson greeted him warmly. This time there was no enquiry about paying respects to Mrs Oswald. The butler led him directly to the conservatory. On entering, his gaze instantly met hers. He smiled broadly. They remained still and silent until Williamson left, then she rose and embraced him. As they broke, he felt cheated, his desire unmet. In the far corner of the stuffy conservatory, the spaniels lay in a jumble, snoozing as the late morning sun poured into the glass-walled room. He sat by her side on the sofa.

'How was Mr Jeffrey? As exquisite as ever?'

'A cross of Adonis with Apollo, tempered by a dash of Narcissus.'

She giggled. 'He's a great performer. That's why the General Assembly invites him every year. The Kirk's version of light theatre.'

Kingan laughed, tickled by the candour of a Moderator's granddaughter. The spaniels briefly raised their heads.

'What's Jeffrey's opinion on Watson's summons?'

'They're as he had expected. A mirror image of mine. The same list of recipients of anonymous letters, the same language, "offensive and disgraceful", "designed to cause great pain", the same reason for damages ("gross injury").' He paused. 'And the same sum, ten thousand pounds.'

Her eyes widened.

'But unlike me, Watson is pursuing the letters. I'm to be fingered as Mr Vinegar.'

'His evidence?'

'Lizars and a "credible witness", presumably Lily Patrick.'

'And Jeffrey still thinks a woman wrote the letters?'

'I'm afraid so. He still believes in Mrs Vinegar. I challenged him again. He was firm. We're definitely not pursuing Watson as the author. Just defending me against the charge.'

She scowled. 'What's Watson's central charge?'

'That claim, I wrote the letters and hatched a plot to divert attention from my guilt. I convinced your brother that Watson was the author and enticed him to carry out the blackballing.'

Her face flushed. 'Ludicrous!' She shook her head vigorously. 'What piffle!'

'Jeffrey's sure they'll use the Vinegar Note to substantiate the plot. Aitken's probably the key witness. And Lawson.' He breathed in then squealed, 'Why, oh why, did I ever write it!'

'Not again, John,' she scolded.

'I can't help but worry about it. They claim it's a fabrication.'

'Which in a way, it is. What more?'

'There's the names of those I spoke to about what a cur he is.'

'As he is. Do you think they can prove what you said is slander?'

'I told the truth about him writing the letters. It's natural to embellish the truth with feeling. One man's satire is another's sarcasm.'

'Who are they?'

He hesitated. 'Hunter—' His voice tailed.

'That's stung you.'

'I know he's an oaf. But he's my oaf.' He looked away. 'We're not as close as we were. But still. It was in confidence.'

He recalled the evening in the Saracen's Head. Hunter's eyes bulging.

'Tell me more!' The fat man's deep cackle at Kingan, mimicking Watson talking with a sore throat. The memory of the evening saddened him. He missed the clubs, the taverns, the inns. They made Glasgow. His head drooped.

'John!' she snapped.

He jerked up. 'Then there's a list of those who'll testify for his good name.'

She snorted.

'Seven. All of rank, an ex-Provost, Magistrates, principal merchants, professors at the college, physicians. Then—' He hesitated. 'Your brother. He's betrayed me.'

'What!'

His expression soured. He paused until sure that he could keep the hurt out of his voice. 'Do you remember that letter I wrote to him at the end of May?'

'The one asking him to help pull you out of the pit he'd dug and pushed you into?'

'Yes, that.' He peered at her. 'Watson has that letter.'

'How?'

'Either James handed it over or someone has secreted it from his keeping.'

She rose and paced to the centre of the room and stood with her back to Kingan. After a couple of minutes, she faced him. 'We'll confront James.'

'I'm not sure it's a good idea for me to challenge him—'

'Not you,' she declared, eyes fierce.

Chapter 29
Lily's Predicament

Lily and Cook sat on their stools, legs out, bellies full, gaping at the embers in the kitchen hearth. By them, on the stone floor, lay the bowls which, a few minutes before, had contained their porridge and soor dook. Lily washed down the stodge with another gulp of steaming tea. Wary ear cocked for the pull bell, she waited her turn of the tub of goose fat, which Cook was liberally rubbing into her knuckles.

Wash day was always worse. It had started with heaving pails of water to the tubs, plunging her hands into the lye-infused cold water, pushing the fabrics around, scrubbing at the blood and sweat and worse. The starching had followed.

An hour later, she had stood heart in mouth at Mrs Cairnie's side waiting on her opinion on the whiteness of her daughters' petticoats. She had forced back a sigh, as two had been rejected. Still, only two. Head bowed, she had thanked the Mistress before hanging the approved clothes to dry in the low November sun. The rewashing had finished an hour ago. Now, she was paying the price for her chilblains.

'Wheesht, Lily,' said Cook. 'Ye'll mak' em bleed.'

'But they itch,' moaned Lily.

'It'll pass. Here, take this.' She passed the half-empty tub.

The maid began working the grease into the bumps on her fingers, occasionally sniffing them, drawing comfort from the rancid odour.

'Ye seem fashed,' said Cook, bending over so that her hands were closer to the dying coals.

'Aye. Ah suppose Ah am.'

'Whit aboot?'

Lily paused. She trusted Cook but she didn't know a servant who couldn't resist sharing a secret.

'Ye can tell me,' whispered Cook. 'Ah'm naw yer bletherin' kin'. Ye ken that.'

That's clever, thought Lily. Now, I need to say something, otherwise she'll think I'm insulting her. 'Ye remember ma visits a while back. They men o' means.'

'The Irishman, then the lawyer, an' yer auld Master.

'Aye. Well, it turns oot ma' auld Master is still at odds wi' Mr Watson o'Linthouse an' they're gaun tae court tae settle it. They say each wan wants ten thoosan' frae the ither.'

'Whit!' screeched Cook. 'Ten thoosan! No, even the King's goat hawd o' that.'

Lily shrugged. 'Whatever. An' Ah, fool ah am, gie a statement tae each back then. Now, they wann anither. An Ah'm telling ye somethin.' She lay the tub at the foot of her chair and glared at the fire 'Ah'm nae gawn tae court fir nae biddy!'

'They can send ye to 'jail fir that.'

'Just let 'em try. Ah'll tell the whole story.'

Cook leaned towards her. 'Whit story?'

Lily swallowed. She'd blabbed too far. There was no way she could tell Cook about the deal with Geordie Bell. The broken deal. She hadn't seen a penny after her statement to Watson's lawyers. Her father had visited Bell at the Watsons' bank a month ago. The jumped-up porter had said Lily would only get her money once she'd repeated her story about the letters to more lawyers. A trial was coming. Bell hadn't mentioned any trial when he had spoken to her the first time. Nobody ever had.

She had considered telling Kingan about the yet-to-be-seen recompense. But it would be her word against Bell's. And would the Auld Master reward her for her information? He and his lawyer had made no offer when they'd visited. She would wait for what came up.

'It's awfie complicated,' she announced.

'So's life. Sealin' yer lips disnae mak' it any easier.'

The bell rang. Lily's head drooped as the day's respite evaporated. 'Can he naw shit at the same time as the rest ae us?' She rose to collect the chamber pot.

#

A week later, Lily was sweeping the backyard when a coach drew up at the front of the house. A minute later, she recognised a voice in conversation with Hall, the foreman. It belonged to that lawyer. Her hands went clammy. *Where's Jock?* she thought, looking around. He could hide her in their place in the stables. *'Ne'er here, when ye wan' him!'*

A moment later, Hall appeared. 'Mr MacDowall, Kingan's Writer and his clerk want to talk to you. You need to come to the dining room straightaway.'

'Whit fur?'

'They have some questions about these letters.'

She glowered. 'Ah've answered them aw' afore.'

'That's what I told them.'

Two hands on the top of the broom handle, she set her feet apart. 'Ah'm no' gawn!'

'They have a court letter. If you don't go, they'll arrange for a constable.'

She considered her options. She had none. She dropped the broom and trudged past the Hall to the dining room. She straightened her bonnet, smoothed her apron and entered. She glared at MacDowell, who was much as she remembered him, fat and sleek like the top hog in the sty. Sitting across from him at the long table was a youth no older than she. She shuddered in the damp air. The backroom only ever saw the late afternoon sun.

'Hello, Lily.' MacDowell said cheerily. 'Take a seat.' He pointed to the chair at the opposite end of the table from him and the youth.

She puckered her mouth and sat down. She noted the clerk's eyes following her. She winked. He blushed. Heartened, she turned to his Master. 'Why dae ye wish tae see me, Sir? I answered aw yer questions last time.'

'I'm afraid Lily that that interview was for another purpose. It no longer stands. There's going to be a trial in Edinburgh. Mr Kingan and Mr Watson are suing each other.'

'Ah heard. Fir ten thoosan poons!'

'The sum's of no import. We believe Mr Watson intends to call you for his case. We've decided to speak to you also. Have you been approached by anyone on behalf of Mr Watson?'

'Mibbe.'

His eyes went icy. 'This is serious, Miss Patrick. We need to interview you formally. According to the rules of the Court. That's why my clerk, Mr Clason, is here to help me. Do you understand?'

She looked at the two in turn. 'Ah'm no gawn tae any court.'

They stared at her.

'That's not advisable, Miss Patrick,' said MacDowall.

'Ye've just told me that ma' last interview disnae stan' now. If Ah dinnae talk tae ye today, ye'll have nothin' tae use in court. So, ye cannae call me.' Under the table, she scratched her chilblains. 'Anyway, I cannae remember anythin' aboot they letters. It all happened sae lang ago.'

'But you remembered at our last interview. I just need you to repeat that now.'

'Well, I cannae.'

MacDowall pinched his lips together. 'What's the problem with going to court? It'll be a day our for you in Edinburgh. We'll pay your costs. And maybe a wee bit more.'

'How much?'

'Your expenses while you're in Edinburgh.'

She squinted at him. He was serious. She waited to see if he would up the offer. Nothing came. 'Ah ken people who've gawn tae court. They hated it. It's where people like you put down people like me in front' o' a crowd o' gawkers.'

'Listen, Miss Patrick,' he growled. 'If you don't talk to us now, there'll be a constable at your door tomorrow.'

Lily folded her arms and said nothing.

'Right!' shouted the lawyer.

The two men rose, put together their papers and left the room.

'Good riddance,' she murmured. She heard them marching up the hall then loud words with the foreman. She clutched her apron tightly when she heard her Master's voice. She steeled herself.

A moment later, the door swung open and a well-dressed, broad-shouldered man in his forties advanced towards her, followed by Hall, their faces grim. She smelled his sour breath as he bent over her. Finger pointing at her now blanched face, her Master barked, 'Listen to me and listen to me carefully. I'll speak just once. I'm not having my door darkened by any constable. Least of all because of a pipsqueak maid like you. You either speak to these men or you're out the door in ten minutes. Is that clear?'

'Yes, Mister Cairnie,' she replied in a quivering voice.

'What's it to be then?'

'I'll speak to them, Master.'

The two men left. As she waited for her two interrogators, her doubts resurfaced. If this was bad, it could only get worse. And the trial!

MacDowall and his clerk took their old places.

'Let's start again,' began MacDowall. 'Did you carry any letters on behalf of Mr Kingan to the post office or to a porter?'

'Yes,' she answered clearly.

'I'm going to read out some names. The same as you heard on my last visit. I want you to tell me if you carried letters addressed to them. Understood?'

She nodded.

'Mr Andrew Spiers.'

'Ah might have but Ah cannae remember clearly.'

MacDowell grimaced. He looked at his clerk, then turned to Lily and said icily, 'Could you, if you were called as a witness at the coming trial, positively swear that you carried letters addressed to that gentleman?'

She held her head high and answered in her best Quality tones, 'I could not, Sir. You see, it's all a very distant recollection.'

As they collected their papers for a second time, her stomach churned.

Chapter 30
Options

Lips curling, Watson threw Cairnie's letter onto his office table. He sat back and pondered its last sentence: 'I'm very inclined to sack her but wait for your advice.' Not only had the servant girl refused to give a statement to Kingan but now also to him. She wanted nothing to do with any trial.

'The little strumpet,' hissed Watson. There was no way he could trust her. But no way he could let her desist. Cockburn had been clear. His case depended on her.

Given that neither he nor Kingan denied having smeared the other, the advocate believed both would be awarded damages. The victor would be he who could best justify his slanders and thus be awarded more by the jury. The letters were central. Such was the stigma attached to their authorship that, if Cockburn could prove Kingan wrote them, the jury was likely to view Watson's attacks on Kingan not only as necessary to defend himself but also public morality.

But now?

He pushed the letter away from the contract papers which he had been examining. He rose, grimacing. His back ached. Stiffly, he exited the room.

He stood at the counter. The bank was busy. In the expanse of the black and white tiled floor, two queues of top-hatted men waited in front of the tellers, their conversations floating up to the high red and yellow coloured glass ceiling. Recognising a couple of those waiting, he nodded to them cursorily. He was in no mood for conversation. He remembered that Gilbert was with an important client. Good. What he had to do, he would do with Bell alone.

He walked over to the guard standing by the front door. The tall, bearded young man's eyes widened as he clicked his heels. 'Sir!'

'Relax, McGregor. Do you know where Bell is?'

'He's taking a letter to Mr Perry's drysalters in the Saltmarket.'

'Go fetch him. Tell him I need to talk with him urgently.'

After McGregor had marched out, Watson recrossed the atrium. He went to his office, his mind stewing.

Last week, pre-trial proceedings had begun with a hearing in Edinburgh. The two sides had agreed that there would be consecutive trials held over two days. Kingan's claim for damages would be considered first. Directly, after the verdict on that, the same jury would be re-sworn to deliberate Watson's case. If possible, witnesses would be cross-examined by both sides, only once, during the first trial, with their testimony carrying over to the second.

The first skirmish had not gone well. The Court had ordered Watson to hand back the anonymous and Kingan's letters and the Vinegar Note. Oswald had resisted Watson's lawyers' request to submit his report to the arbiters. The Court had declined to command him to do so.

More worryingly for Watson had been Cockburn. His earnest delivery had been convincing but dull compared to Jeffrey's flair. A week later, Watson could still remember whole sentences of Jeffrey but only a few words of Cockburn.

Now, on top of this, the accursed Lily. He imagined what she looked like. A foxy sneering face appeared, crossed eyes glinting at her prey. Him. His eyes grew hard, his fists clenched. A pressing desire to thrash her flowed through him. Then, as he had trained himself over the years, righteousness blocked aggression's surge. In a quiet voice, he recited, 'Hide Your face, Lord, from my sins and blot out all my iniquity. Create in me a pure heart, O God and renew a steadfast spirit within me.'

The psalm drew him into a stillness. Her image went. He pondered whether to advance her reward. He would wait for Bell's advice.

#

Fifteen minutes later, there was a knock on the door. Bell entered and stood with his felt hat in his hands. Watson pointed to the chair. 'Sit down, Geordie.'

The porter did so carefully, keeping his eyes on his Master.

'I received unwelcome news this morning,' started Watson. 'Which would be best kept between ourselves. About our little wastrel.'

'Lily?'

'Who else?'

'What's happened, sir?' asked Bell, frowning.

Watson related the contents of Cairnie's letter, finishing with, 'What do you think?'

Bell remained silent for a moment. 'I can go to Denny to speak to her, if you require, Master.'

'Will it change her mind?'

'I doubt it. She's as stubborn as a mule.'

'Should I give her part of her money to secure her cooperation?'

'She could run off with it or worse, go to Kingan and tell about the reward. It's high risk.'

'There's a risk in whatever we do with her. Are you sure there's no one else saw Kingan writing these letters?'

'I tried to find someone when I got Lily. No one came forward, Master. It'll be worse now. They're scared to be caught on the wrong side.'

'Try again. There must be somebody.'

'I've been through Kingan's old servants.'

'The street porters? That type is always looking for commission. They're even less trustworthy than servants.'

'True, Master but that's the problem. Some have come good for us, but others have let us down. Remember Ferguson. He could spin a tale.'

'Perhaps our motivating featured a little bit more fear than fortune in his case.'

'With all due respect, Master, he deserved his beating.'

'Alright. But fortune is more appropriate than fear in the current circumstances. We need another witness. And quickly. Understood?'

Bell nodded. He looked down and tugged at his hat. After a moment, his eyes returned to Watson's. 'It'll need money, Master.'

'I'll arrange that.'

Bell nodded. 'And Lily?'

Watson exhaled loudly. 'I'm minded to have Cairnie fire her.'

Bell thought for a minute. 'I don't think you have a choice, Master. Mr Cairnie should refuse her a reference. I'll speak to the hiring agencies and the mills so nobody'll touch her. She'll have no choice but to fall back on her family—or to walk the streets.'

Watson's jaw tightened, his eyes harsh. 'Then, she'll find herself not in front of an Edinburgh judge but before Him who is the Highest Court of All.' He inhaled deeply. 'Go to her family. Give them an advance, five pounds. Not her. Promise them another five if they let us know if she turns up.'

'The family may ask more. Almost everyone knows you're seeking ten thousand from Mr Kingan.'

'Ten pounds is fair for a cobbler,' growled Watson. 'If we disburse more to the Patricks, we'll have every vagabond in Glasgow at our door.'

#

Cairnie sacked Lily without references. Bell visited Govan and paid five pounds to her father. Lily moved to her sister Martha's house in Goosedubs in Glasgow. Finding no job, she was soon on her brother-in-law's nerves. Every couple of days, either her father or mother visited, each grumbling about the impact of his failing eyesight on his cobbling. Why couldn't she collaborate with kindly Geordie?

Her father told Bell where she was. Bell decided on fortune over fear. He took her every day to a nearby inn for a glass of claret, then another. At the fourth visit, she bent. He guaranteed her fifty pounds would come after the trial. If she repeated to Watson's agent her previous statement about the letter, a post was available at the estate of one of Watson's clients, Mrs MacLean Clephane, of Torloisk on the Isle of Mull.

Chapter 31
The Theatre

Wonder flooded the theatre. Half-crouched, Kingan gasped. The Monster seemed upon him. A pain shot through his hand from her grip as she and the whole row jumped up at the bang. Her scream flowed into the chaotic cacophony. An avalanche of white fluff cascaded down on the contorting Monster, engulfing the shining pistol hovering over him and its bearer, Dr Frankenstein.

Their senses returned to this reality, they stayed standing after the curtain closed then joined in the thunderous applause, as the cast took their bows. The aroma from the roses in her hair enticed him to angle closer. From behind came a loud 'Tut!'

He stiffened and then turned. The eyes of Miss Winifred Anderson, Nancy's chaperone and cousin, starched black bonnet sealed to her head, drilled into him. He moved back to his space but kept hold of Nancy's hand, disregarding the tap on his shoulder. On the next, much firmer, he pondered his quandary. The people-watching would soon start. He decided to let decorum reign and let go of her hand. He lifted his still warm hand and smelled her lavender scent.

His continued moral burning had made theatre going in Glasgow impossible. The news that Mr T.P Cooke's production of *Presumption; or, the fate of Frankenstein* had been coming to Edinburgh had excited him and Nancy. They had planned their visit with great care, travelling separately, residing in different locations, keeping their liaison at the theatre secret to everybody except Mrs Oswald who had divined her daughter's true purpose. The old woman had insisted on a chaperone.

He looked over to the box above the stage at the Edinburgh Theatre Royal where earlier he had spotted Jeffrey, resplendent in a dark blue frock coat and gold waistcoat. He was talking to a plump and attractive woman whom Kingan took to be his wife. She was vigorously fanning the air heated by the profusion of candles and the press of a few hundred bodies.

Kingan sighed as the sight of his defender brought back his predicament. Their meeting that morning had gone well. The trial was a week away, the pretrial proceedings having finished the week before. Oswald had been forced to hand over his report to the arbiters. It still wasn't clear how supportive he would be at the trial.

On the plus side, Walkinshaw had agreed to testify for Kingan. He would tell of the pressure Watson had placed him over the business letters. The great unknown was the maid. Her refusal to provide a statement on his behalf still infuriated him. She was still missing, presumed hidden under Watson's guard.

Nancy interrupted his reverie. 'That was wonderful!' she exclaimed, sweeping a fallen ringlet from over her eyes.

'Magnificent!' he blurted.

He laughed and grasped her hand. The coughing behind began. They turned to face their vigilante.

'Cousin Winifred,' said Nancy, half shouting above the bustle of the exiting crowd. 'Did you enjoy it?'

'Some,' she brayed. Stick-thin, black-dressed, she stood out from the mosaic of theatre finery.

'Which parts?' asked Kingan, stooping over her.

'The opening overture.' The lines on her long, pale face tightened as he and Nancy burst out laughing.

'Nothing of the rest?' he asked after a moment.

'The unintelligible cavorting of an undressed man. I think not, Sir. The whole affair was beyond any strand of normal belief.'

Nancy couldn't suppress her mirth. Miss Anderson's face reddened. Kingan decided to play on her discomfort. 'But it could all happen. Through science, we are understanding more and more about galvanism and its effect on our bodies. Soon, we'll be able to use it to restore health to afflicted parts. Would you like that?'

The chaperone's eyes blazed. 'The ability to dispense the force of life rests solely with Our Maker and He Alone.'

'Well, he must be awfully busy with all His wains,' sighed Kingan.

As Nancy giggled, her cousin turned away and exited the now empty row.

The couple drew back and let a little distance grow between them and Miss Anderson as they went down the stairs. As they passed a recess on a landing, Kingan guided her gently into it and kissed her, her lips soft, tasting of the claret they had drunk at the interval. He pulled her to him. They kissed harder and deeper.

'It's been a lovely evening, John,' she whispered on their breaking.

Kingan looked around. There was only an uninterested straggler nearby. They were out of earshot. He said softly, 'It's a shame it has to end.'

Nancy blushed. She stroked her ringlets and eyes smouldering, said in a voice infused with an intensity he had not previously encountered, 'What I feel for you won't ever end, John.'

He didn't return her words, but his eyes signalled his yearning.

They remained silent as they descended to the foyer where Miss Anderson stood, her eyes burrowing into his with unbridled Presbyterian rectitude.

'Soon,' he whispered to Nancy as she left for her cousin.

Chapter 32
Lily's Escape

Lily plodded through the Canongate's narrow wynds, the black mass of the castle looming overhead, heading for her brother's flat in the Pleasance. She gripped her once-white cloth bag. Inside were a change of clothes, a hairbrush and a purse with a thimble, pincushion, pencil and scissors. Her fine cambric handkerchief, found after one of Mr Kingan's dinner parties, was stuffed into her cleavage.

She dodged through the idlers, some pressing snuff up their noses, others passing around a whisky bottle. She'd never seen so many meagre, pallid beings. Encouraged out of their damp cells by the warm sun, it was as if the graves had disgorged their corpses. After Mull, the stench of the sooty air was overpowering. A puce-faced ogre beckoned her to come. She tightened the grip of her other hand on the pocket which she had sewn into her mud-stained frock, containing her savings, five pounds in coins. Face grim, she moved quickly on.

She had spent much of what little she had to arrive in the city. Her journey had started with a hidden parting from her Mistress in Mull. She had taken advantage of an amorous coachman to cross the island to the ferry, leaping onto the departing boat as he had cursed her for sharking on their deal for returned favours.

Eventually, she found the Pleasance and her brother's close. Robbie, a year older than her, was the only member of her family she felt close to. She could trust him. He would help decide what to do.

Outside the entrance to the stairwell was a pool of urine ejected from the chamber pots of the inhabitants of the tenements enclosing the dank alley. A couple of ragged boys had been waiting for the opportunity. The fatter of the two threw his boulder first. The other followed. She let lose her crudest epithets, drawing a protrusion of bonneted heads from the small windows above, some yelling at the miscreants, most joining their laughter.

She put down her bag and wrang her dress as best she could then mounted the slime-covered, worn steps. She chapped on the door she understood to be her brother's repeatedly until the voice she reviled sounded from inside.

'What're ye wannin'?'

'It's me, Peggy,' she shouted, resting her bag on the stone landing. 'Lily!'

'Lily?'

'Aye, Robbie's sister.'

Silence ensued, followed by a rustle. A moment later. Peggy Patrick opened the door, glaring.

'Ye no lettin' me in?' asked Lily.

'Ye're meant tae be far away.'

Lily didn't respond. 'Is Robbie no in?'

'He's at the stables.'

Lily sat down on her bag. 'Ah'll wait fir him.'

Lily pulled her dark grey shawl together. Her red hair straggled to her shoulders. Despite her shabbiness, she exuded a superior air.

From inside came a girning.

Lily raised her head. 'Ye hae anither?'

'Aye. A couple o' weeks past.' She eyed Lily coldly. 'If ye're oot much longer, ye'll stick tae the wall.'

They entered directly into the single room. On the left was a small hearth with a few dimming coals. Facing the door, a small single-paned, mould-encrusted window let in a half-hearted light. In an alcove by the hearth sat an infant girl in a once white, patched smock on a perfectly made bed. Lily tried to remember her name but couldn't. The infant smiled. Lily waved and then went to the cradle at the side of the bed. There, swaddled in flannel, was the new arrival awake but quiet now.

'She's lovely. What's her name?'

'It's a he, Robert.'

'Like his faither 'n' grandfaither.'

'Whit hae ye done tae yer frock?'

Lily looked down at the bright yellow spots. 'Twa laddies ambushed me.'

'Them twa. They're a'ways waitin' by the golden gutter. Some pay 'em tae keep watchie fae the factors. Ye'll need t' change or ye'll stink oot the hoose.' She pointed to the bed. 'Tak' that blanket tae cover yersel'. Ye've anither?'

'In ma bag.'

#

Two hours later, Lily was playing with Rina, the infant, when Robbie returned. She rose and hugged him. He showed her to the small table where Peggy sat breastfeeding the latest Robert. She took the baby off the breast and lit two candles, then went to rekindle the coals, adding at his command, a few more for his sister.

As she changed the baby on the bed, Robbie took Rina on his knee and fed her some cold porridge, Lily felt her stomach grumble as she watched the infant greedily swallow every spoonful. At last, Peggy came with two warmed cooked potatoes, one for Robbie the other split between the two women. Robbie put his daughter to bed. Lily wolved her half down.

'Why did ye leave, Mull?' asked Robbie on finishing his dinner.

'Mull!' shrieked Peggy.

'I couldnae hack it oot there,' replied Lily, keeping her eyes on her brother's. 'Naebody tae natter wi'. They aw spoke the Erse. It got tae me.'

'But why here? Is it tae dae wi' the trial?'

She hesitated, aware of Peggy staring at her. She had no option. 'Well, there's that n' aw.' Her eyes moistened, 'Ah dinnae ken whit tae dae,' she implored.

'Ye better hurry. It's next week.'

'Ah ken. Mistress MacLean tellt me. She goat a letter fae Mr Watson. They wir comin' tae pick me up.'

'So ye ran aff?'

'Aye.'

'Ye cannae hide fae the powers o' the lan'. Bell'll be oot lookin' fir ye right now.'

'That's why Ah came tae Edimbra no' Glasgae.'

'Ye daft? Ye cannae run frae the powers o' the lan'. Quality like Watson'll have chums in the Quality here.'

'Naebody's seen me here. Ye can put me up.'

'That'll be right!' spat Peggy.

'Wheesht!' He took his sister's hand. 'They'll find ye wherever ye gaw.'

'Yer ain faither'll see tae that!' scorned Peggy.

Lily looked down, tears in her eyes.

163

'Ah ken it's difficult,' said Robbie, squeezing her hand gently. 'But it's tae far gawn noo. Faither's dependin' oan that money.'

'Ah ken! He put me up tae it. It's no fair!'

'Fairness goat nuthin' tae dae wi' us, Lily. It's fae the Courts. They twa hate each ither. Whit have they done fir us?'

'Mr Kingan wis a guid Master.'

'He's goat mair money than hawff ae Scotlan'. Ten thoosan'. Men who can stan' tae lose that, can affor' tae help oor family. Tak the fifty fae Watson.'

'Ah'm nae sure Ah'll ever get it,' she moaned. 'Ah dinnae trust them.'

'Ah bet they'll trust ye efter runnin' awa,' hissed Peggy, taking their plates. 'It's nae right!' she shouted as she put them into a basin of cold water.

The baby started crying.

'Wid ye turn fifty doon?' challenged Robbie his wife. 'She's nae job n' nae prospects.'

'Whose fault is that? She keeps gettin' put out.'

Lily shrivelled into her shawl. Peggy was right. She wasn't cut out to be a servant. But put herself through what was coming? She shivered.

'Ye need tae mak' yer mind up quick, Lily,' said Robbie. He looked at the dimming fire. 'Let's leave it fir the night.'

Peggy hauled a wooden trunk from under the bed and extracted a grey flannel blanket. She threw it to Lily. 'Here, tak' this 'n' sleep on the flair.' She lifted the damp rinsed dress from the bed where it had been laid to dry and threw it to Lily. 'Use this as yer pillow.'

#

The next morning, Peggy took the bairns out for some air. On coming back, she busied herself with changing little Robbie. Lily took Rina. A firm rap on the door made both jump. Peggy's smirk alerted Lily. She opened the door. There he stood, scowling, black felt hat in hands, red spotted kerchief round his neck. She breathed in. 'Mr Bell! Please come in, Sir.'

As he brushed past her, she chirped, 'make yourself comfortable. Mrs Patrick, do you have a glass of your best claret for our guest?'

'Very funny;' he growled.

She looked at Peggy, the baby in her arms like body armour. 'Treacherous hussy!'

Chapter 33
Cover All Bets

Watson checked his pocket watch. He had a few hours before he had to leave for Edinburgh to finalise with Cockburn preparations for the trail. Where was Bell?

Weary from reading it since his breakfast, he put down his Bible and shuffled to the bay window of his study. The morning sunlight slanted over the rolling lawn down to the river. His eyes fixed on the sloping slate tiled roof and the light brown harling walls of the old edifice of Stobcross, his childhood nemesis.

'I shall have peace, though I walk in the imagination of my own heart,' he whispered. 'My privilege will animate me to win this fight in the city of life and carry me replenished to peace eternal.'

The business with the maid had shredded his nerves. He had been going into the bank less and less. Merchants, aware of his plight, had become more difficult to deal with. Hiding his anger had tired him. Kingan probably had something to do with it, kindling their demands, knowing that more than ever, the bank needed income. If the jury awarded Kingan ten thousand pounds, it would bankrupt him. The necessity of winning bore down on him more and more. In his anxiety without respite, friends had become enemies, servants, spies.

A few minutes later, Bell arrived, still dusty from the journey back from Edinburgh. Watson looked him up and down before motioning the porter to stand in front of him.

'Master.' Bell's response lacked its usual military brio. His face showed a trace of surliness.

Watson held back from reproaching him. 'Well, was she still there?'

'She was, Master.'

'And we have her secure?'

'Andrew Boyd is with her in the hotel.'

'She'll testify?'

Bell shifted in his chair. 'I think so.'

'Think?'

'I worked on her. Boyd's keeping pressing. Her father's on the coach to Edinburgh now. I'm confident she'll act as we order.'

'And if she doesn't?'

'I've hinted what might happen.'

'But no threat of violence.'

'No. Nothing Kingan might use.'

Stony-faced, Watson looked away. *Why can't he just give me a guarantee about her?* he thought. He glanced at Bell, discerning the beginnings of a smirk. Watson's face set rigid. 'And the porters?' He spat.

'There's progress, Master.'

Watson stiffened. 'Yes?'

'I've been working with Connie O'Neill. Do you remember him?'

Watson nodded. O'Neill, once a livery stabler for Watson's horses in the city, was a well-known rogue. 'What does he do now?'

'He has a pub in Goosedubs.'

Watson's lips curled at the mention of the pit of low life.

'His lad was waiting for me at the coach station. Said a porter'd turned up from Edinburgh. Used to work out of Leckie's stance around the corner from Clyde Street. McPhail by name. He told O'Neill that he had carried letters for Kingan. Between the right dates. He's at O'Neill's now.'

Watson's eyes narrowed.

'Are you not pleased, Master?' asked a surprised Bell.

'I've never trusted O'Neill.' *And now you*, he thought. 'Mull was supposed to be a prison. But a simpleton maid just walked out.' He pondered. 'This discovery of a porter is very convenient after the rollicking you got.'

'Go to O'Neill. Speak to this McPhail. If you think his tale stands up, take him to the bank. I'll interview him about the same names as for the maid.'

'But you're going to Edinburgh.'

'Oh—' Watson rubbed his face. 'Get Renny or McCoist to do it. Or one of their people.'

'I saw them leaving at the coach station. Two coaches full.'

Watson bit his lip. He pondered his quandary. *I need this porter,* he thought. 'The maid's totally untrustworthy. If the man's tale's true, it'll swing the trial in my favour.'

'Bring the porter here. Henry will interview him.'

Bell blanched at the mention of Watson's son. 'Wouldn't Mr Gilbert be better? He's a writer.'

'He's in Edinburgh already. My son will take the statement. If he judges it can be used in evidence, he'll send an express rider with a note to me in Cockburn's chambers in Edinburgh. I'll decide with Cockburn if we use him as a witness. I'll send back Renny to take the formal statement and we'll submit it to the court first thing.'

Bell grimaced. 'There are too many ifs and buts, Master, at such a late stage.'

Watson bristled. 'Such as?'

'Your son talking to McPhail will link him directly to you. We never do that with informers.'

Watson's eyes protruded. In a shaky voice, he yelled, 'I pay you for carrying out my orders. To the letter! Not for your counsel. You understand?'

Bell jerked to attention. 'Yes, Master!'

Watson looked him over. No sign of cheek, only obeisance. 'Now, go!'

#

The initial surliness on Bell's face stayed with Watson throughout the long, bumpy journey to Edinburgh. He arrived at Cockburn's chambers, exasperated. Details hadn't been attended to as required. He had explained to Henry what he had to do, itemising each step, getting him to note each question, how to look for contradictions. Finished, he had asked him to repeat the tasks. The reproaches had grown louder with his son's each error. Then, another repetition and for a semblance of satisfaction, a third time, which seemed to last forever given the reappearance of his son's stammer.

His mood wasn't improved when, having been shown to the meeting room, among the twenty people milling about, he spied Gilbert in raucous laughter with one of the Edinburgh agents who had obviously just cracked a joke. He marched over and pulled his brother aside. 'What are you doing?'

Gilbert freed his arm from his brother's grasp. 'I was receiving a report from Howatt,' he replied testily. 'He took the maid's precognition this afternoon. It's deposited at the Court.'

'And that's funny!'

Gilbert stood back and studied Watson. 'Are you alright, Robert?'

'No!' snarled Watson moving off to greet Cockburn.

Four hours later, the planning session was ending. Watson was beside himself waiting for delivery of a note from his son. He could hardly concentrate on Cockburn's droning on about some legal manoeuvre when the door opened.

'I thought I said we weren't to be interrupted, Stewart,' said Cockburn.

The blonde-haired, good-looking youth bent over and whispered into the advocate's ear. Cockburn looked at Watson. 'A rider has just arrived from Glasgow with an urgent message. I hope it's nothing serious. With your family.'

'No,' said Watson, rising. 'I was expecting it.'

'Oh—' blurted Cockburn.

Watson found the rider in the hall. He grasped the letter from his outstretched hand, turned and read it. A smile came over his face, then a shaky laughter. 'My privilege,' he whispered. 'My privilege!' He turned and strode to the room. All eyes were on him as he sat down.

'Sirs, some most germane and welcome information has just arrived,' he announced. 'A new witness had come forward unexpectedly to substantiate that Mr Kingan did indeed write these letters. A porter who carried letters written by Kingan to the three recipients we know received anonymous letters but never any signed by Kingan himself.'

Gilbert and a couple more gasped. Cockburn eyed his client warily. 'Can I see?'

Watson pushed him the letter across the table. None spoke as Cockburn read it, his bald head motionless over the text. He lifted his head and delved into the pile of papers in front of him. The only sound for the next seconds was a quiet rustling as he rummaged through the papers. He pulled out and scrutinised three documents. After an age, he stared at Watson with an expression of distaste.

'The witness statements by these three all say that the anonymous letters were delivered by the post office.'

Chapter 34
The First Day

MacDowell pushed through the crush outside the Court of Session. Behind him came Kingan. Conscious of the whispered comments from the queuing spectators, he flicked the specks of dust off his best black frock coat. The grey classical buildings of the old Scots Parliament pressed on him, their solemnity increasing his apprehension.

Kingan stopped at the open double doors to Courtroom Two. At the far end of the high-ceilinged, wood-panelled room, on an elevated platform, stretched a mahogany table. At its centre was a red-leathered padded throne, flanked by two high-backed chairs. Shafts of light from the high windows caught the gold and silver insignia of the Crown in Scotland with its motto, *Nemo me impune lacessit.* 'How apposite,' he rued.

Below the platform, at two surprisingly small tables, huddled two sets of bewigged advocates. He spotted Jeffrey, talking animatedly with Moncrieff and Jameson, his other counsels. At the other table, the conversation was being led by a tall, erect figure with a solemn, thin face. His dark eyebrows contrasted with the wisps of grey hair extruding from under his wig. Kingan baulked as Henry Cockburn's penetrating stare met his.

MacDowell noticed and guided him to the chair reserved for the pursuer of damages, in a row behind his advocates. Kingan saluted his other three solicitors.

Eyes bright, Jeffrey approached, 'Mr Kingan, our day has come!'

'At last,' responded Kingan, more in relief than expectation.

'How do you feel?'

'Hopeful. But, cautious.'

'Good signs, Mr Kingan. Signs of a general who has marshalled his troops well. Let me introduce you to my colleagues.'

Kingan shook the hands of his other advocates. As he did so, he spotted Watson with his agents in a row of seats behind Cockburn. For the first time since the saga had begun, he set his eyes on his foe.

The eeriness of the moment was soon replaced by alarm. His skin tingled as the febrile loathing in Watson's glare split asunder his equanimity. He took a deep breath and returned to his enemy what he had practised for this moment during the long hours between waking and leaving his lodgings at the New Club, a brazen smirk. Watson's neck corded, his eyes darting sparks of black hatred. Cockburn took his client's arm and turned him around. Kingan's heart raced as he mouthed, 'Yes!'

A clamour made him look up. Spectators were rushing to get the best seats on the balconies on three sides of the room. He spotted Nancy and the po-faced Miss Anderson at the back of that behind him. She was wearing the infamous printed gown, judiciously covered by a green tartan shawl. She waved. Smiling broadly, he returned the gesture. It would be their last such exchange for the day. They had agreed in their last note to avoid each other's eyes so as not to draw attention to their relationship.

The room quietened as the twelve men of the jury entered the benches to the right of him. He scanned their well-fed faces. He was met with indifference and curiosity. The lack of empathy discomforted him. His life was in their deliberations. He swivelled to focus on the front bench as McDowall had instructed.

He stood to attention as the three judges, in grey shoulder-length wigs, red cloaks lined in white fur and gold pendants of authority, took their places. MacDowall squeezed his arm and whispered his and Jeffrey's chorus, 'don't worry.'

Seated erect on his throne, Lord Adam, the Lord Chief Commissioner, red-faced and stout, cleared his throat and, in a booming voice, began the trial. He outlined the main issues for the jury. He then invited Jeffrey to set out the pursuer's case.

His eyes keen and firm beneath his wig, the advocate took up centre stage in front of the jury. He stood still, nodded courteously to them, then in a clear gentlemanly voice, began his peroration.

'Gentlemen, upon the part of Mr Kingan, I shall not have to trouble you with any considerable detail. There will be no difficulty in making out that the defender, Mr Watson, did impute to Mr Kingan the writing and transmission of these abominable letters; that he did so repeatedly in all places where he went, scenes of festivity, the haunts of business, in company, on the streets, in houses and on highways, scattering his accusations with a persevering malevolence, a cruel industry wholly without example.'

'I have the most unbound confidence, that before the trial proceeds far, the evidence to be laid before you will be of such a nature as to destroy every shadow of a pretext for this foul accusation and to leave you in such a state of astonishment that so rash, false and groundless charge should have been preferred.'

Punctuating each significant point with a fixed stare on a single member, he described how he would dismantle Watson's allegation that his actions had been justified by Kingan's smearing; would disprove that Kingan had plotted to conceal his true authorship of the letters by displacing his guilt onto Watson and would make evident that Kingan had considerable grounds for damages whereas Watson had none.

After finishing the exposition of his intentions, he signalled to the Clerk of the Court. The small, bald-headed official strode to the jury and, with a display of overwrought courtesy, presented them with copies of some Vinegar letters. They read each with care.

Kingan sat through Jeffrey's performance in admiration at his concision and panache. His anxiety transformed to resolve. The witnesses were to follow.

Jeffrey then requested the clerk to read out his first evidence, Mrs Oswald's deposition. It made clear that it was her family who had first concluded that Watson had written the letters, not Kingan. James Oswald was then called. Head high, chest out, he marched to the witness box. Kingan felt nauseous. He sought contact with Oswald's eyes but the erstwhile friend stared straight ahead.

Oswald answered Jeffrey's questions in the voice he used for political meetings. He confirmed that he had received anonymous letters, three. Kingan's eyebrows rose. Two more! He was on the point of looking at Nancy but drew back.

Oswald confirmed that his family were the instigators of the belief in Watson's guilt and that at first, Kingan had disbelieved this. The blackballing had been his decision alone. He had never and still didn't entertain any suspicion that Kingan wrote the letters. Lizars' opinion was not credible, tainted by his association with Aitken's bank. He no longer believed, however, that Watson had been the author.

'In your report to the arbiters, submitted as item I-23,' continued Jeffrey. 'You placed great store on a note of an encounter between the pursuer and the defendant sent to your sister Miss Agnes Oswald, by the pursuer, as having been proof of your then belief in the defender's guilt. Why?'

'Because the note describes Mr Watson's surprised reaction to the suggestion that he use vinegar for a sore throat.'

'Why was that important?'

'I met Mr Watson earlier that day at the foot of Jamaica Street. I noticed that his voice was hoarse and commented on this. He replied that his throat was very sore. He told me he was heading back to Linthouse. He left me, heading across the bridge to the Clyde footpath.'

Kingan's eyes widened. *'Where had this come from?'*

'I found it somewhat curious that Mr Watson, afflicted as he was by a sore throat, had been surprised by Mr Kingan's use of the word, Vinegar. It's a common remedy for such an ailment. I wondered why? The only reason I could find, which I now recognise as fallacious, was that the word "vinegar" had another meaning for Mr Watson, not as the common liquid but as his "nomme de plume".'

'His surprise was due to Mr Kingan having known about this signature. This conclusion was reinforced by Mr Rowan's next letter received two days after, again signed "Vinegar". It started with the words, "I see you have been showing my letters." At the time, the concurrence of my encounter with Mr Watson, the Vinegar Note and the second Vinegar letter demonstrated proof that Mr Watson had written the letters.'

Relief flooded Kingan. Nancy's words came back to him. 'We will confront him.' Whatever confrontation had taken place, probably led by Mrs Oswald, it had worked. His eyes moistened.

'Are you sure that you met Mr Watson the same day as Mr Kingan's encounter with Mr Watson?'

'Positive. I was going to the Broomielaw to catch a boat to Helensburgh. I was passing some days with Mr Rufus Dennistoun at Cambuseskan. He can vouch for me.'

Jeffrey thanked him.

Cockburn rose. His manner was more of the elder statesman than the mercurial Jeffrey. 'As you well know, Mr Oswald,' he began. 'We have substantial contrary evidence about the veracity of the Vinegar note, which I will demonstrate tomorrow. Why did you not mention your meeting with Mr Watson in paper I-23, your report to the arbiters?'

Kingan held his breath.

'I thought the Vinegar Note and the other letters provided sufficient detail.'

Cockburn glared at him. 'Strange that you avoided any mention of such an important encounter with Mr Watson on the same day, on which, according to the tale you put so much credence to, he had his purported encounter with the pursuer.'

His stare haughty, Oswald bristled. 'The evidence I've just given is factual, true—and verifiable. I believe I mentioned my meeting Mr Watson to Ruffy Dennistoun, my host at Cambuseskan. He will vouch for me.'

Cockburn turned his stare on the jury but addressed Oswald. 'Mr Kingan is well known for his taste in merriment. Do you not consider the Vinegar Note to be a prime example of him inventing a story to satisfy his incorrigible lust for malicious amusement?'

Oswald shook his head. 'Mr Kingan has a well-founded reputation for joking. But he is intellectually and morally incapable of doing what you suggest, writing these letters, casting Mr Watson as their progenitor, falsifying the encounter. You only have to read one of these letters and I have read many, to know that the wit in that trash, if you can call it wit, is as far from Mr Kingan's style as Bonaparte was from God.'

Kingan's face beamed. He felt like running to the witness box and hugging his old friend.

Cockburn's mouth twisted into a sneer. He turned to the witness and said icily, 'Thank you, Mr Oswald.'

Nancy came next. He forced himself to look straight ahead. She went through the printed gown episode and the Vinegar Dialogue with a calmness which carried on through Cockburn's cross-examination. As she stepped down from the box, they couldn't help but share the briefest of glances. The warmth in her eyes stayed with him for the rest of the day.

Margaret Oswald told of the George letter, Miss Hutton of Watson's comments about the boy. She corroborated the Vinegar letters, as did Mr Rowan.

Jeffrey kept the focus on refuting Kingan's authorship of the letters. A couple of longstanding residents and letter recipients testified that only someone with intimate knowledge of Govan could have written them. Kingan was not known in the Parish. Coachmen and clerks told of them having been with Kingan far from Glasgow on the dates anonymous letters had been postmarked by the Glasgow Post Office. Four experts lengthily opined that his handwriting was totally different from that of the Vinegar letters.

Next appeared the witnesses of Watson's slanders. Monteath, appearing under duress, related the blackball and Watson's attempt to have Kingan barred from the Western. Walkinshaw, his voice occasionally breaking, told of how Gilbert Watson had coerced him into surrendering his 'revered' partner's letters.

The shadows in the court grew longer, the crowd in the balconies thinner. Candles were lit, giving the long room a spectral character. Kingan's head began to ache. He forced himself to concentrate.

Led by Finlay, the character witnesses went last. Jeffrey asked each if they had ever received an anonymous letter or a letter signed by Kingan. Recipients of both testified that the Vinegar letters were in no way like his. The last witness, Mr Robert Dalglish, a fellow member of the Monkland Canal Company board, finished at eleven. The courtroom was empty apart from the officials, judges, lawyers and the two plaintiffs. Lord Adam dismissed the proceedings.

Kingan, clutching his frock coat lapels together in a vain attempt to conserve heat, looked across. Watson was rising stiffly, leaning on his agent who took his arm. Kingan grinned.

Chapter 35
Lily Waits

The morning the trial started, Lily lifted her outstretched fingers to the window. The stubby puffiness of the chilblains had gone. She raised the hand so that the light caught her glinting nails, twisting her hand right, left, then back again. She chuckled at the sparkle, chuffed that her harangue of Boyd had made him cough up for the bottle of oil from the stall on Princes Street. He had taken her there for her daily supervised walk. Who would have thought it? Oil for your nails.

She rose from her chair by the window overlooking the crowded High Street. She'd passed much of the last two days looking down from the hotel's fifth-floor window at the motley array tramping underneath her. The first day, it had been enjoyable but yesterday, tedious. The sights didn't compare to Princes Street with its true quality.

A knock sounded. She exhaled. 'It's him,' she said to herself. 'As welcome as ma chilblains.' She heard the key turn and the door opened. Andrew Boyd walked in.

A leering smile spread across a fat face dominated by a broken nose and two squirrel eyes. 'Guid mornin' Lily,' he said in a squeaky voice. 'Sleep well?'

She kept her face sullen.

'Dreamin' o' me agin?'

'Aye. I woke up wi' the colic. Had tae fart ye oot.'

He burst out laughing. 'C'mon Missy. Let's get some victuals intae ye.'

As she passed him, he patted her shoulder. 'Soon be over. The trial starts today.'

She shivered. Tomorrow she would be up before them. Today, more badgering awaited about the list of those who had or hadn't received these damned letters. It was worse than school.

He guided her downstairs to the dining room and thence to their table as if she didn't know how to reach it after their three days in the hotel. The long room was crowded and dim. The aroma of lard from the incessant frying clung to the space. The windows were kept shut to keep out the cacophony outside.

They sat down. Boyd did all the ordering. She looked around. Almost all the tables were filled with men in couples, some conversing, others studiously avoiding each other's eyes, paired by their need for a quick repast. Most were middle-aged and pudgy. Her eyes alighted on an exception and lingered there. *Now, he's braw 'n' bonnie*, she thought, *'N' he knows it.*

He lifted his head from his porridge. His pale blue eyes caught hers like they had known them for years. They were asking a question to which only she knew the answer. It flowed through her, "yes". Her stomach fluttered.

A waitress cut across her vision. Her porridge was laid in front of her, accompanied a moment later by a plate of fatty bacon with a bannock plonked in front of Boyd.

'Gawn' n gie me a bit o' yer bacon,' she pled.

'Aw right. Tak' this.' He passed the rawest rasher to her plate with his knife.

'Dinnae be mean. A piece o' yer Bannock n'aw.'

'Ye gonna leave me some porridge?'

'Awright.'

Boyd completed his part of the trade.

She looked across at Mr Braw 'n' Bonnie. His tablemate had started to talk to him. She tried chewing a morsel of the lump of lightly smoked fat with the grace she'd observed at the Clephane Macleans but her jaws were immediately chomping and grinding. To her mortification, he looked at her. She didn't know whether to spit out or swallow whole. In the end, she did neither. It sat in her slightly open mouth like a gumshield. Head back, he laughed. She waited until his attention returned to his tablemate, then spat the chunk onto the plate.

A minute later, she turned to Boyd, engrossed in his bacon. 'Ah'm in need o' relief.'

'Ah'll come w' ye.'

'D' ye mind!'

'Aye, Ah dae. Ye'll be aff.'

'Here.' Under the table, she pulled up her skirt and extracted her coins from the concealed pocket. She placed them on the table. 'That's aw I have. I cannae get far wi'oot those.'

He looked at the coins and then at her. 'Ye'll need tae gie us a feel o' yer skirt.'

She glared at him, aware that her charmer had finished his tea. 'Keep yer hauns tae the fabric.'

He did.

A minute later, she was in the corridor outside the dining room, her heart thumping. Then, he appeared, looking even better standing full figure, his dark blue frock coat adding a form to his broad shoulders.

'Enjoy your bacon?' he asked in a well-modulated Edinburgh accent.

She liked that. A toff with a sense of humour. 'Better for the jaws than the stomach.'

He laughed, his open gaze engulfing hers. 'Is that your husband?'

She wrinkled her nose. 'Him! He's auld' 'nuff tae be ma faither.'

'Just teasing,' he said without conviction. He moved closer to her. 'I'm here on business. It'll be over by noon. How do you fancy an afternoon at Portobello Sands?'

'A bit cauld,' she blurted. 'Anyway. Ah cannae.'

'Why not?'

'That auld man's ma guardian.'

'Guardian?'

'He's lookin' efter me. Ah'm due tae marry his nephew in England. We're gaun tae Leith tomorrow tae tak' the boat.' She smoothed her skirt. 'They don't want me to get into any trouble afore the wedding night.'

His eyebrows rose. 'You?'

She laughed. They stood still for a moment, his world hers. Then she jumped.

'Hey!' There was Boyd, mouth tight, running to her. 'Whit're ye daein?' He turned to face her beau, 'N' you. Get alang w' yersel!' He reached out and grabbed her, his hand clenching her arm.

'Oi!' she screeched.

Braw 'n' Bonnie thrust his body between hers and Boyd's. Two waiters, who had come running from the kitchen, separated them.

Boyd, eyes ablaze, turned to Lily, 'You!' he shouted, pointing upwards. 'Up the stairs!'

'Ah've nae finished ma porridge!'

'Get up these damned stairs!'

'Ah was gonna leave ye some!'

He moved threateningly towards her.

'Awright.' She straightened herself then, her head held exaggeratedly high, ascended the stairs, glancing once to see if Braw 'n' Bonnie was still downstairs. He wasn't.

Boyd pushed her into the room, then locked the door. He went down to reception. A note had arrived for him.

He returned two minutes later. 'Ah've been called tae see Geordie. He's in a session wi' Gilbert Watson. Ah've tae gaw n' get instructions fir taemorrow.' He shook his head. 'You're a real one, you. Ah cannae tum ma back. Whit wis he promisin' ye?'

'Portobello Sands. Ye better it?'

He slammed the door.

She lay on the bed, enjoying the feel of the pillow against her back. She brought her legs up to her stomach. Then she felt the bulge under her skirt. Half empty. Boyd had gone with most of her money. 'Ah need that,' she hissed. 'If Ah dinnae get it back, they can say guidbye tae any talk aboot they letters.'

A knock on the door interrupted her resentment. A posh voice sounded. 'Lily!'

She thought about not replying but he obviously knew she was in the room. 'Aye?'

'It's me, Alfie?'

'Alfie? Ye English?'

There was silence, followed by, 'My Mother was.'

'She deid?'

'Yes,' he sighed. 'Can I come in?'

'It's locked. Ah dinnae have the key.'

The sound of the lock turning startled her. A moment later, his head poked around the door. 'Can I come in?'

'Naw. Ye cannae. Ah'm a single lady.'

'We don't have much time. Boyd'll be back soon.'

'How d'ye ken his name? N' mine?'

He didn't wait for an answer and sauntered to the foot of the bed. 'Lovely room, Lily. One of the best here.'

'D'ye work here? Is that how ye goat the key?'

He smiled at her, but his previous warmth had vanished. 'I was looking forward to taking you to the Sands, Lily. Shame.'

She pushed back against the wall, knees up, pillow clutched between them and her chest. 'If ye try, Ah'll scream the walls doon.'

'I've no interest in that,' he snapped. 'I'm here on behalf of Mr Kingan.'

She yelped like a cowered pup.

'I'm here to give you some advice.'

Silently, she cursed Boyd's absence.

'Do you know what the perjury is?'

'Aye.'

'Then tell the truth tomorrow. If you don't, we'll pursue you through every court in the land until we see you inside a jail.'

She sat still, hugging herself. When would this nightmare ever end? Her father had been here yesterday with his sob story, Boyd egging him on.

'Do you understand?' repeated Alfie.

'Ah dae,' she sneered, stretching herself.

He was about to lean over the bed but stopped as she froze. 'And don't tell anyone of this little chat or you'll have to explain how I got into your locked room. Whom do you think they'll believe? A gentleman or a maid?'

'Whaur's the gentleman?'

Chapter 36
The Second Day

After a second minute of thumping, there was still no response. Gilbert opened and put his head around the door. His brother lay on the bed motionless, an open Bible on the rumpled sheets. For a moment, Gilbert feared the worst until a rasping snore filled the room. He went over and shook the unconscious form until it moved. His brother's head slowly lifted from the pillow.

'Gilbert,' he croaked. 'What time's it?'

'Seven.'

'Oh—'

'Are you sickly?'

'No,' he said, rising. 'Weary.' He pulled the covers back and then froze. 'The maid?'

'She's locked in her room. Her mother and father are here. They stayed with the brother last night.'

'And the three who received at least one letter she carried but never one signed by Kingan.'

'They arrived last night. Bell says Boyd has her word perfect on them.' Gilbert shifted on his feet.

'What is it?' asked his brother.

'Someone contacted her yesterday, but Boyd chased him away.' Gilbert related the events finishing with, 'it was one of Kingan's men.'

'What?' He put his head in his hands. 'Bell—the porters, now this! Useless clown.' He sighed. 'I'll be down soon.'

As he watched his brother leave, yesterday's debacle came back to him: Jeffrey's surefootedness, Cockburn's plodding, Oswald's lying. How had all these well-paid lawyers not found out about him concocting a meeting on Jamaica Street? He turned again on Bell. 'What's happened to him?'

Then, the image of Kingan's smirking face came. Tears of rage ran down his cheek. His hand frenetically searched for the Bible among the crumpled bedclothes. He found it and his eyes fixed on the last page he had read in the hour before dawn.

Truly, my soul finds rest in God; my salvation comes from him. Truly, he is my rock and my salvation; he is my fortress, I will never be shaken.

The words took the edge off his desperation.

He dressed in his usual sober garb. The dining room was full. Chandeliers provided light to complement the weak, early sun. Gilbert was wolfing down toast and smoked herrings. He ordered the same but then couldn't face them.

Gilbert pushed his empty plate away. 'Is Cockburn recalling Oswald?'

'No. He told me it's not worth another argument. Says we have no corroborated evidence to disprove his tale. And anyway, Oswald didn't directly say he saw the Vinegar encounter taking place, just pointed to its likely veracity.'

'He'll have Dennistoun lined up as an alibi. You know how they are.'

'I spoke with Hunter last night at the Sheep's Heid. He said the city has divided into Watsonites and Kinganites. We're in a clear majority.'

Watson's expression remained impassive.

'Most are of the opinion that Kingan's satire is to blame for the whole affair. I told him about Oswald's testimony. He's very suspicious. Thinks Jeffrey and Oswald have some Whig plot to save Kingan.'

'And will he write that?'

'I doubt it.' Gilbert fixed his eyes on his brother. 'Whatever comes out today, Robert, I'm sure it will be in our favour.'

Watson looked away. *If I could only believe that*, he thought. He tried to marshal his thoughts, to review his options as he had done every day of his life since adolescence. But, for once in his life, attention to detail was beyond him. Faith in The Spirit was carrying him.

#

An hour later, he was sat with his agents. The courtroom was even more crowded than yesterday. He took care not to look at Kingan.

The court hushed as the three judges entered. A minute later, Cockburn rose to face the jury.

After reminding them of the dual nature of his mission, to defend Watson against Kingan and to pursue Kingan on Watson's behalf, he continued as if preaching to his congregation.

'You see in front of you, a man. Mr Watson, whose mind and conduct are regulated by a strong Christian code. A gentleman living peacefully in the bosom of his family, his character unbreathed upon, respected and esteemed by the public as well as by a numerous circle of friends. A gentleman who has been thrown into a state of agitation and distress from which he has not yet, indeed may never recover, by a series of events designed to result in open and public indignation against him, his ejection from society and his extinction as a gentleman and citizen.'

He moved closer and in a conspiratorial tone, said, 'now this attack on Mr Watson was not begun directly by the pursuer but by his friend, Mr Oswald. The same Mr Oswald who has completely and formally exculpated Mr Watson from having written these letters. The same who has acknowledged that he suspected Mr Watson on grounds which he has admitted to have been totally fallacious. We have proof that Mr Oswald's chief reason for suspicion was communicated to him by Mr Kingan in what is referred to as the Vinegar Dialogue. Which I now present to you.'

He nodded to the clerk who took the Vinegar Note to the head of the jury, who then passed it around to the other eleven members.

On the last member having completed his reading, Cockburn moved to take the note. He raised it in front of the jury and proclaimed, 'No such dialogue ever took place. It was invented.' He paused then said in an even louder voice, 'by Mr John Kingan with the sole intention to poison Mr Oswald's mind so as to hide that he and he alone, was the real author of these vicious letters!'

He turned and pointed to Kingan who was sat, eyes glued on the judges. 'I am sorry that Mr Kingan has rendered it necessary for me to advert to the elements of his personal character. Mr Watson says and I will prove that there is no individual in Glasgow so likely to have committed the offence of having written these letters; no one more addicted to personal satire, sarcasm and jocularity. Kingan is their master in the West of Scotland, verbally, in writing, in prose and in verse.' He paused, nose wrinkling, lip curling. 'He is nothing but a common Glasgow joker!'

He quietened and gingerly put the Vinegar note back down on his desk. He pointed to the pile of evidential documents. 'It would have been unpleasant for you to read yesterday such examples of obscenity. But you cannot have read them with a feeling of greater disgust than that which I have had to endure in the exercise of my professional duty to my client.'

'By the end of my case, you will have heard from direct evidence, circumstances which will dispel all notion of the innocence of the pursuer in having written these letters. Listen closely to my last witness, Miss Lily Patrick, once a faithful and trusted maidservant of the pursuer now the main agent of his unconcealment.'

'Listen to the evidence of the arbitration. Listen to the evidence of the pursuer's propensity to manufacture lampoonery. All will lead you to the same conclusion as mine. That Mr Watson was and is totally justified in entertaining that belief that Mr John Kingan was the author of these letters and should be the recipient of substantial damages!'

For the next few hours, Watson listened to his witnesses, each one replenishing the stock of hope swept away in yesterday's torrent of self-doubt. Lawson's emphatic denial of the riverside encounter, followed by his certainty that Kingan had been thrashed by Hagart after Miller's ball. According to him, Mrs Miller's letter was "the peak of the gross and obscene allusions and dastardly insinuating entirely typical of Kingan."

Aitken related how he had reached his unshakeable belief that Kingan had been the letters' author at their meeting at Oswald's. He would regret all his life having remained silent about Kingan's smears of Watson until after he blackballed. Everything was due to the Joker's propensity to low wit, which amongst bankers was well known. He vehemently rebutted Jeffrey's charges of having stage managed the arbitration to obtain revenge for Kingan's jokes.

MacIntosh affirmed his now firm belief that Kingan was the author based on a careful appraisal of the evidence at the arbitration. He regretted not having stated this clearly in the arbitration report.

Watson's spirits rose further when Cockburn announced his turn to focus on Kingan's addiction. An ex-Provost told of having received an anonymous humorous poem lampooning a fellow Tory politician, very much in Kingan's style. MacIntosh's son told of a dinner party where he had heard Kingan reciting a poem ridiculing that same politician.

When he had challenged Kingan to send the poem directly to the politician, "the Joker" had responded, 'What a great idea! I could fire off an anonymous!' To MacIntosh's son's response, 'But he would put it straight in the fire,' Kingan had declared, 'But an anonymous produces great effect on first reading!'

His denigration section complete, Cockburn supervised the setting up in front of the jury of an easel with a large board on which were engraving of lines of text from the anonymous letters paired with lines from Kingan's. Through frequent use of a pointer, Lizars identified the similarities between the two. He was followed by three other experts, all with the same message.

The gentry witnesses followed. As instructed by Watson's agents, each testified that the banker's actions were well merited by the damage Kingan had done to him. Among them were the three recipients of Vinegar letters who had never received a letter signed by Kingan: Spiers; Donaldson and Chalmers. Cockburn elicited from them their suspicions that Kingan had been the author.

#

The court broke for a brief repast at four. Cockburn and Gilbert joined Watson.

'You look haggard, Mr Watson,' said the advocate.

'I am on the outside,' admitted Watson. 'Inside, I am heartened like the distressed wrestler who became the victorious triumpher; the beaten soldier, the resplendent conqueror.'

Cockburn smiled. 'You know your Binning, Sir.'

'I do indeed.'

'Our witnesses have done well.'

Watson nodded.

Robertson, the junior advocate, came across. 'I've just heard that Lord Adam is opening the court tomorrow.'

'But it's the Sabbath!' cried Watson.

Robertson looked at Cockburn who said firmly, 'It's highly irregular, Mr Watson. Very much a measure of last resort. But we have no choice but to accede. There is pressure on the courts.'

'Then, I won't come tomorrow!'

A frosty silence ensued. Gilbert broke it. 'But Robert, Scripture tells us that in extreme times, The Lord makes exemptions. In war, if a soldier is attacked on the Sabbath, he has a licence to defend himself. This is our war.'

Watson glared at his brother, who repaid his stare. *Why is he betraying me?* he thought. Then, the absurdity of his question hit him. He is my brother, my ally. He's right. 'We have no choice.'

Cockburn nodded gravely. 'The maid is next.'

Chapter 37
Lily in Court

Sat on a hard bench, back against the damp, whitewashed wall, Lily checked the sheen on her nails again. The thin sunlight almost extinguished, she shivered in the foosty air. She regretted not putting on her other shawl, the tartan from Mull. She would have draped it under the treasured Paisley patterned shawl she had on, bought in the backroom of Buchanan's Inn. She pulled it tighter and straightened her recently starched bonnet, 'Sunday – best for the courtroom.' She peered up at the tiny, grille-enclosed window ten feet above her. *It must be soon*, she thought. Every hour since arriving at ten, Bell or Boyd had opened the double-locked locked door to offer words of encouragement. She had rebuffed them with her usual acidity. At least, Boyd had returned her coins.

Despite having tried to shrug him off, the posh oaf Alfie had disconcerted her. Money or truth? From the faint recollection of some Sabbath came, *He who takes a bribe to condemn an innocent person is as guilty as a paid assassin. He is to be cursed for life.* She looked around the cell usually used as a waiting room for the debtors' court. 'Tell me about curses,' she murmured. 'What faces me if I give up on the money? Or ma faither? A real curse, the pauper's misery.'

The door opened and in walked Bell. He stood in the middle of the room, a cheap smile and cocky eyes on her. She kept her eyes off him.

'Almost there, Lily?'

She trembled.

'I've come to talk to you before you go on.' He sat down on the bench beside her. 'I know it's difficult for you,' he said gently.

She stiffened.

'I'm not here to talk about the names or anything like that.'

Aye, that's right, she thought.

'I have your money.'

Her head twirled towards him. He raised a small leather bag. She put her hand out to grab it, then paused, ready for him to snatch it away. But he didn't. Eyes wide, she whispered, 'I don't believe it!' She grabbed it and then felt the coins inside. Untying the cord, she let them fall onto the bench. Even in the dull light, the gold glinted. All goosebumps, she stroked the embossed figure of St George killing the dragon. *He's got no clothes on*, she thought. She counted thirty. 'Ah wis promised fifty.'

He stood still in contemplation for a minute, then pulled another bag from his coat pocket. 'You'll get the rest tomorrow. If you get the names right.'

'Ah ken them better than ma family's. Since that first time ye telt me.' She looked at him tenderly, then began to calculate, the thirty and the twenty coming against Kingan's pursuit of her for the rest of her life. 'Ah need fifty mair.'

Bell laughed. 'Come on, Lily. Be thankful for what you've got.'

'Naw. Ah mean it. Master Kingan's man came tae me yesterday. If Ah dinnae tell what they're callin' the truth, they're gawn tae spank the tan o' ma hide in e'vry court in the lan'. An' they're nae kiddin'. Ah need money tae run as far frae them as Ah can.'

'When did he see you?'

'Yesterday at the hotel.'

His eyes shot to the ceiling. 'I thought Boydie saw off your fancy man.'

'He came back.' She smirked. 'Ye ken men. When they're smitten, they cannae stoap.'

His eyes rose to the ceiling. After a moment, he turned and fixed her with a calm stare. 'Here ye are.' He handed over the second bag.

Her jaw dropped. She emptied the coins onto the bench and counted. There were twenty sovereigns. 'Yer Master's awright wi' me getting them noo?'

He shrugged. 'Who cares?'

Her eyes opened wide at his ennui. 'Ye fallen oot?'

His eyes clouded. 'Aye.'

She moved the coins around the bench like a child at Christmas. 'Fifty pounds!'

'That'll take you far from Mr Kingan.'

'Tae America.'

'You can get a cabin on deck for that.'

'Naw. Ah'm nae gaun tae throw it aboot. Ah've tae give some tae ma faither. The rest Ah'll need tae get a good start. In New York.'

'New York. I have a sister there. She could help you.' He hesitated. 'Me too.'

She eyed him boldly. *Ye're an interesting one,* she thought. She looked him over, his expression expectant, his posture to attention. *Nae bad*, she thought. *'Mibbe better than Ah thoat.'*

She heard a knock on the door. Bell helped her scoop the coins into the first bag. Then she pressed both bags into her secret pocket. She smoothed her skirt, hoping the bulge wasn't too evident. Eyes fixed on Bell, she swallowed hard.

'She's ready!' He shouted.

She took a deep breath and opened the door to 'Good luck, Lily!'

#

The usher, a small old man, led her to the courtroom. As she entered, she was overwhelmed by the miasma of sweating bodies, the babel of a hundred pressing faces which hushed as she took the witness box. She searched for a reference point. She spotted her parents, their expressions as if they were on trial. She waved. Her mother responded wanly, her father a tad more forcefully. She touched her skirt. The coins were there.

In the witness box, she put her hand on the proffered Bible. She looked past the Clerk of Court and was amazed by the rows of white wigs, only seen before by her on the footmen at Shieldhall. They glowed in the gloom of the candlelit courtroom. She spied her old master, his eyes cool on her. Her heart thumped. Beyond him, behind another row of wigs, a small man looking as if he had a colic, peered at her. She recognised him from the Kirk. Mr Robert Watson. She turned away and swore her oath to the truth. Whose version? It didn't matter now. She knew her escape.

A stern old man, wig atop, approached. She kept her eyes on his as she answered his question about her name. 'Miss Lillias Patrick,' she said clearly.

'Now, Miss Patrick,' he began after a pause. 'I will focus on your employment with Mr Kingan. Can you tell me the period of your employment and your duties?'

She reeled off her oft-practiced response.

'Between those dates, did you ever see Mr Kingan write any letters?'

'Aye, Sir, Ah did. Aften.'

Cockburn grimaced.

She remembered Boyd's coaching. 'Talk proper like the Clephane Macleans.' 'I did, Sir. Often.' She accentuated every vowel.

'Did you carry any letters written by Mr Kingan while you were employed by him?'

'Yes, Sir.'

'Did you take them directly to their intended recipients or to the post office or to a porter for onward carriage?'

'Just the last two, Sir. Mr Kingan didn't like being without a maid in the house for too long.'

'Did you know for whom the letters were intended?'

'I did, Sir. I read the addresses.'

'Can you remember carrying letters to the following names?' He read out twenty names, all of which she had memorised. To fifteen, she answered yes.

She braced herself for the test: the three names.

'Are you sure that you carried a letter addressed to Mr Alexander Spiers?'

'Yes, Sir,' she announced in a high voice. 'I remember reading that address on a letter passed to me by Mr Kingan.'

Advocate and witness repeated the same question and response for the other two names.

Cockburn moved in front of the jury. 'You'll recall that earlier you've heard from these three witnesses. All testified that they had received at least one anonymous letter but never, to their knowledge, a letter directly from Mr John Kingan.' He nodded to Lily. 'That'll be all, Miss Patrick. Thank you.'

Whit nae smile, she thought. *'Efter aw that.'* At the corner of her eye, she caught sight of Kingan glaring. *'Dinnae blame me. Ye brought it awn yersel.'* She felt a chill as the man Boyd had warned her about arrived in front of her. She looked him over. He seemed to have drawn to him all the courtroom's scanty light. *He wears his wig better than the last yin,* she thought. *But Ah dinnae like his eyes. They see tae much.*

He smiled warmly.

She stilled. *'Whit's he up tae?'*

'Miss Patrick.' He uttered the name as if he had just bumped into her on Princes Street 'I have a few questions for you,' he paused. 'You've testified that you can read and write properly. But yesterday, we were presented testimony from your once colleague, Mrs Hunter, that she had to read the addresses of Mr

Kingan's letters and put them in order so you knew which to take to a porter and which to the post office. Are you sure that you can read?'

Her nostrils flared. *That auld bitch!* she thought. 'Of course, I can. I was at the Govan School for two full years. There should be a letter here from Mr Gibson, the teacher, about my record.'

'I have it here. Item-C44 of the Court papers. Mr Gibson states that you attended the Kirk school for two years and had reached a level of basic competency in writing. There is no mention, however, of your reading ability.' He hesitated. 'I wonder why. Do you know?'

'You'd have to ask him that.'

He looked at her, his clear blue eyes drilling into her.

'Mrs Hunter was always dreaming up tales about me. That's why I had to leave Mr Kingan's service.'

'Mmm—' He moved to his table.

Her fingers began to itch. She restrained the urge to scratch them.

'I have here another of the Court papers, Item I-65.' He strolled over and presented it to the head juror who read it and passed it to his neighbour who did likewise. Jeffrey stood like a head waiter waiting for a diner to finish their main course.

What the hell's oan that paper? thought Lily.

On their finishing, Jeffrey retrieved the page. He made a play at going to present it to her before having second thoughts. 'This document is a record of a statement you gave to my learned friend, Mr MacDowell, dated 15 June 1826, in Denny. This is your signature?'

He shoved her the page. She recognised it from her first meeting with the writer in Mr Cairnie's house. Her stomach churned. 'They tellt me it wouldnae be used. They needed a new statement fir this trial.'

'Just answer my question, Miss Patrick. Is it your signature?'

'Yes.'

'Mr Cockburn asked you about certain names to whom you may or may not have carried letters for onward remittance. You have a good memory of those to whom Mr Kingan wished to send the letters you carried for him?'

'I do.'

'I believe you do as well. Now, there is a name in your signed voluntary statement which lies in front of you, of a gentleman to whom Mr Kingan wished to send letters written by him. You affirmed in the statement that you subsequently carried these to a porter. That gentleman's name is Mr Robert Dalglish. Did you carry a letter addressed to him?'

She sighed. She did remember a letter. Auld Bitch Hunter had known of him, had called him "a mean auld nyaff".

'I did. He lives in St Vincent Place.'

'His name didn't feature on Mr Cockburn's list. Do you know why?'

She hesitated. *There's somethin' behind this which is nae guid.* 'I've no idea.'

'Might it be that the tale of your carriage of letters for Mr Dalglish was invented by you?'

'No, Sir. Ah ne'er invented anything.'

'Then, how do you explain the presence of Mr Robert Dalglish's name in the statement you gave in Denny but not in your most recent given to Mr Watson's agent and presented to this Court by my learned friend, Mr Cockburn?'

She peered into his scowling face. Bell and Boyd had never prepared her for this. 'I've been asked a lot of questions about a lot of names. I carried a lot of letters. I don't think being one out constitutes much.'

'I beg to differ. Veracity derives from accuracy.' He paused. 'Are you aware that Mr Dalglish testified yesterday that he'd never ever received any letters from Mr Kingan. Nor had he ever received any anonymous letters.'

It was as if she had been kicked by a mule. *I definitely remember a letter,* she thought. She looked over the crowd, searching for Bell. He wasn't there. Only her father looking like he'd swallowed an apple whole. Her hands went down to her skirt. She stroked the coins.

Head erect, she fixed her eyes on Jeffrey's. 'I'm not aware of his testimony, Sir. I've no idea why he would give such an account. I only know that I carried a letter addressed to him by Mr Kingan to a porter.'

'I ask you again. Did you—'

'I've already answered that question, Sir.'

Chapter 38
The Verdicts

Next morning, the court was replete with the irreligious and the righteous muffling their conscience. The judges' arrival hushed the hubbub but couldn't dissipate the edge in the air. Lord Adam rose, his steely stare scanning the room. Hands on the table, he stooped slightly forward and addressed the jury.

'Good Morning. Today, the pursuer's advocate will sum up his case in the first trial. I will then give you brief guidance on considering its merits. You must then reach a verdict. Please separate in your minds the first case, Mr Kingan as pursuer, Mr Watson as a defender, from the second, the reverse, when reaching your verdict. After your verdict on the first trial has been given, you will be re-sworn for the second. Do you understand?'

They nodded.

Hunched in his chair, Kingan ran his hands through his hair. He hadn't slept all night, trying unsuccessfully to scour his mind of the opprobrium directed at him in court. Sure that he was going to lose, he wished they'd given him his sentence yesterday. The waiting was awful. He squinted at Jeffrey, who was rising.

The advocate moved to the centre of the room and spread his arms wide. 'Well done, Sirs!' he smiled broadly. 'I congratulate you on your indefatigable fortitude.' He let his arms drop. 'Over the last two days, you've listened to the testimonies of forty-seven witnesses, read a plethora of documents, studied a series of charts and engravings and digested the complex pleadings of my learned friends, the best legal minds in our country.'

'I am conscious that time bears heavily on you, today being our blessed Sabbath. I will, therefore, now abridge the key details of the pursuer's case and guide you to the conclusion at which you must infallibly arrive.'

He smiled again. Kingan studied their faces. Though none smiled, he discerned warmth in many expressions. He relaxed slightly.

Jeffrey continued, 'Mr Kingan's claim for damages rests on two issues. Firstly, that he was libelled by the defender and secondly, that Mr Watson had no justification for his actions.'

'The first issue is a question of fact, totally independent of probable cause and compensation. We have provided to you, testimonies of repeated occasions on which Mr Watson has accused Mr Kingan of being the author of these abominable letters.' He set out the instances. 'These are the most public acts of libel which could be committed verbally.'

He paused. 'Let me turn to the second issue: the justification which with no great prudence or proprietary, the defender has insisted upon, that Mr Kingan wrote the anonymous letters and then caused others to believe that Mr Watson was their author. Yesterday, My Learned Friend, no doubt unintentionally, has misrepresented the history of this case. Let me explain how.'

Jeffrey started with how Cockburn's claim of a plot instigated by Kingan had been "totally destroyed" by the Oswalds' evidence. The real plot was the arbitration set up by Aitken, whose "much vaunted proof of the pursuer's guilt was as worthless in itself as the disgraceful method resorted to obtain it was unjust and inexcusable". He moved on to Lizars' opinion on the handwriting. Mr Kingan's experts had completely contradicted it, as had some of the defenders. Whom could you trust? The majority, who had exculpated the pursuer.

His voice took on a darker timbre. 'Let me now proceed to the all-important question, has Mr Watson established that Mr Kingan was the author of these letters. Why is my attention on the defender? Because the onus of proof undoubtedly rests with him, to make the pursuer's guilt as clear as the sun at noon. His proof should be undoubted and unimpeachable, not one whit higher than if we were in a criminal court.'

For the next twenty minutes, he itemised how Watson's case had been debunked, Govan residents insisting no one outside of the Parish could have written the letters; Kingan, having been out of Glasgow on many postmarked days; how Watson's witnesses to Kingan's authorship had only come forward after the banker had approached them.

He stood more erect. 'My Learned Friend attempted to provide a motive to the pursuer by most woundingly attacking his personal character. But, you have heard from the most esteemed of Glasgow that Mr Kingan lives in the very best of society, uniformly received with kindness and regard by the most respectable, many of whom, like him, are in the habit of making good-humoured jokes. Do you believe that a person with his joyous temperament could be guilty of something so mean, despicable and malicious?'

Kingan flushed. He waited for a murmur of assent, but none came. His angst returned.

'Yet they said they had proof of his letter writing,' continued Jeffrey. 'From whom?' He paused. 'A servant girl of the name of Lillias Patrick!'

Did she say she had seen Mr Kingan writing any anonymous letters? However willing, she made no such statement. No, this witness Patrick was brought forward to prove she had carried letters from Mr Kingan to those who had received anonymous letters.

But the pursuer was fortunately enabled to meet her testimony in the most decided manner. She swore that she had taken letters for an onward carriage to a gentleman by the name of Mr Robert Dalglish. He declared in this very courtroom that he had received neither anonymous letters nor any ever from Mr Kingan. She stated that she can read yet we have produced evidence, she can't. She has been contradicted by so many important particulars that her evidence is worthless.

And lastly, the famous or should we say infamous "Vinegar Note".

Kingan braced himself.

'The question as to the fact that the dialogue actually took place has been disputed by the defender. So how do the facts stand? It has been established that Mr Kingan and Mr Watson both set out walking with destination home around the same time. Mr Oswald attested that Mr Watson was hoarse, as did Mr Lawson, who noted that his cousin had had a bad cold at church the next day.'

'So, two parts of the story are completely proven. Mr Lawson had no recollection of the encounter with Mr Kingan. Did Mr Lawson swear it had not taken place? No, merely he could not recollect it. Does an unsworn set of positive evidence of its non-occurrence overturn two sets of circumstantial evidence pointing to its occurrence? Is it possible, therefore, to say the Vinegar encounter did not take place? No, is the answer to both.'

'I have exposed the groundlessness of the accusation that my client wrote these abominable letters. His character has been purified by an abundance of the most honourable testimonies. And Mr Watson's plea of justification? He has completely failed to make it good.

I have my total confidence that you will find a verdict for the pursuer with such a level of damages as leaves no doubt of the sense of injury you feel he has sustained.'

As Jeffrey sat down, Kingan felt giddy. His head bowed. 'Was that enough?' he asked himself. He looked up blankly. The eyes of the jury were on Lord Adam, who was charging them to provide a verdict. He caught the odd phrase, "very peculiar case", "banish from society", "the pleas of justification". Then the jury rose as one and left.

#

MacDowall led him to a small room where the legal team were clustering around a small table on which lay a tea set. Jeffrey's clerk poured as the advocates took off their wigs and stretched their legs.

The lawyers' banter began, about the jury, about the opposition team, about the judges. At first, it passed Kingan by but soon it irked him. 'Do you think we'll win?' he interrupted in a brusque voice.

Jeffrey turned his sympathetic eyes on him. 'I'm sure, Mr Kingan.' There was a weariness in his voice. 'Now, even more. And probably with substantial damages.'

His demeanour brought relief. On receiving his cup, however, Kingan's hand shook so much that the hot liquid splashed over him. After the fuss of wiping him clean had subsided, everyone sat quietly. He had just reached a state of approaching equanimity when the usher appeared. The jury was ready. 'So soon?' he asked Jeffrey.

'A good sign.'

#

In the courtroom, they waited for the judges to reappear. Once they were seated, Lord Adam reminded the jury of the two issues, on which they were asked to give a verdict: 'did the defender falsely and calumniously state or insinuate to various persons that the pursuer was the author of the anonymous letters' and 'whether the pursuer did write or cause to be transmitted such letters, knowing the content of the same.'

Kingan grasped MacDowall's hand as the hush of expectation seemed to suck the air out of the room. His burning eyes tried to capture those of the head juror who had risen. The well-dressed, grey-haired gentleman, though, was staring straight at Lord Adam to whom he announced in a loud clear voice, 'we find for the pursuer John Kingan Esquire on both issues. Damages, five hundred pounds.'

The air appeared to rush back in, sweeping him into a place of happy stillness. He was vaguely aware of movement and pressure around him. His arms started to be pulled. Then, MacDowall's eyes penetrated his, followed by the sound of, 'we've won! We've won.' He extricated himself from the hug only to enter a series of other embraces. His eyes met Jeffrey's who shook his hand. Only then did the tears start. He searched the crowd for Nancy but couldn't see her.

The sound of the gavel impelled him to sit down. He looked over. Watson lay slumped in his chair, his brother Gilbert crouched in front of him. Kingan sighed, his first expression of sympathy for his foe since the saga's onset.

After checking with Cockburn that Watson was fit to continue, Lord Adam moved to start the second trial. The same jury was re-sworn. Adam reminded them that this new trial was about whether the pursuer, now Watson, had established that the Defender, Kingan, had written the anonymous letters, plotted to charge the pursuer as having been their author and slandered him accordingly.

The two lead advocates indicated that they had no further evidence to bring forward. The Lord Chief Commissioner dispatched the jury.

#

Kingan returned with the legal team to the same room. This time, he paced the floor. Despite Jeffrey's warnings of its unlikelihood, he was desperate that the jurors would dismiss Watson's case and award no damages. Then, victory would be complete. An hour later, they were called back to the courtroom.

Kingan strode in and took his place. A few minutes later, the head juror read out the second verdict. 'We find in favour of the pursuer, Robert Watson Esquire, damages one shilling.'

Chapter 39
By the Well

In contrast to the cheering of the first verdict, Kingan, like the spectators, met the second with confused silence. Subdued, he had thanked Jeffrey for his masterly performance and then lauded each member of the legal team. Now, three hours later, lying on his bed in his room at the New Club, his equanimity returned. He went over the events.

He had been confident that Jeffrey would dismantle Lily Patrick, less so with the Vinegar Note. Nancy had rescued him, thank the Lord for her. He must find out what threat her mother had made to her brother. More than ever, he missed her, still cheated by the lack of her arms around him at the moment of their victory.

A knock on the door sounded. He shouted, 'enter!' A tall footman in the New Club's green livery brought in a silver tray. Kingan rose and picked up the card on it. He dismissed the servant and eagerly opened it.

Mon Palamon, meet me at the St Bernard's Well at four. L'amour de ta vie.

'A tryst on the Sabbath?' He laughed.

#

Thirty minutes later, he was marching down a steep street, the austere silver-grey buildings of the New Town closing in on him, towards the valley of the Water of Leith.

He found it difficult to believe. Free! No more concealing their sweet togetherness. His longed-for blessings were within reach. His heart swelled. And the dinners, the clubs, the balls! He would need time to see the lay of the land: But soon. He doubled his pace.

On reaching the steps down to the muddy path by the brown flowing river, he surveyed the scene below, marvelling at the number of people taking a stroll on the Sabbath, couples chatting, children playing. *Episcopalians*, he thought.

He descended, cursing that his boots were now splashed with earth. After a short walk on reaching the bottom, he spotted her by the well's columned temple with the golden pineapple on its dome. He stopped to admire her. She was watching a group of elderly gentlemen standing by the spring, drinking its water from pewter jugs. She still had on the black and silver velvet gown he had seen her wearing that morning, a matching bonnet and a tartan shawl on her shoulders. Her handsome features thrilled him.

His nose wrinkled as the smell of the spring's sulphur got stronger. She turned and saw him. Her eyes radiated a light which filled his soul with a longing for her intimacy. She ran to him, arms outstretched. As they took each other, his top hat dropped to the ground. She pressed her face to his chest, then a minute later raised it in expectation. They kissed, then broke, then kissed again.

Someone tugged his frock coat. He turned.

'You're blocking the path,' said a small boy, eyes fiery, resplendent in a short red velvet jacket with a white frilly collar. A few steps behind him, stood a woman younger than Nancy, dressed in widow's black, averting her eyes.

Kingan looked at Nancy. They giggled.

'Let's go,' he said.

He retrieved his hat, put it on at a jaunty angle, then took her hand. They walked away from the well, in the opposite direction of most of the strollers, hand in hand, gently swinging their arms, two playmates wrapped in the cocoon of their enchantment.

'How does it feel to have won, John?' she asked as they approached a weir in the river.

'Like I'm free. A full man again. Validated. My guilt dissolved. So many feelings. I'm awash.' He grasped her hand tighter.

'Life will be different now that the world has seen how Watson made you suffer by his calumny.'

'You know, I've hardly thought about him since the trial finished. I've no wish to ever see him again. The Court will handle the collection of damages from him.'

'I may not have that choice, although perhaps he'll move from Linthouse.'

'I doubt it.'

They walked a little more in silence. His moistened eyes would catch hers, then look away, amazed and frightened by the depth of affection. Her face seemed younger, her eyes brighter. Then, arm around her waist, he led her to a small glade some yards from the path. His heart raced. They stopped by a large rock in a thicket of spruces. He let go of her.

'I'm so happy, Nancy. I don't know what to say and if I did, how to say it.'

'Then don't,' she said, placing a finger on his lips, which he kissed lightly.

He gently pulled her head to his. They kissed deeply. His senses tingled. He put his hand on her breast and pushed himself against her, but she froze. He stilled. Voices were approaching. They separated then eyes afire, let their breathing calm as another couple passed nearby, probably looking for the same as them.

'I don't know how I would have survived these last months without you, Nancy,' he said huskily.

'You would have, John. You're strong.'

'No, I'm not. Not without you.' He took both her hands and raised them to his lips. As he gently drew them to his chest, eyes tender, he whispered, 'I love you.'

Tears ran down her cheeks as they embraced, squeezing the breath out of each other.

As he freed himself, he asked, 'Will you marry me?'

She raised her glowing eyes to his. 'Of course, John. Oh, of course!'

They kissed, his tears on hers.

'You'll have to speak to James for permission,' she said quietly as they moved apart.

The mention of her brother dampened his ardour. He remembered Oswald's growled words about his sister Lillias' wish to marry Andrew Mitchell, one of the family's lawyers. 'Share her bed with that little secessionist? Never!' After months, he had relented. Mitchell had had to give up his lay preaching and promise none of their children would be raised in his church. His marriage to Nancy would be worse. He hadn't spoken to him since his dinner party.

'Hopefully, it'll be easier with him now that the trial is over,' he said wistfully.

'Leave it till after we speak with Mother.'
'When should I come to Shieldhall?'
'The day after tomorrow. In the afternoon. I'll prepare her.'

Chapter 40
Eager Was the Wait

For weeks, the anticipation had been building. The warring parties' agents had interviewed so many of the Glasgow Quality (the "dismal ransacking") that the Vinegar Letters had become the *topic du jour*. By a wide margin, the sympathy lay with Watson. The blackballing had wrongfully shamed him, leaving him little choice but to defend himself. It was Scotland's supreme expert on handwriting, not he, who had discovered that Kingan was the writer. Then, it had all seemed to fall into place. Who else could have been the author but the master of the jape, the wizard of the anecdote? John Kingan Esq.

The scatter gun quizzing had also affected servants, porters, coachmen and clerks. Tales of huge rewards had stoked the labouring classes' interest. On the street corners, the jousting over smears had become known as the 'Ten Thoosan' Gemm'. That its outcome hinged on a simple maid had caused great pride.

From the Western Club to the quoit games on Glasgow Green, wagers had begun to be laid. As the trial approached, they had become heavier. By the end of the first day of the trial in Edinburgh, a Friday, hundreds had been placed on Kingan to win but far more on Watson.

The morning of the trial's second day, a crowd gathered outside the Buck's Head, disregarding the heavy showers, waiting for the arrival of the Edinburgh stagecoach. Passengers were stopped as they descended for news of the trial. Odds were amended according to their usually invented titbits.

Come the afternoon, the excitement grew. Kinganites and Watsonites gobbled the greasy food sold by widows and children who had descended on the throng. At the sound of coaches' blowing horns, they jostled to be the first to hear any gossip. But they only learned that the trial continued. After the same tale from passengers on the last stagecoach at nine-thirty, most dispersed.

A few souls, however, mainly layers of large bets, waited at the foot of Nelson Street for the last mail coach. Their curses were loud when they heard the verdicts would not be given until the following day. There were no coaches on the Sabbath. The wealthier than clubbed together and agreed to hire a horse and rider to bring back the verdicts from the Court of Session. He was to return immediately after having learned it, to the Tontine.

On Sunday morning, the Tontine was thronged, the crowd spilling onto the street. The multitudinous bells calling the faithful to Their Maker's Service failed to move them. They were oblivious to their Ministers declaiming the wilful lapse into sin.

As the day went by, a sense of frustration grew. Catcalls were exchanged between the two groups of supporters. On a couple of occasions, individuals had to be parted before fists began to fly. Then, at two, the messenger and his frothing horse arrived. The gathering immediately mobbed the mud-splattered rider who yelled out the two verdicts.

An outburst of confused mumbles arose. Both had won? Then slowly, then loudly, the minority Kinganites cheered. Some hugged. Top hats flew into the air. Dumbfounded, Watsonites glared at their opponents, their murmurs swelling to shouts of disbelief and then derision.

'Damned jury, a parcel o' low life!'

'Wretched ignoramuses!'

'Whit dae ye expect. They're aw fae Edimbra.'

Soon, their outpouring was turned onto Kingan, especially by those who had lost heavily from wagers.

'He's done it agin. The Glasgow Joker. Duped them aw.'

'Goat the charms o' Auld Nick, that yin!'

'Aye. Learned them frae that Mrs Hagart during their secret trysts in the rooms at the back o' the Sarrie Heid.'

'Mair likely, fae yin o' his housekeepers. Ye ken how he likes tae get them blootered efter the midnight hour.'

The Kinganites responded with their own insults, mainly about Watson's Holy Joe airs and penny-pinching ways. Altercations started, the fisticuffs cheered by an ever-growing legion of urchins. The Constabulary, ever wary of becoming involved with the gentry, had no choice but to intervene. The crowd was dispersed. For the rest of the Sabbath, Glasgow was ablaze with the news, whispered between the Psalms, burbled at the end of a silent, cold repast.

By Monday, there was only one topic of conversation. Kingan's victory had deepened the rift with the Watsonites, who were strident in their proclamations of its injustice. Their bitterness towards the victor grew.

#

During the Monday, most participants on the second day of the trial returned. Among the last, was Mr Robert Dalglish, whose evidence had been so crucial to Kingan's victory. On arriving at his house, his son, Stevenson rushed to embrace him. The young man had returned from Liverpool on Saturday after a spell working in the family company's sub-office.

'I heard the verdict,' said the youth, breathlessly. 'It all must have been so exciting!'

'Exciting?' replied Dalglish, taken aback by the ferocity of his son's hug. 'The whole episode was horrendous. Hours waiting as they prattled on about these atrocious letters. My word against a maid! If I ever hear about these letters again, I think I'll vomit. Thank The Lord, I never received one! Nor anything from Kingan.'

Stevenson moved two steps back from his father. 'Oh—but you did, Father.'

'Eh?'

'Two years ago. When you were in London. I received a letter addressed to you. From Mr Kingan. It was to do with the dissolution of the surgical practice, Shaw and Cowan. Cowan's Kingan's nephew. It was a minor affair. Our investment in the practice was minimal. I dealt with it myself. It totally skipped my mind when, after you came back, I recounted what had happened during your absence.'

Stiff with disbelief, his jaw rigid, Dalglish's eyes burned into his son's. After a moment, he shouted, 'Skipped your mind! Like your turn to order at a bar!' He marched directly in front of the quivering youth, now a boy again. 'You fool!'

Many and loud were the tearful, but guiltless son's apologies. They made no difference, however, to his father, who stomped out of the room, slamming the door.

For the next ten minutes, Dalglish sat in his drawing room, cursing his son. His sense of relief had been blown away. Then he went for a walk. He stewed over what to do. Initially, he decided to keep his information quiet, but he didn't trust his son's ability to keep so weighty a secret. Whom to tell, Kingan or Watson?

Chapter 41
Salvation

Watson gawped at his wife, her face pale, her eyes bloodshot. She was at the foot of their bed onto which he'd dropped fully clothed last night. Words were stumbling out of her mouth and then vanishing.

She breathed in and said slowly, 'Mr Dalglish is downstairs. He's come with a very important message. He's insistent. Something about an unforgivable error.'

'What's it to do with me?' he rasped, his tongue furred, his head throbbing from last night's whisky, his eyes half shut.

She bent over him. 'He wants to tell you himself. He's stubborn. I can't get rid of him.'

Watson closed his eyes and let his head fall back into the pillows. After a moment, he engaged his usual self. Dalglish was one of the city's richest men, active on the city council. *I need to see him*, he thought ruefully. He took her outstretched hand and pulled himself up out of the still made bed. She smoothed his rumpled jacket and straightened his cravat.

A minute later, he descended gingerly on her arm to the drawing room. Sitting uncomfortably in an armchair was Dalglish, his deadpan eyes staring from a round fleshy face, below a shiny bald head, above a full pink nose and lips. Watson halted and looked him over. This was a man who, a couple of days ago, had been sworn in as his enemy.

Dalglish took the initiative. He stood up and addressed Watson, 'I won't be long, Mr Watson. I've come to let you know about a dreadful mistake. It concerns my son.'

'Sit down,' said Watson, who took the chair opposite. His wife stood behind him.

In a dispassionate voice, Dalglish retold what he had learned earlier, finishing with a promise to make a formal statement on the matter.

Watson remained silent as his gasping wife lowered herself over him to grasp his hands. His embarrassment stirred him to respond. He freed his hands. Softly but firmly, he proclaimed, 'Thank you, Mr Dalglish! You are indeed a messenger from above!' He raised his eyes upwards and intoned, 'Thanks be to our Lord in Jesus Christ, the Great King above all gods, for giving us this hallowed message. A perfect donation, which as every blessing, descends from Him and Him Alone.'

'Amen!' shouted Iris, hands to heaven, tears streaming.

Hands clasped, head bowed, Dalglish mumbled, 'Amen.' then rose. 'I'll leave you, Mr Watson.'

Watson clenched his hands and shook them forcibly. 'Thank you! Oh, thank you!'

After God's messenger had exited, Iris left to call his sons. In a couple of minutes, eyes wide, they ran to him and hugged him. Iris led him to the dining room. A few minutes later, he supped a couple of cups of beef stock with two slices of bread and butter. After, he sat at the table in contemplation.

That Kingan had avoided his due punishment, embittered him. It was nothing, however, compared to the hurt of the derisory differential in damages awarded. He detested the injustice. Cockburn had opined most jury members hadn't believed that the merchant had written the letters.

The reasons were clear to Watson. The Oswalds. The mother, Kingan's fancy woman, Nancy and the lying, popinjay brother. And Bell. How hadn't he picked up on the link with Dalglish? The maid had faltered but that was because Bell hadn't prepared her properly.

Cockburn had reassured him that the trial had destroyed Kingan's reputation. But that offered no succour. For the last two nights, Watson had lashed his soul with the shame of forsaking His Maker. God had given him a privilege, but he had let Him down.

But now, a revelation had come. His Maker had seen his penance and awarded him salvation. Why? To follow through on his privilege.

#

Three hours later, Watson walked into the atrium of his bank. Sunlight streamed through the ceiling's portals reflecting off the tiled walls. Except for a few gasps, all sound drained out of the queues. He looked around. The numbers were as usual for a Tuesday morning. A glow of relief came over him. He took in the applause, a few claps at first, then a rush, echoing throughout the high space. Behind the counter, the doors of the offices opened and out came Gilbert and the clerks. His spirits surged. He was back. Head high, he passed the tellers to receive his brother's embrace.

In his office, he started to tell his brother about Dalglish but like most of the Glasgow gentry, Gilbert already knew. Their smiles broke into laughter.

'What are you going to do?' asked Gilbert, on it subsiding.

'Secure a retrial.'

Gilbert frowned, then tried and failed at presenting a heartening smile.

Watson's eyes probed his brother's. 'A re-trial troubles you?'

Gilbert looked away, scratching his deformed forearm. 'It does,' he said softly. 'The expense. Our profits have much lessened over the last few months. The merchants have either held off from us or gone elsewhere.'

'That's temporary. Look at today.'

'Our capital is much down. Three advocates and four agents are high-cost. Then, there's Bell's outlay.'

'They're investments.'

'Will we win a second time? Do we need to? After Dalglish, Glasgow is with us. They say even Finlay doubts Kingan. Oswald's nowhere to be seen. They think he's in Edinburgh. Some servant he keeps is in childbirth. Our standing's high. A second trial could undercut it.'

'No,' growled Watson, shaking his head. 'Our standing will be firm when we are seen to win. And, we'll only truly win when Kingan is publicly punished for his calumny and our damages are paid in full and his are rescinded.'

Gilbert went to reply but his brother continued, 'We must start the attack this time. Not the common Glasgow Joker. To win, we need further proof. That housekeeper he had. What was her name?'

'Mrs Copperthwaite.'

'Yes, her. She must know something.'

'We tried. She showed us the door.'

'Perhaps he's been as thick with her as Hagart's wife. That woman in Ardrossan whom he stays with when he takes the waters.'

'She's his cousin.'

'So?' He paused. 'We need to retry porters, servants, any underling.'

'That almost finished us last time. Cockburn was most unhappy.'

'Damn him!'

Gilbert's eyes widened.

'Forgive me,' muttered Watson, as surprised as his brother at his blasphemy. He swallowed and then continued. 'We might consider another advocate.'

'He and Jeffrey are the best.'

Watson hesitated. 'Let it go. That's for later. First, we need more evidence.'

'The maid, Lily?'

'We have all we need from her.'

'But she'll be useful in establishing grounds for a new trial.'

'How so?'

'She was interfered with. Remember Kingan himself met her at Denny when she gave that statement they used. Then, one of his men approached her in Edinburgh.'

Watson pondered the suggestion for a minute. 'But will she talk? Look at the trouble last time. And Bell has already paid her. She'll want more.'

'We can ask him to get in touch with her.'

Watson wagged his finger. 'No! Not Bell!'

'Not Bell?'

'Not Bell,' he repeated, glaring. 'That fiasco with Dalglish was the last straw. He's incompetent.'

'But it was Dalglish's son who was incompetent.'

'Bell should have spotted Kingan's play in the run-up to the trial!'

Gilbert grimaced. 'But he's our main man on the streets. Has been for years. He can sniff information in the air.'

'Not anymore. Look at the porter, McPhail. Either Bell was duped or worse, was betraying me.'

'It was Henry who interviewed McPhail.' He hesitated. 'Bell's no traitor.'

'You sure? Pay him off. Boyd can take over.'

'But he's not in the same rank.'

'He soon will be.'

Gilbert stared at his brother. 'Are you sure about Bell?'

Watson breathed in. *'Why so many questions?'* He asked himself. Then answered. *'Because he's incapable of making a decision. He's always been like that, lounging in the dreamer's haven of "what ifs".'* He faced his brother. 'We pay Bell off. Handsomely. I have the impression he's waiting for it.' His eyes turned fierce and penetrated his brother's. 'Arrange it.'

Chapter 42
No, Not Again

The Monday after the trial, after spending two uncomfortable nights with her brother, Lily caught the first coach to Glasgow. She had heard the verdicts with a rueful smile. Justice had out, neither had won. The trials' indeterminate outcomes dispelled any lingering doubts about the rightness of her actions. She was going to leave her past, come what may.

From Glasgow, she walked to Govan. Her parents welcomed her at their front door like Wellington entering London after Waterloo. Within thirty minutes, the negotiations began. She started by announcing, to their astonishment, her intention to leave for America as soon as possible.

She confidently rebuffed their half-hearted exhortations to stay and fulfil her daughterly duty to care for them in old age. Then the barter started. She forced down her increasingly angry father's demand for thirty to twenty pounds. The chill in their cottage was fearsome for the rest of the day. She wasn't bothered. It was more money than he had ever had.

During the night, her mind fizzed with the strange newness of her situation. For the first time in her life, she had money. And money brought options: whether to pay for a steerage or deck passage, whether to buy new clothes before embarking or wait until America. But with options came a sense of solitariness. Everything was now down to her, not a Master. The thought of enacting her opportunity scared her. For the first time in her life, she began to pine for a companion.

Early the next morning, to her displeasure, her mother woke her, breathless with the gossip. 'Word's aw' aboot the well. The gemm's tae start again. Mr Dalglish's took back his story. He did receive a letter fae yir Auld Maister, after aw.'

'Ah taul' ye. Ah didnae fib!' Then the realisation of the news' import hit Lily. 'It cannae aw be aboot tae start agin,' she moaned.

She spent the rest of a long day avoiding the neighbours. The blether in the village was that a new trial was certain.

'Ye better get ready,' said her father. 'Mair cash could be comin'.'

Her mood darkened at the prospect of yet more humiliation by a posh rogue.

#

The whistle had just sounded for the end of the day at Pollock's Silk Mill. Her mother was blowing on the coals to take the chill of the single room's air when Lily heard Bell's voice.

She startled him, her parents and, most of all, herself with her hug. A broad grin on his face, he freed himself. To her father's displeasure, he insisted on taking her and her alone, to the backroom of Buchanan Inn.

In a booth away from the main concourse, they sat bent over the worn table, their heads almost touching, aware of but disregarding inquisitive looks. After their first glass of claret, she asked, 'N' yer Master?'

'I no longer work for him.'

'Ye left?'

'Na. He fired me.'

'Why?'

'The old fool blames me for losing the trial,' he spat. 'Hadn't the guts to get rid of me to my face. Left it to his "head in the clouds" Brother, Gilbert. I had to ask him to stop apologising. The Auld Master had ordered him to make me take an oath on the bible. I refused. Gilbert didn't force me. But I had to sign a promise to keep quiet about what I did for them. As if a signature ever meant much to them. Then I got my guineas.'

Her eyes rose. 'How much?'

'That's for me to know. I took my savings from the bank safe as well. Good riddance to the lot of them!' His eyes sparkled. 'You'll never guess who's taking over from me?'

Smiling in anticipation, she looked into his eyes. Then it dawned. 'Boyd?'

He nodded.

She laughed. 'Him!'

'I know.'

'He's as useless as a cat that cannae jump.'

They spent the next ten minutes deriding the 'hopeless fool'. She hadn't had a laugh like this for weeks. His eyes told of the pleasure he found in her company. She played with her hair and greeted his every word with at least a warm chuckle. After a moment, they paused, both exhilarated by the other. He squeezed her hand, then before she could speak, rose and went to the bar. He returned with another carafe.

'Now, we're almost ready,' he said on refilling the glasses.

'Fir whit?'

'For this.' His hand went to his inner jacket pocket, from where he extracted two folded papers. After pushing their glasses to the other end of the table and then wiping the surface with his sleeve, he laid them down.

Her eyes focused on the outline of the sailing ship. Head over the page, she made out her name in copperplate script. But try as she might, she couldn't decipher "New York".

'Whit's this, Geordie?' She put her finger under the word, which she then enunciated slowly, 'Mawn—Treel—'

'Montreal,' he said. 'Don't worry. It's a hop and a skip from New York.'

Eyes filling with tears, she gasped. The puzzle that had been in her life these last months was resolved. She could escape. With him. A deep sense of thanksgiving came over her. She leaned across the table and kissed him.

After a moment, they broke. She dried her eyes. 'How much?' Her hand went to touch her coins.

'Later.'

'When do we go?'

'Midnight.'

'But ma maw—' She felt an emptiness in the pit of her stomach.

'They're going to come looking for you for a new trial.'

She exhaled loudly. 'Awright. Where?'

'At the Cross.'

'Better at yin. Auld Willie the scavenger, dis his roons at midnight.'

She didn't ask where they'd be going. For the first time in her life, she trusted someone outside her family.

Chapter 43
A Strange Visitor

Kingan lay on the chaise longue, curtains closed, the tea tray untouched. Outside, mid-morning was breezy, in his study, clammy. And fetid from his continued presence there since Dalglish's debacle. Blythswood Place had become the new Clyde Street, despond the new blindness. He had ordered, 'No visitors.' Not even Miss Oswald.

The laudanum two hours before had brought respite, submerging his thoughts deep into a pool of blankness, well below the surface of his self-loathing. He had lingered thus for a further hour before his burden had begun to reassert itself, provoking a slow debate about whether to return to the presence of the day. He had decided, no. Now, he was on the point of ringing for a top-up of the solace-bringer when a knock on the door sounded. The maid entered.

'He's come back, Master.'

Her voice sounded afar, the words travelling solitarily to him then taking a few moments to coalesce into meaning. Even then, he had no idea what she was talking about.

'What?' he croaked.

'The porter who's come from Edinburgh, especially to see you. He's returned.'

His dizzy head flopped onto the velvet-covered bolster. What was she thinking? If he had told her to send a card turning down Nancy's plea to see him, why hadn't she understood that he wanted no one near to him. Least of all some vagabond. His anger spurted. 'Send him on his way.'

A minute later, she reappeared. 'What should I do, Master? He won't go!'

He sighed in exasperation. 'Get Welsh to get rid of him!'

'He left last week, Master. We're waiting for the replacement. The man says to tell you Geordie Bell sent him. He has information of use in the new trial.'

The dread of the last phrase cut through Kingan's ennui. Conscious enquiry returned to his mind. 'Geordie Bell?' He grappled with the name. A memory came. MacDowall in his office uttering the words, "henchman", "ruthless". He turned onto his side. He couldn't escape. He would have to re-engage.

'Take him to the kitchen. Give him something to eat. Then come and clear these.'

He flapped at the rosewood table with the empty decanters and glasses. 'I'll ring when I'm ready to see him. In the drawing room. Is he clean?'

'No.'

'Then in the hall. Set out two chairs.'

She nodded. 'Will you change, Master?'

He looked at her. Her eyes were on the crimson satin robe he had bought with Oswald on one of their expeditions to London. He looked down. Its lapels were smeared with the silver stains of dried saliva. He sighed. 'I will. I'll do it myself.'

An hour later, after some tea, he walked to the oak-panelled hall, his thoughts grappling with the situation, a porter sent by the agent of his nemesis. Why? His thoughts turned to Nancy. Her image brought a smile to his lips for the first time in days. *'If only she were here to support me.'*

He paused to scrutinise his visitor. Seated sloppily on a wooden chair from the kitchen was a jangly, rough-cut man in the most worn of clothes who he had learned from the maid, was called Donald McPhail.

He stood up as Kingan approached. They shook hands. Kingan took the gilt-caned chair facing McPhail and rested his forearms on the armrest. He looked over the silent visitor who was clutching tightly a patched brown felt hat, his porter's trademark kerchief loosely knotted at the neck. Grey-blue lines formed a half-moon under the bags below his eyes, which had a vacant look. *He's as wasted as I feel*, thought Kingan.

The porter began to cough. Kingan nested his recently cleansed fingers in front of his mouth and waited. On the fit stopping, he asked politely, 'What can I do for you, Mr McPhail?'

'Thank you for seeing me, Master Kingan,' replied McPhail in a surprisingly educated voice. 'I hope you're keeping better.'

Kingan raised his eyebrows.

'Your maid told me you were unwell.'

'I'm better now, thanks.' Kingan stared at him. 'You say you're a porter, but you sound better than that.'

McPhail breathed in. 'I've been a porter these last five years. Before that, I was a clerk to Mr Robertson in the Gorbals. Do you know him, Sir?'

'Vaguely. How did you end up in Edinburgh?'

'Debts, Sir. People looking for me here.' He cast his eyes down. 'The drink, sir. It has affected me with a vengeance.'

Kingan studied him. 'Is Bell one of those looking for you?'

'No, Sir.' He raised his eyes, now radiant. 'I've no debts with him. He came to see me in Edinburgh. Told me to come to you. Didn't he tell you?'

'Fortunately, I've never met the man. I've no idea why you're here.'

McPhail's mouth slackened. 'They've tricked me again,' he mumbled. He looked away.

'Who are they?'

'Bell. O'Neill. McVey. Mr Henry Watson.'

Kingan leaned forward. 'Mr Henry Watson? The son of Mr Robert Watson?'

'Yes, Sir. The very one. I met him at his father's bank.'

'About what?'

'About testifying at your trial that I'd taken letters from you to Mr Spiers, Reverend Leishman. Some others.'

'What?'

'I was to go to the trial.'

'I caught that.' Kingan looked him over. The porter showed no sign of connivance or anxiety. 'But you didn't.'

'No. The lawyers blocked it. Left me stranded in Glasgow without a shilling. Took me a week to raise the fare to return to Edinburgh.'

'No. I didn't mean that. I meant that you didn't carry any letters from me to Mr Spiers or the Minister because I didn't write any for them.'

McPhail put on a grave expression. 'I did carry letters written by you. I was at the stance on the corner of Clyde Street for a while. Your maid took them to me. Lily. The one at the trial. I used to come to the basement for payment.'

'But not to them! I wrote no letters to anyone in Govan Parish!'

'Yes. That's true.'

'Then why did you say it?'

The porter shifted in his chair. He stared at the wall. 'McVey told me what to say. O'Neill instructed him. He promised us that Bell would get the Watsons to pay us. Handsomely. Said they were desperate to win the case. They didn't trust the maid to come good. But it all fell through.'

'Thank God,' stuttered Kingan. 'Who are O'Neill and McVey?'

'O'Neill is close with Geordie. He owns a bar in Goosedubs. McVey was my friend. A porter.'

Kingan stiffened. The residue of the afternoon dissipated. 'Could this be a Watson snare?' he asked himself. 'Using this scoundrel to plant a false story of a porters' plot. Getting me to bribe him. Then organising a statement from him to show how I fabricate evidence.'

'What did Bell say to you in Edinburgh?'

'He found me outside Dowie's where I share a stance. Took me for a dram. He told me that the whole rigmarole between you and Mr Watson was going to start again. Said you would be interested in what had happened with me before the last trial, putting together the story of the letters, meeting Henry Watson. You could use the facts in a new trial to show how the Watsons work. He said you would give me a reward. Will you?'

Kingan disregarded the question. 'What's in it for Bell?'

'Revenge, I think. He said that Watson had fired him, had greatly made badly of him, blamed him for our tale not having been used in court. After how he's been treated, Geordie doesn't want to see Mr Watson win any new trial. He gave me the fare to here. Told me I should tell you what I've just told you. Then wished me the best and upped and left. He's getting out of Scotland. Where, I don't know.'

Kingan frowned. He didn't know what to make of this self-confessed drunkard with the unsettlingly strange air. Why would such a creature come all the way from Edinburgh if there was no truth in his story? He didn't know what to do but one thing he was sure about, he wasn't going to pay McPhail until he knew it wouldn't prejudice any future defence against Watson. He needed to speak to McDowall about his options.

He rose and paced the floor behind McPhail, rubbing his neck, sore from having been cricked for hours during his stupor. *I have to say something to this ne'er do well*, he thought. *But what? I can't frighten him away. I need to give some form of retainer.* He turned and sat back down.

'I thank you for what you've just told me, Mr McPhail,' he said firmly. 'But before I make a decision on what to do, I need to discuss it with my lawyer. Are you willing to make a signed statement to him?'

'For a small sum, Sir.'

Kingan grimaced. He thought for a moment about refusing but decided needs must. 'I can't promise that until after I meet with him.'

'When will you know?'

'It's late now. They'll be closing their offices. I'll endeavour to see one of them this evening. I promise to let you know by tomorrow noon at the latest.' Kingan stared at him. McPhail's eyes didn't flinch. Perhaps he was telling the truth. 'Do you have somewhere to stay?'

'I'll look for lodging in the Briggait.'

'Do you have enough for it?'

'In truth, no, Sir.'

Kingan felt in the pockets of his frock coat, which he hadn't put on for many months. In the side pocket was a coin. He took it out. To his surprise, it was a sovereign. McPhail's eyes lit up. Kingan felt his waistcoat and trouser pockets. There was nothing. He hesitated, then handed the coin to McPhail who bowed, saying, 'That's very generous of you, sir?'

'Come here tomorrow morning.'

'I will, Sir.'

They rose and shook hands. Kingan accompanied him to the front door and then watched the porter walk jauntily down the street. *In a hurry for the first bar*, he thought.

He turned back in and closed the door. On the table by the entrance lay three cards in Nancy's handwriting. He opened the top, dated that morning.

My adorable John

To say your refusal to see me these days has cut me to the quick, underestimates the deep hurt I feel.

On reflection, I understand. Only a deep anguish provoked by the turn of events caused by that misanthrope, Dalglish, could have led to your flight from my love.

Do not be lonely, my love. Remember our joyful hour by St Bernard's Well, our precious feelings for each other, the openness in our hearts, the hope in our souls. May that memory bring you courage!

Oh, my adorable John, take care. The Fates have militated against you. But your life is so much more than this struggle. Do not let the endless defence against Watson's perfidy corrode your spirit. This is pointless.

Madly eager to see you again.
Nancy

An hour later, his reply was on its way to Shieldhall.

My beloved Nancy
I apologise with every atom within me for the distress I've inflicted on you. In these last two days of confusion and anxiety, I have not been myself. That is not an excuse but an explanation. Your note of today penetrated my isolation. It brought hope, exactly what my soul yearned.

My Love, you are right. This never-ending dispute is crushing my volition for life. Without you, I cannot withstand any longer its dead weight on my soul. If it does have a point, it is that its ending will bring us together and thus fulfil the single-most desire I have, for us to be joined so that before we die, we may at least say our days have been blessed with happiness.

Madly eager to see you again.
John

Chapter 44
O'Neill

The next day, Kingan was with MacDowell in his study. The late March weather had taken a turn for the worse. The black sky signalled snow. A fire raged. Even so, the two huddled close to it for warmth.

By early afternoon, after a light lunch, there was still no sign of McPhail. As the lawyer studied papers which he had brought to prepare for a forthcoming court case, his host paced the room.

'Where might he be?' asked Kingan.

'Sleeping off last night in some den, I imagine,' replied MacDowall.

'He mentioned O'Neill's in Goosedubs. Do you know of it?'

'No. Do you think we should try there?'

'Better than sitting here twiddling our thumbs.'

'Let's go before dusk.'

'I'll get the maid to call a gig.'

#

Thirty minutes later, their capes splattered with snow, they walked down the long, narrow lane of Goosedubs. Kingan raised his muslin handkerchief to his nose; glad he'd perfumed it. O'Neill's was at the far end of a row of drinking dens—cheap liquor, warm bodies and bawdy ribaldry. On entering, he looked around at the smattering of drinkers in the different booths, mostly men, a few attentive women. There was no sign of McPhail. He and MacDowell stood out like dukes at a dunghill.

He marched up to the bar. The solitary, fresh-faced barmaid, barely a woman, stiffened. 'Hello, my dear,' he cooed, eyes twinkling.

'What you fir?' she barked, suspicious eyes wandering all over him.

'Some information, my dear.'

'That's no' on the slate.'

'Not from you.' He hesitated, then asked, 'What's your name?'

She scowled. 'Whit's yir name?'

'Mr John Kingan.'

Her eyes widened. 'You're the gent frae the Ten Thoosan Gemm?'

'I am indeed.'

'Ah'll hae t' speak wi' ma faither. Wait here.'

'But your name, my dear?'

'Betty.'

'How lovely!'

Her face turned even stonier. She turned, opened a door behind the bar and left.

'She knows why we're here,' commented MacDowell.

Kingan nodded.

A moment later, Constantine O'Neill opened the door, followed by his daughter. Rolls of stomach protruded over his belt, stretching his creased shirt to busting. Below it stuck two legs, surprisingly short for its bulk. Topping a neck which merged into his shoulders was a rotund face with an even redder bulbous nose between a pair of squeezed green eyes.

He extended his hand. 'Mr Kingan,' he intoned. 'An honour.' He turned to the lawyer and repeated the welcome. He pointed to an empty booth. 'Why don't we sit over there? We can have some privacy.'

They refused his offer of drinks and took their places, side by side, on a wooden bench by a scarred table. O'Neill, huffing and puffing, sat down opposite them.

'My daughter said you wish for some information.'

Kingan and MacDowell looked at each other. The latter went first. 'We're making enquiries about a legal matter concerning my client, here, Mr Kingan.'

'The new trial with Mr Watson.'

Kingan glared at the suddenly business-like publican.

'There's no new trial with Mr Watson,' retorted MacDowell.

'Yet,' replied O'Neill.

'What's it to you?' intervened Kingan.

O'Neill pursed his lips and fixed his eyes on Kingan. 'To me, I reckon it's about fifty pounds.'

'For what?'

'For information. That's the going rate.'

'I've never paid any informant that sum in my life.'

'Your competitor does!'

'You were expecting us, Mr O'Neill?' asked MacDowall.

'I was.'

'Donald McPhail was here last night?'

'He was. With his shiny gold sovereign. Many a toast, many a happy face taking his company, many a happy song.'

'And where is he now?'

'He left with a woman of many favours. He had plenty to choose from. They were like a pack o' dogs on a fox.'

MacDowell's lips curled.

Kingan looked at MacDowell, who sat arms crossed, waiting presumably for some instruction on whether they were going to make O'Neill an offer. Kingan chose another tack.

'Mr McPhail told us about a plot you and he were involved in to incriminate me. You, Geordie Bell and Henry Watson were its ringleaders. We're on our way to collect Mr McPhail to take him to the Fiscal,' he announced.

'In that case, I've nothing more to say to you.' O'Neill pulled himself up.

'Wait!' shouted Kingan.

O'Neill stopped, placed his hands on the table and, leaning over, peered down at Kingan, who met his stare with steel in his eyes.

'You're at risk, Mr O'Neill,' he declared. 'We'll seek from the Fiscal a charge against you of attempting to pervert the course of justice. If you cooperate with us, however, I guarantee there'll be no charge against you. Mr Henry Watson and Mr Geordie Bell are whom we want. After they receive their just deserts, I promise you a substantial gift as a token of my affection.'

O'Neill's eyes went to the ceiling. After a minute, he sat down. 'Geordie's gone. You won't get him.'

'Where to?'

'To London.'

Kingan exchanged glances with MacDowell, who nodded. He turned to O'Neill, whose fat face was sweating. 'Well?'

'I'll help you.'

'Tell me about your dealings with Bell and Watson.'

For the next ten minutes, O'Neill spoke about the porters' plot. Kingan asked most of the questions. MacDowell took a note. On completing his tale, the publican agreed to come to MacDowell's office to make a formal statement the next morning.

O'Neill offered them a whisky. This time they acceded to his invitation.

While he was at the bar, Kingan rested his arms on the table, let his head droop and breathed out loudly. 'Thank God!'

'Well done, Sir,' said MacDowell, patting his weary ally on the back.

'Thank you.'

'We need to secure McPhail and quick.' He looked around. Half a dozen faces turned away.

Kingan nodded.

As they supped their drams on O'Nell's return, MacDowell asked him, 'Do you know where McPhail went yesterday?'

'He left with Maud Tait. She lives not far from here in a close behind the Saltmarket.'

'Do you have her address?'

'I don't. I can get someone to take you, though.' He looked around. 'I think I've seen that fellow over there with her. Wait.'

He rose and went to a booth at the opposite end of the dim room. There, nursing a tankard, was a small, hunched bald man with a wizened face. After a brief conversation, he nodded, O'Neill returned.

'He'll go. He's charging a sovereign and wants a solemn promise you won't tell anyone of his association with Maud. He's not giving you his name.'

'Tell him, I agree.'

O'Neill stood up and nodded to the expectant man who returned the gesture.

As MacDowell rose, Kingan asked O'Neill, 'How did you know Watson is paying fifty pounds?'

O'Neill smirked. 'Do you want to outbid him?' He nodded towards McDowell. 'Not worried these lawyers will drain your pockets?'

'Don't worry, Mr O'Neill. I have deep pockets.'

'I know because it's what Lily Patrick received.'

'How do you know that?'

'Geordie told me.'

'Where is she now?'

'In London. With Geordie.'

Kingan stilled. The image of her scuttling across his kitchen in Clyde Street, being chased by a screaming Mrs Hunter, ladle in hand, came to him. It seemed a century ago. Despite his bitterness towards her, he grinned. *She always knew what she wanted*, he thought. *And she got it. Good on her.*

'Will you testify to that effect?' asked MacDowell to O'Neill.

'I will. If you keep to your side of the bargain.' The bar owner paused. 'Fifty pounds is what Boyd's dangling in front of the porters now.'

'Who's Boyd?' asked Kingan.

'The new Geordie.'

Kingan let out an ugly laugh. *Watson never gives up*, he thought. 'I guarantee you at least fifty pounds, Mr O'Neill. At least.'

Chapter 45
Find Him

The morning Kingan and MacDowell were waiting for McPhail, Watson was in his office at the bank, on the point of leaving for a celebratory lunch at the Western Club. He had prepared a few quips about the Glasgow Joker, revelling in his new disappearance. Was this one due to another thrashing? He would steer clear, though, of ribaldry about Kingan's illicit liaison with Hagart's wife. The husband was attending.

There was a knock on the door. 'Who is it?'

'Mr Boyd, Sir.'

'Come in.'

This had better be good, he thought. *'I've to be out of here at eleven.'*

Boyd entered, cap in hand, heart fluttering. 'I've to be out of here in ten minutes,' he grunted, glaring at Boyd. 'What is it?' He'd already had to berate the "new Geordie" twice yesterday for his semi-coherent excuses about not locating Lily Patrick.

Boyd twitched. 'I've some news from my investigators.'

'About the maid?'

'No.'

'A porter?'

Boyd shifted on the high-backed chair in front of Watson's empty desk. 'Sort of.'

Watson grimaced.

'It's about the last porters. The ones that came forward about carrying letters from Mr Kingan to Govan.'

Watson leaned forward.

'Donald McPhail has reappeared in Glasgow. He's the one who spoke to Master Henry about the letters.'

'I remember. The liar.'

'Yes, him. He was in O'Neill's last night, with a sovereign.'

Watson's lips curled.

Boyd hesitated. 'McPhail was very big-hearted with his favours. The sovereign drew a large company. At first, he refused to answer how his luck had changed. But later, when he was well fu', he let go to the company. In it was a woman we use occasionally.'

'A harlot?'

Boyd flushed. 'Yes.'

'I told Bell to stop paying these hussies after Walkinshaw.'

'He didn't tell me.'

Watson's face went puce, his eyes protruding. 'Go on.'

'The woman, Jessie McPherson—'

'I don't wish to know her name.'

'She came here looking for Geordie fifteen minutes ago. I saw her. She told me that McPhail said he had received a gold sovereign from Mr Kingan. Later, he left with a woman, Maud Tait.'

'I told you, no names!' Watson's nose wrinkled as his good cheer about the imminent lunch drained completely. 'Bell told me McPhail had returned to Edinburgh.'

Boyd kneaded his felt hat. 'I presume his appearance in Glasgow has something to do with the prospect of a new trial, Master.'

'Obviously,' hissed Watson. The new trial was his to win, the damages reversed, Kingan finally punished. Most of his fellow gentry wanted to see Kingan out of Glasgow. He was certain Oswald wouldn't stop him this time. Rumour had it he was most unhappy at his sister's dalliance with the Joker. All he needed to secure his triumph was a more complete set of evidence. But now this.

Kingan would use McPhail, perhaps even go to the Fiscal. And the involvement of Henry. He shook his head. That was a grave mistake, he rued. A heaviness came over him.

He turned back, eyes flinty. 'Find McPhail. Bring him here. Or else—'

Boyd winced. 'The woman is waiting outside the back door to take me to—where McPhail went last night.' He paused, then mumbled, 'I need to pay her if you want her help.'

Watson scratched the back of his head. Bell had never pushed him into this type of dilemma. '*Can I use the services of a harlot for higher ends?*' he asked himself. He scoured his memory of sacred works for guidance.

Then he sat back. Rahab, the brothel keeper of Jericho. '*Had she not served God by helping Joshua and the Israelites defeat the sinful Canaanites? Was she not praised as a person of good faith in the Book of Hebrews?*'

He looked at Boyd. 'Stay here. I'll get a couple of florins from the desk.'

'She'll want more. McPhail had a sovereign.'

Chapter 46
A Murder

Just beyond the open front door of the flat, head between his knees, Kingan held his breath and waited. His fallen top hat had landed on the top stair just beyond the pool of his vomit. After a minute without retching, he picked it up, straightened and ran his hands through his wavy, grey hair, checking that it covered his temples. From the inside of the flat, he heard voices. He wondered about going back inside. But the prospect of seeing the smashed and splintered skull in its glistening halo of blood repulsed him.

An urge to escape came over him. He picked up his hat, wiped his mouth with the back of his white kidskin glove and stumbled down the stairs into the alley. He cursed as his patent leather shoes hit the open sewer. The splash covered the hem of his ankle-length suede cape. He began to trot up the cobbled space between the high tenements looming over him, blocking the low winter sun.

After a few seconds, he stopped, chest heaving and looked around. A barefoot child in rags gaped at him. Then, a fleeting memory came to him of the last time he had been here many years ago, before the neighbourhood's descent into what the Ministers decried as "the squalid abyss of vice". Try as he might, he couldn't remember what he was doing here or who he was seeing.

After he didn't know how long, he felt a tap on his shoulder. Cowering, he slowly twisted his head. He sighed in relief. It was McDowell.

'We've covered the body, Mr Kingan,' said the lawyer, his florid face stern. 'What now?'

He took a step back, mumbling, 'I don't know.'

McDowell stared at him.

Behind them, a repeated thud sounded. Kingan turned and saw their guide stamping his slush sodden boots to warm his feet.

'You need to decide something, Mr Kingan,' said MacDowell as they stood freezing.

'What?' quivered Kingan.

'You need to tell me as your lawyer what you want done.'

Kingan's disgust at the sight of the cadaver had morphed into a stunned confusion. 'He's been murdered,' he muttered. 'McPhail. What do I need to tell you?'

'Normally when I become aware of a serious crime, I inform the Fiscal. But I'm acting on your behalf just now. You need to tell me if I should proceed in the same manner,' he said in a voice which appeared eerily calm to Kingan. 'Before you answer, you need to be aware that his death has legal implications for you. It may complicate your defence against any court case that Watson may mount against you. Who knows? You may even become a suspect.'

'Me, a suspect?' Kingan's voice quivered. 'But I could never have done anything like that. We found the body. This gentleman will testify to that.'

As he turned round to see their guide from O'Neill's, he heard MacDowell shout a loud 'hey!'

The small man was scarpering up the street. MacDowell gave chase for fifty yards, but he was no match for the fleer. He returned breathing heavily, his face crimson. They waited until the effects of his unwelcome exertion had passed.

'Do you think that he'll come back?' asked Kingan. 'I mean to confirm that we found the body.'

'I don't know.'

'And the woman?'

'Tait? If she's alive, she'll have scarpered.'

Kingan began to shiver. He was on the cusp of crying but with an effort, controlled himself.

MacDowell's eyes filled with concern. 'You're deathly pale, Mr Kingan. We need to get you out of the cold. A brandy will help. Let's go back to O'Neill's. I'll find out there who our guide was.'

'And then we go to the Fiscal?'

'Do you want that?'

Kingan hesitated, nonplussed by the question. *Is there a choice? This is murder.* 'Yes,' he whispered.

'I agree. But we need to pull ourselves together and work out our story.'

'We don't need a story. We have the truth. Everything points to Watson being behind this.'

'Truth is precious, Mr Kingan, but often wounds the teller. You've just come out of Glasgow's most infamous trial in years. On paper, you won but your reputation was thrashed as is unfortunately now after Dalglish, your credibility. There's a chance Watson will successfully incriminate you for this murder. It's important we engage the Fiscal before Watson. But we need to be clear what we say.'

Kingan found it difficult to discern his lawyer's meaning.

'Let's not go into these matters now,' said MacDowell. 'We'll go to O'Neill's. There we can hire a gig to the Fiscal. We'll talk during the journey.'

MacDowell took his client's arm and led him back down the alley past the entry to the close. A small crowd had gathered. It silenced at the unusual sight of two Quality approaching. Kingan trembled as he pushed through the sullen faces. Once they had passed, the murmur restarted again, an anger in their gravelly utterances.

'Don't look back,' hissed MacDowell.

#

Five minutes later, they were at the door of O'Neill's pub.

McDowell placed his hand on Kingan's arm. 'This place will be agog with the murder. It's better you let me do all the talking. I'll go and speak with O'Neill after obtaining you a brandy. You sit by the fire.' He opened the door and then turned. 'Remember, don't speak to anyone while we're here.'

Kingan nodded, his mind on his lawyer's.

The heat hit him first, then the fading of the hubbub to a hush. He slumped against the door side. The dizziness had not totally left him. MacDowell steadied him and then guided him to the raging fire. He ordered a burly drinker to leave the chair he had taken beside it. The man rose, cursing. MacDowell plunked down the wobbly Kingan.

A minute later, Betty came with a glass of brandy. She stood over Kingan like a guard as he supped it slowly, conscious of all eyes on him. Slowly, he strengthened to a point where he felt a modicum of resolve. *I've acted honourably,* he reassured himself.

Five minutes later, MacDowell reappeared, a glass of brandy in his hand. He downed it in one. 'Let's go.'

'And O'Neill?'

'I spoke to him upstairs. He'll take care of Moir. He wants an advance. We'll organise that later.'

'Moir?'

'Our guide.'

'Oh—'

Kingan took Betty's hand and stood up.

'Thank you, my dear,' he said with a feeling. 'What's your name?'

She shook her head.

#

In the gig, MacDowell explained that William Moir, had already been in the bar, announced the murder and had fled. O'Neill though, was certain he would not go far and, with inducement, would collaborate. Maud Tait, McPhail's company, hadn't been seen all day. There was a chance Moir might lead O'Neill to her. O'Neill's sent his son out looking.

Kingan sat slumped. The clacking of horses' hooves on the cobbles filled his head. He thought of his predicament. *'A court case about the murder would devastate me,'* he concluded. *'And Nancy.'* Remorse surged through him. Then, the image of McPhail's shattered head in its pool of blood, the Devil's halo, came back. 'He's the victim, not I.'

He bent over to MacDowell, sitting opposite, his mouth close to his ear so the driver could not hear. 'We must tell the Fiscal everything we know about McPhail, including that Watson is behind his murder.'

'We have no proof of that.'

'But there are reasonable grounds for suspicion.'

'There also are of us.'

'But you've just said, we'll find Moir.'

'O'Neill assured me of that and I believe him.'

'Then, there's no impediment to us being frank with the Fiscal—Is it still George Salmond?'

'Yes.'

'Good. I know him. He's a fine and reasonable man. He's not of Watson's party.'

'But he is close to our Chief Magistrate, Archibald Lawson. And we know what danger he presented to you at Court.'

Kingan went quiet.

'Listen, Mr Kingan. This is my advice. As you say, we must be frank with the Fiscal. Not being so will lead to suspicion as to our motives. But only up to a point. That point is our suspicion of Mr Watson's involvement.'

'Eh?'

'In my opinion, a murder trial is not in your interest. If the Fiscal uncovers that one of Watson's men is the murderer and there is evidence that Watson is implicated, you would be called as a witness if we tell the Fiscal all what McPhail has told you. Any trial would be viewed as an extension of that which finished last week in Edinburgh. Most of the Glasgow gentry, from whom a jury will be drawn, would not see the Crown prosecuting Watson but you.'

His eyes grew harder. 'My firm recommendation is that we tell the Fiscal of our meeting McPhail but withhold our knowledge of his involvement in Watson's plot before the trial and ensure through O'Neil that those who hold such knowledge also keep it to themselves. We say that McPhail promised us information of use in any new trial but wouldn't provide it until paid. You, as was the case, promised not to pay him until you'd spoken with me. The Fiscal will investigate. If he finds one of Watson's men implicated, that has nothing to do with you. If Watson claims to the contrary, you rebut it as more of his grievance.'

'But all at the O' Neill's Bar know I gave McPhail a sovereign.'

'Just say it was out of pity.'

'But it's a murder.'

'A murder of whom, Mr Kingan? A drunk. An idler. A debtor. A lecher who died in a harlot's den. A plotter in a criminal conspiracy against you. A man with no known family. Is such a life worth the devastation a trial would wreak on you? I don't think so!'

'But you're a lawyer!'

'Of many years. And this is what I've learned. The law is in the hands of the victors. What chance do you think there is of a successful prosecution against Robert Watson? He's careful. Any evidence of his wrongdoing will be scanty. He has power, access to the best of advocates. He has respect, a former magistrate whose standing has been enhanced considerably by recent events. I tell you that there is no chance of a successful prosecution against Mr Robert Watson. And upon whom would the failure to secure a sentence rebound? You.'

'And on justice!'

'That's not in your interest. I doubt if your health would survive a second, even more vitriolic battle. You would certainly relinquish any prospect of acceptance back into good society.'

Kingan felt squeezed by MacDowell's rationality and the nausea churning in his gut. The light-headedness returned. Then, an intense anxiety came over him. What would happen to Nancy? To their chances of marriage? He pressed his lips together. 'What do we do then?'

MacDowell sighed. 'We use this murder to our advantage.'

Kingan squinted at him as if from behind a barricade. To his advantage?

'I know this is difficult,' said MacDowell in a placatory voice. 'But what's just happened could be a way to extricate you from a new Vinegar trial. End this endless affair.'

Kingan shifted uneasily. 'How?'

'We threaten Watson with telling the Fiscal everything we know about his porters plot. Look at what we hold against him. McPhail's evidence about the plot, especially Watson's son's involvement. Then, there's what O'Neill just told me. Bell maintained a roster of the impure for choice gossip. McPhail's bedmate, Maud Tait, was probably one. O'Neill's sure that another of them will have already spoken to his new man Boyd about McPhail. They're the steps on a path linking Watson to the porter's murder.'

'But we never obtained a statement from McPhail.'

'I'll squeeze a statement about the plot out of O'Neill. No doubt for a high price. He's promised he'll try to find out which harlot is talking to Boyd. When he's found her, I'll take a statement from her incriminating Boyd. We'll find this woman Tait. She might have something on Boyd.' He paused. 'We'll offer Watson a deal: we'll not inform the Fiscal of our hand against him if he agrees to stop seeking a retrial.'

Kingan frowned. Seeing Watson in prison would rid of his pestilential presence from his life. Then Nancy's phrase returned. *This is pointless.*

He turned to MacDowell. 'And if Watson doesn't agree?'

'We go to the Fiscal with our evidence about his involvement with McPhail.'

'You've just said the Crown will lose against Watson.'

'That's the most probable outcome. Will Watson want to take that risk? I doubt it. If he does, he's a fool.'

Chapter 47
Manoeuvres

Nobody wanted to tell him.

The backdoor guard had been the first to hear. The gossip had started a couple of hours before. Kingan had been seen in the close of the "hoor Maud's hoose" where "a deid body" had been found. Then, it had turned out that the Joker hadn't been there first. 'Billy Boyd n'aw wi' that wimmin Jessie.'

'That Maud must hae been awfie bissy!' Another tasty morsel came later. 'Kingan's at the Fiscal!'

At the bank, the tellers debated who should inform the Master. He hadn't been seen since Boyd had marched, head down, out of his office.

'Let's wait for Billy Boyd.'

'But where is he?'

As the clock clicked towards closing, they decided it would be safer to tell Mr Gilbert and let him do the talking. 'Surely, he'll be back soon.'

'These literary lunches.'

#

All eyes upon him, Gilbert arrived, flushed. Ross, the chief teller, pulled him to one side. As he spoke, Gilbert's eyes widened. He asked Ross to repeat himself. On receiving a negative answer to his inquiry about his brother's knowing, he inhaled and braced himself.

Robert Watson was seated with his head over his work bible, which lay on the otherwise empty desk, mumbling Psalm 121, 'I lift up my eyes to the hills. From where does my help come? My help comes from the Lord, who made heaven and earth.' He looked up, startled by Gilbert's entry. His lips turned down on recognising who it was. 'What is it?'

Gilbert shivered. The fire was unlit; the room was freezing. 'May I sit down?' Watson pointed to the empty chair.

'My apologies for interrupting your prayer,' said Gilbert, placing his hand over his mouth to hide a burp.

Robert Watson kept his eyes on his brother, whose voice, thankfully, he hadn't heard for hours. *'Where's he been?'* he asked himself. Now he smelled it. *'Quaffing with his versifying friends.'* 'Not praying,' he snarled. 'Seeking sustenance in God's Words.'

Gilbert tried unsuccessfully to suppress another burp.

'Too many oysters?' sneered Watson. He didn't wait for an answer. 'Would you please tell me why you're here? I'm waiting for someone.'

'Billy Boyd?'

Watson's face tightened. 'Yes. How do you know?'

'Ross told me.'

'How does he know?'

Gilbert disregarded the question. 'There's been a murder. This morning of a certain Donald McPhail in a whore's room in a tenement near the Saltmarket. Boyd was seen coming out of the close. As was Kingan. But after Boyd. Kingan then went to the Fiscal.'

Watson's face turned ashen. His hand trembling, he shut the Bible as if God couldn't take any further bad news. He slumped into the chair. What was happening to his salvation? Where was his privilege?

'Is it the same McPhail who came forward claiming he carried Vinegar letters from Kingan?' asked Gilbert.

'Yes.'

'And did you ask Boyd to find him?'

Watson nodded. 'We heard he'd gone to Kingan. Had told him of his involvement with us before the trial.'

Gilbert's eyes widened. 'This is serious,' he paused. 'And the others involved with McPhail?'

'Bell never said who the others were. Boyd did say Bell was linking with O'Neill who used to keep stables in the Gallowgate.'

'I thought he'd left Glasgow. Some unpaid debt.'

'He's back. Owns some low-life tavern.'

Gilbert paused a moment. 'I've always found it strange that it was Henry who interviewed McPhail. It was one of Bell's rules to keep his informants away from us.'

Watson froze over the error, with which he had been berating himself this last hour. 'It was on my instructions.' He put his head in his hands.

Gilbert moved towards him, but Watson put out his hand. They both sat in still silence.

After a couple of minutes, Watson said hoarsely, 'We need to find Boyd. Before the constables. He was setting out to O'Neill's.'

'But Boyd's our man for these things. Who else do we have? Maybe we can get Bell to come back.'

'No!'

They fell silent once more.

'I can speak with Davidson. Ask to use his agents,' said Gilbert. Davidson was a Writer often commissioned to represent the bank in court proceedings for debt recovery.

Watson pondered the suggestion. *Boyd'll squeal to the Fiscal like a pig before slaughter,* he thought. 'Involving lawyers in his capture. I don't know.'

'Kingan probably already knows of the murder. And if that's the case, so will the Fiscal. They'll claim that you had a motive to order the murder and Boyd was your killer.'

Watson's head drooped. Gilbert sat hunched.

'We have no choice, Robert,' announced Gilbert. 'We must see Davidson.'

Watson, his expression vacant, nodded.

#

They decided not to hire a gig and walked to the Blythswood Estate. The bustle in the gaslit streets might as well have been on the moon. As they turned the corner into the street of Davidson's premises, Watson stooped rigidly. On the opposite pavement striding through the slush was MacDowell.

The enemy raised his top hat and shouted, 'Good afternoon, Mr Gilbert and Mr Robert! I trust we'll meet soon.' He smiled and continued on.

'Cur!' hissed Gilbert.

'Why's he here?' quavered Watson. Suddenly, Kingan seemed everywhere.

Gilbert shrugged.

To a frozen Watson's relief, they finally reached their destination. The premises were light and airy in contrast to those of most of the city's lawyers who grouped together on the gloomy upper floors of old Glasgow tenements. They waited in a high-ceilinged hall, its walls decorated with paintings of Highland landscapes. They spoke little, Watson still amazed at his quandary.

Davidson himself came to greet them, shaking their hands heartily. Gilbert's old friend had retained his youthful demeanour, his light brown curly hair free of grey, his visage free of wrinkles, his smile free of regret. 'Let's go into my lair,' he said cheerily. 'I'll order some tea.'

Watson rose stiffly. Gratified that the office was warm, he settled into a plush armchair by a rosewood coffee table. Gilbert sat opposite him. After a few minutes, a maid brought the tea. Davidson drew up a chair facing the brothers. While Davidson and Gilbert exchanged chitchat, Watson watched the maid pour the tea.

As soon as she had left, he began. 'We saw MacDowell on the street outside.'

'He just visited me on behalf of Mr Kingan,' replied Davidson, to Watson's irritation, smiling.

'Why you?'

'He knows I often act on your behalf. He asked me to take a highly confidential message to you.'

'Which is?'

'It's about the murder of a certain McPhail. Do you know of it?'

Watson looked at Gilbert. 'Yes.'

'Poor man,' sighed Davidson.

Watson eyed him suspiciously. A soft-hearted lawyer?

'The Fiscal's looking for his killer,' continued Davidson. 'That's why you're here.'

Watson glared.

Gilbert nodded. 'Do you know if our porter, Billy Boyd, is a suspect?'

'McDowell didn't mention that. He knows Boyd is acting for you as someone called Bell once did, but he didn't refer to him as a suspect. He spoke more about McPhail himself.'

He faced Watson. 'According to him, yesterday, McPhail told Kingan that you had been going to bribe him to falsely testify at the trial that he had carried some of these Vinegar letters from Mr Kingan to identified recipients. His tale, however, hadn't stood up with your advocate. McPhail promised Kingan that he would tell the Fiscal about this so that a criminal charge be brought against you.'

'He was due to return to Kingan's to make a statement to MacDowell this morning to that end. When he didn't turn up, they went looking for him. They found him murdered. MacDowell says he has evidence from a certain O'Neill who was involved with McPhail in the plot. It implicates one of your staff named Bell—and your son in the procurement of falsified evidence.' He looked over at the pale Watson. 'Now, you tell me, that this Boyd may be a suspect in a murder. Why?'

Watson remained speechless.

'We found out about McPhail blabbing,' intervened Gilbert. 'A prostitute told Boyd. We asked him to locate McPhail. We then heard that Boyd was spotted where McPhail was found dead, in the room of another prostitute, I believe, before Kingan's visit.'

'Oh—' Davidson nested his fingers and rested his chin on them. 'MacDowell didn't come just to tell me what I've recounted. They want an agreement with you, Mr Watson.'

'About what?'

'You give up on the retrial and they hold on to their evidence of the plot involving McPhail. If not, they'll tell the Fiscal and incriminate you in McPhail's murder.'

'Eh?' exclaimed the two brothers in unison.

'MacDowell and Kingan haven't told the Fiscal anything about Bell or your son's dealings with McPhail. They claim never to have mentioned anything about this Bell, or for that matter, Boyd. Simply that McPhail had come to Kingan with some information about a maid's whereabouts. Lily something.'

'With all due respect, Mr Davidson,' spouted Watson. 'You don't know John Kingan like us. He's an inveterate liar with immense powers of deception. This is a trap. His end is to get me. Why wouldn't he and MacDowell just tell the true story instead of this concoction?'

'To use it as a bargaining counter in this proposed trade.'

'But MacDowall's admitted to you that he's misleading the authorities?' asked Gilbert.

'If they don't get what they want, their line to the Fiscal is that they only learned the whole truth after further speaking to O'Neill. He'll corroborate that.'

Watson's lips curled. 'That bastard's the Deil's spawn!' he bellowed. 'Give up on him? Never!'

Davidson winced. He turned to Gilbert, who asked, 'Robert, are you sure? The Fiscal will be looking for Boyd.'

'Of course, I'm sure! After everything he's put me through. No!' He stilled for a minute, saying to himself, *'They need to understand.'* He breathed in. 'I have a privilege from Our Maker. To release this world from Kingan's calumnies. I cannot desist.'

Gilbert shrunk back.

Davidson looked at Watson intently, then eye cocked, said, 'but if the Fiscal finds Boyd and they tell the whole story, you're done for.'

Watson was about to decry their cowardice when Davidson spoke again. 'I sympathise with you, Mr Watson. You have indeed been most unjustly wounded by Mr Kingan. But today's events have made a new trial to obtain just retribution for your wounding over these letters, most unlikely. Any criminal proceedings will take precedence over a civil trial. And what is likely to be presented in court would make the chance of a successful outcome to a retrial for damages practically nil.'

'And Robert,' said Gilbert. 'Kingan is finished. He's a pariah. No one of any worth in Glasgow is letting let him darken their door.'

'That's not enough,' affirmed Watson. 'Divine Justice demands the Joker is branded guilty by the Courts. And I repeat, I have received the privilege of ensuring it.'

'He's already been found guilty, Mr Watson,' said Davidson. 'You won your damages.'

'But not enough.' The stoniness in the other two's features made him pull back. *They can't see the sacredness of retribution*, he thought. *'MacDowell's won Davidson over to Kingan's cause. Gilbert's allying himself with his crony.'*

'Boyd's still out there, Mr Watson,' reminded Davidson.

'He'll betray me like you.'

'Nobody's betraying you, Robert,' said Gilbert gently.

'I think someone already has,' declared Davidson.

Watson's eyes sparked. 'Who?'

'MacDowell told me it was your man Bell who told McPhail to go to Kingan.'

Watson's flinched as if punched in the groin. 'Judas,' he whispered, then chanted, 'woe to that man through whom the Son of Man is betrayed!' His head drooped. *Victory had been near,* he thought. *But the Devil is wily. His principal Marshall, Kingan, cunning. He's probably had Bell on his side for years. He's set up McPhail's murder to escape the retribution which he merited. But the privilege still rests on my shoulders.* He glared at Davidson. 'I'm not giving up.'

Chapter 48
The Endgame

Points of light from two candelabra and a chandelier played on the table, fighting the late afternoon gloom which dulled the white acanthus cornices, turquoise walls and oak-panelled doors. Pale blue velvet curtains draped high windows. Under a white marble fireplace with Corinthian columns, a fire raged.

Kingan looked across at the white-faced Watson, whose bloodshot eyes burned into the long, polished walnut table. The banker's hair was bedraggled, his clothes crumpled, his hands drumming the table in an uneven. staccato rhythm. Kingan thought Watson seemed on the brink of a breakdown. The thought didn't bring satisfaction but heightened the apprehension he had suffered all day while waiting for the meeting.

By midday, with no word coming about Watson's engagement in an agreement, MacDowell had had to send Davidson a note. By then, O'Neill had found Boyd, who was now hiding upstairs in the bar. MacDowell had indicated that what happened with Boyd next depended on the outcome of the proposed Kingan/Watson meeting. Davidson had responded that Watson had just agreed to meet, but only to judge if an agreement could be reached. Kingan had totally rebutted this.

Time was pressing; the Fiscal had constables out. There had had to be an agreement or Boyd would be arrested. Then two hours before, Davidson's reply had arrived. His client had acceded. The two lawyers had then met to draw up a draft agreement, two copies of which now laid on the table, one in front of each party.

'Many thanks for coming,' announced Davidson, sat at Watson's side, facing MacDowell beside Kingan. 'I hope you find as I do, the setting suitable for our task, to achieve a harmonious resolution to what has been, I think we all agree, a most arduous and lengthy dispute.'

Kingan kept his eyes on Davidson. *What a popinjay!* he thought. 'Dressed like he's going to a ball.' He glanced at MacDowell, reassured by his usual sobriety.

'Shall we go through the agreement paragraph by paragraph?' asked MacDowell.

'I recommend that,' said Davidson. 'Gentlemen?'

'That would be most useful,' said Kingan.

Watson swivelled and glared at Kingan. 'Before that, I have a letter for you which I wish you to read. Hopefully, you will agree on the contents and we can both sign it.'

'But Mr Watson,' cried Davidson. 'Mr MacDowell and I have already drawn up a draft agreement!'

'That's to do with not seeking a retrial. This—' He extracted a page from his frock coat pocket. 'Concerns the letters.' He pushed the page across the table.

Kingan looked at MacDowell. 'Do I need to read it?' he asked.

'We're not going to advance until it's considered.'

He looked at Watson, whose eyes oozed malice. He turned away and read the scribbled words in the first line:

I, Mr John Kingan, do most humbly apologise for the—

He read no further and pushed it back to Watson, who, to his surprise, looked genuinely shocked.

'It's to be confidential,' blurted Watson. 'Appended to any agreement. I guarantee no publicity.'

'I have no reason to apologise to you for anything.'

Watson shook his head. 'You most certainly do! You know you wrote these letters and Dalglish's admission proves it.'

'It does nothing of the kind!'

'You deny it still!' shrieked the banker. He pointed to the letter. 'If you will not give me justice on your authorship of the letters, at least finally withdraw your evil charges that I wrote them.'

In no way was Kingan going to bend the knee. Yet he swithered. His hand went to his inner pocket, where he had stuffed Nancy's letter. The delay in Watson's response to their offer had enabled him to send a card to her, explaining the situation. Her reply had reached him just as MacDowell had arrived at his home to accompany him to Davidson's. As he fingered it, he remembered her final sentence, *Stay strong, Palamon!*

'We are not here now to repeat the trial but to avoid a new one,' he said calmly. 'Let me remind you that your man Boyd is in our keeping. We've arranged a witness of easy availability, Jemma Wood who will act as an alibi for his whereabouts at the time of McPhail's killing. Boyd was most thankful. If you do not accede to our request for an agreement, he's agreed to inform the Fiscal of your command that he use the web of harlots you've been maintaining for years, to find McPhail.'

Wright, MacDowell's partner had visited the Fiscal at noon. There was no sign of Maud Tait, McPhail's liaison. She was now the authorities' prime suspect in the murder. MacDowell had told Kingan not to divulge this information in the meeting.

Watson froze, eyes raised to the ceiling. After a moment, the irregular drumming started. No words came.

MacDowell took the initiative. 'I'll start on the agreement. Here's the first section.

'We, Robert Watson Esq. of Linthouse and John Kingan Esq. of Blythswood Place, Glasgow do today 7 April 1828, as witnessed by Mr Peter Angus Rupert Davidson, Writer and Mr Francis McDowell, Writer, honourably swear in strictest confidence that:

"With regard to a motion for rule to show cause that a new trial should be granted in the case of Kingan vs Watson and Watson vs Kingan heard on March 21 and 22, 1828 at the Court of Session, Edinburgh, both parties will desist from pursuing any legal proceeding with this as an object from now until both are deceased."'

MacDowell hesitated, then looked at Watson, then Kingan, 'Agreed?'

'I agree,' said Kingan.

Watson's head was still turned away. After a moment, he turned and looked at Kingan, his bloodshot eyes burning with disdain. Kingan glowered back. *Cede*, he thought. Their eyes moved off each other.

'Agreed,' blurted Watson.

MacDowell breathed in then continued, *'With regard to the murder of Mr Donald McPhail, Porter, Edinburgh, both parties will desist from providing to* the Procurator Fiscal evidence which may incriminate either party as having been involved in or having given rise to the involvement of other parties in, actions which may have indirectly led to or caused directly this crime and may therefore lead to one or both parties being prosecuted in a criminal court.'

'Do you agree to the clause, Mr Kingan?' asked MacDowell.

'I do,' Kingan muttered.

'And you, Mr Watson?' asked Davidson.

'I do,' he grunted.

'Given the highly confidential nature of this document,' MacDowell continued, *'And the high-risk which it presents to both parties, there will be no other copies made of it. These two identical documents will be held in a double-locked safe, in a secure building to be defined by both parties' legal representatives alone i.e. without the prior notification of the parties.*

'A single key will be made for each lock. One legal representative will hold one key, the other representative the other key. On the occasion of either of the legal parties' retirement or demise, the key will pass to a nominated successor, details of whom will be sent to the other legal representative prior to such event's occurrence. Should access to the document be required, by one party, his legal representative should inform the other's and a joint access contract drawn up prior to the document being released from the safe.'

'You don't trust me,' growled Watson.

'We do, Sir,' replied Davidson. 'This is simply a safeguard.'

'Against what?'

'Against continuation of the dispute.'

'Do you disagree with the clause, Mr Kingan?' intervened MacDowell.

'I'm challenged by it, to be honest,' replied the merchant, surprised by Watson's apparent ignorance of the condition. 'It suggests that neither I nor Mr Watson can be trusted to give up on our—' He hesitated. He was going to say feud but then considered the word belittled the struggle of the last years. 'I think you called it, "dispute", Mr Davidson.'

Davidson was about to reply when Watson shouted, 'Dispute! It was no dispute!' He pulled himself upright. 'It was a battle of the soul.' He pointed at Kingan. 'You, Sir, are evil!'

Kingan had been girding himself for Watson's covenanting zealotry. In her letter, Nancy had written how Miss Catherine Hutton had come over to Shieldhall that morning. She had heard that Watson had appeared at first light at the Govan Manse, requesting Reverend Leishman's blessing for today's meeting. The Minister had desisted, not wishing to be seen taking parties in the affair. Watson had then burst into a hysterical harangue about God having given Watson the privilege to punish Kingan, Glasgow's most corrupt and irredeemable perpetual sinner. Leishman had slammed the door.

'I am not evil, Sir,' Kingan responded icily. 'Like all, I may do evil. Our peers in court made a judgement on my actions and found some had wounded you. I apologise for those. But I'll never apologise for the letters because I did not write them. Accept the verdict of the courts!'

'No, Sir! There is a higher court in life than that in Edinburgh. The natural office of conscience. The most-high God placed it as his deputy within every man's breast. God has given me the privilege to use it. It is this which I use to accuse you.'

'Evil is more than the sum of a man's actions. It is a state within. In the heart, the mind, the soul. In you, these are as sepulchres painted without but putrefied within. Your evil leads you to refuse to acknowledge His infinite goodness. It helps you flee from the responsibility of your choices. What happened in Edinburgh was a failure to punish that flight.'

What self-deluding gibberish, thought Kingan. *'He insults me to receive an insult back to fire up his lust for revenge.'* He breathed in and with effort, took the emotion out of his voice. 'This is pointless.'

MacDowell and Davidson remained hushed as Watson stiffened and glared at Kingan, his eyes full of savage loathing. But the absence of a riposte, the lack of a blow against blow for the first time in years, fulfilled its purpose. He remained speechless.

Kingan, conscious of MacDowell's restraining hand on his arm, continued staring at him but remained silent, bathing in the satisfaction of seeing his enemy's passionate desire to hurt go unrequited.

After a minute, Watson turned again. He wasn't finished. 'Do you think Glasgow is unaware of your idolatry of the female flesh?' he said in a trembling but quiet voice. 'Mrs Hagart. Mrs Copperthwaite. Miss McCall, your very cousin. And now, Miss Agnes Oswald.' His voice strengthened. 'Do you think that your liaison with her shows your once friend in a good light? The man from whom you've to obtain permission for the misguided marriage you're planning?'

Kingan gasped. *'How does he know?'*

'Take care, Mr Kingan. I'll never forget the evil you inflicted on me and my family. And, as My Maker is My Judge, I'll make sure you never do.'

Kingan's heart raced. He strained and constrained the impulse to fling a wounding barb. The foreboding, which he had submerged all morning, reasserted itself. Watson would never change his views. Further inflaming his poisoned mind would only lengthen their pointless struggle. He turned to MacDowell. 'Can we please continue the proceedings?'

MacDowell nodded. 'Mr Kingan, do you agree to this last clause?'

'I do.'

He turned to Watson, who was seated staring blankly. 'Mr Watson?'

There was no answer. Kingan flinched.

Davidson repeated, 'Mr Watson?'

From the mouth of the rigid banker came an embittered rasp, 'I do.'

Epilogue

Kingan raised his head out of the water and let go of his nostrils. As the sulphur fumes pinged against the back of his throat, tickling a cough, both hands ascended to smooth his hair, making careful strokes to clear his forehead of any strands. They then descended underwater to cover his genitals. His manhood protected, he lay back in the salty, almost viscous water. Sunlight streamed through the rotunda's windows, reflecting off the water onto the white marble statues of figures from Greek mythological females encircling the pool.

He arched his neck and took in his fellow takers of the waters in the Montpellier Spa Bath Room. On Men's Unclothed Morning (Members Only), most of his dozen or so fellow bathers, of a certain age like him, also had their hands over their groins, occasionally lifting one or both to take a couple of lazy strokes.

He spotted Colonel St Clair, one of the many military men who passed their days in Cheltenham, either in retirement or between commissions. He waved at him, shouting, 'see you this evening!'

The normally pale now crimson square-faced Highlander barked like an order to his infantrymen, 'bring your joke book!' before emitting his high-pitched, staccato laugh, which Kingan never failed to find disconcerting.

That evening, both were to attend a dinner for General Sir Archibald MacLaine, the Hero of Matagorda, at the Royal Hotel. Kingan was due to give one of the toasts to Her Majesty's Navy. Captain St Clair, the Colonel's brother, was to reply. It was Kingan's main dinner that week.

When he had judged his dose of immersion sufficient, he signalled to the attendant stood erect by the door. The athletic, handsome guard nodded and immediately went to a press at his side and extracted a fluffy white cotton bathrobe and three similarly opulent towels, one for the head, one for the groin, another for the hands.

He strode to the steps down to the round pool, extended the largest of the towels while balancing the robe over his shoulder and the other towels on his forearms. As he did every week, Kingan synchronised his ascent of the steps with the attendant's actions. After a flurry of whiteness, he exited the pool room, snuggly draped in towelling.

He luxuriated in the feel of the cotton against his skin. It was so much better than the sodden flannel he had to peel off at the Sherborne Spa, the site of his other two immersions per week. Tomorrow was a Pump Room Day. He would imbibe his measured three pints of the Spa water and pass on to the masseur for vigorous feet and leg rubbing.

As he dressed in his changing cubicle, he gave his silent thanks to Dr Montagu, recommended to him by his nephew Cowan. His Priessnitz principles worked. Neither his gout nor eye problems had returned since twelve months before. He had arrived in the pretty, hill-circled town to recover from the travails of the last two years. He had hoped to return to Glasgow after a few months, but Nancy's and Finlay's letters had advised waiting. Watson's relapse into severe despond had stoked the Quality's antipathy to him, the cause of his nervous exhaustion.

He strolled to his rooms at the Queen's Hotel, nodding to the promenaders. As the months passed, the fashionable and mannerly bustle of the spa town had sustained his mood of renewal. His bitterness at the moral burning had receded.

Men's Unclothed Morning heralded the arrival of his weekly mail from Glasgow. He expected his nephew Cowan's weekly package of selected periodicals and a letter from Nancy. It would contain news about their plan.

#

His mind turned to their tearful goodbye at the Glasgow coach station two weeks after his agreement with Watson. The wrench had been almost unbearable. Two weeks later, Mrs Oswald suffered the first of her strokes. Her speech slurred but her intellect undiminished, she now required constant nursing. Nancy's laments about her mother's fate had filled him with remorse about his distance from her. But he couldn't have faced Glasgow.

Three months later, he had received another shock: news of Margaret's engagement to the recently widowed Dr Alexander MacFadzean whose hydropathic facility was near Oswald's summer house in Ardrossan. James had promptly approved the betrothal in contrast to his belligerent rejection of his and Nancy's pleaded request. Her sister's wedding had severe consequences for Nancy. She had to assume the role of dutiful daughter and oversee her mother's care and her nieces' upbringing.

He had tried to keep up her spirits, but he could tell from the bitterness in her letters that she had been close to despair. Then, the week after the wedding, to his surprise, had come her plan. She would visit her sister-in-law, Elizabeth Anderson, in London to propose that the two girls, Mabel and Mary, now fifteen and thirteen, come to live with their mother. This would free Nancy from one of her duties.

With Mrs Oswald's tenuous state of health, the second would surely pass soon. They could then marry with or without James' approval. She would keep her brother in the dark about the plan. Despite having had major doubts about the plan's prospects for success, to give her hope he had agreed. He would come to London to meet her after she had made the proposal to her sister-in-law.

#

He picked up his mail from reception and ascended to his suite. He read Nancy's first. It was finally safe to travel. The cholera epidemic which had swept through the country was abating. She would be in London in two weeks.

A broad smile broke over his face. 'At last!' He opened Cowan's package and turned first to his now preferred newspaper, *The Scots Times*, the *Herald*, eschewed after Hunter's treachery. The paper was full of the unrest which was sweeping the country. The King had blocked the Whig's act to reform the voting system. He had invited the Duke of Wellington and his Tories to form a government. The main article was about the response in Glasgow.

A crowd of over a hundred thousand had gathered on Glasgow Green. Hundreds of black flags flew high with slogans, "Liberty or Death", "We are Prepared", "By the Bones of our Fathers, We Shall Be Free". Kingan' lip curled as he read the introduction to the main speaker 'Oswald of Patriot Father—Patriot Son!'

In a voice loud and clear, his nemesis had pledged to support "with all my energies, the measure of Reform unmutilated and unimpaired". At his finale, arms outstretched, he had proclaimed, 'we are ready, if necessary, to lay down our lives in defence of our rights and the liberties of our country!' He had closed the meeting by leading a mass singing of *Scots Wha Hae.*

Kingan put down the newspaper. The words in Nancy's letter returned. *He's unbearable now. He talks of nothing else but politics. He hardly touches the businesses. Thank God, I hardly see him.*

#

A month after her letter, they met in Anderson's drawing room, wiping away tears of joy and relief, embracing and kissing deeply. The next two hours were the happiest of Kingan's life. Speaking a little, smiling much, they held each other tightly and kissed. When desire had impelled them for more, they broke and stood apart.

Conscious of the coming tea with the Andersons, Nancy breathed in. 'Elizabeth was much taken by my proposal. Indeed, relieved. The girls' marriage prospects are so much better here in London.'

'And their dowries.'

'That's true.'

'Now, I have to face James,'

'If he'll deem to see you.'

'You read about him?'

'In the Scots Times.'

'You've heard about the Clique?'

Wellington's government had fallen to be replaced by Earl Grey's Whigs. The Reform Act was being passed. In preparation for the first election under democratic rules, Oswald had formed a group, termed the Clique by Hunter's Herald, with his Whig cronies.

'I did.'

'They're plotting to take control of Glasgow politics with him as the next MP.'

A chill came over the room.

'He'll never let us marry, Nancy. Not now, when he's on the point of realising his ambitions.'

'Don't say that!' Her eyes filled with tears. 'Let's elope, John. What do we have to lose?'

He hesitated. At first, on the journey to London, he had come to the same conclusion. Then his doubts had surfaced. He had much to lose. Acceptance. The moral burning was a distant memory. No one now moved to the other side of the street when he went for a stroll. His wit had returned and with it, the invitations. Cheltenham had given him back his soul.

She stiffened at his delay in responding.

'Let's not rush,' he said soothingly.

'Why? The waiting is destroying me.'

'Let's be patient. If he agrees to the girls' move, then—' he hesitated at mentioning her mother's likely demise. 'it won't be long.'

'It already is long. Too long. You can't understand how much I suffer. Alone up there in Shieldhall.'

He took a step back. 'You have your friends.'

'Not many. The only one I see regularly is Catherine. Each Sabbath after the service. I'm tired of talking about our woes!'

He grimaced as her accusing eyes raked him. What he had hoped wouldn't occur was.

'You don't want to elope, do you, John? You've become comfortable in Cheltenham.'

'I can't go back to Glasgow, Nancy. You know that.'

'I'll join you here, then.'

'I'd love that.' He moved closer. 'Believe me, I do. But we couldn't settle in Cheltenham after an elopement. People would talk. We'd be excluded.' He shivered. 'I couldn't go through that again.'

Her head dropped. She began to cry. He took her in her arms. She rested her head on his chest.

He waited until she had stilled. 'I have an idea.'

She looked up at him, eyes doubtful.

'To get your brother to drop his opposition.'

She shook her head. 'He won't.'

'If I were to apologise publicly to Watson and he was to accept it, there's a possibility James would reconsider his disapproval of our match.'

'Why?'

'Letting bygones be bygones would signal the end of the affair. It would erase any cloud hanging over James from it. Appearances are all in politics. Especially at this time.'

'And how do you intend to apologise?'
'Through a letter published in the newspapers.'
She frowned and pulled back slightly from him.
'What other option do we have?'
'Elope.'
There was a knock on the door. Tea was ready.
'I can't do that, Nancy,' he burbled.
She fled from the room.

The rest of their time in London, the visits to the galleries and Bond Street shops were pleasant, but a restraint entered their closeness. He strained to recapture their intimacy, cracking witticisms at every opportunity. She laughed but with a boisterousness which wasn't natural. The heightened feelings of the first hours of their renewed tryst had dissipated by the time they separated the day before her return to Glasgow.

#

His next weeks were tinged with shame at his lack of courage to elope. He dreaded the arrival of her letter. He wasn't surprised. Discretion had entered her words. Effusiveness had escaped from them except when referring to her brother. Oswald had refused to accede to the girls' move. Glasgow would be safer for them. Kingan worried about the depth of the bitterness she expressed in her words of reproach. He mused that Oswald might be a lightning conductor for her feelings towards him.

He put off his reply. His lowered mood brought back the Vinegar letters. The trials' outcome still rankled. He replayed the events in the courtroom, selecting snippets of testimony which, in turn detracted, then reinforced from his status as the loser.

At first, he found it difficult to concede that the jury had found truth in both his and Watson's charges. But the more he thought, the more doubt entered his mind. He looked back on his own belief of Watson's guilt, which Jeffrey had refused to submit: the printed gown, George, Mr Gingham. It came to him that it was all a convolution-based on supposition. Watson hadn't written the letters.

The realisation freed him from his depression. He had no doubt. He had to issue an apology to Watson, stating clearly that he no longer believed that he had written the Vinegar letters. The problem was, he had to do so without it reopening the question of his own guilt.

He wrote to Nancy, announcing his firm intentions. Her reply was short and frosty to the edge of scorn. Shocked, he wrote remonstrating his ultimate end to expedite their marriage. There was no reply.

Saddened, he moved ahead, hoping that results would remove her misgivings. He hired a well-known journalist with the Edinburgh newspaper, the Caledonian Mercury to elaborate a report showing how he could not have written the letters, using the evidence from the trial. It made no reference to the Porter's plot, McPhail's murder or the agreement with Watson. Its last paragraph was:

In conclusion, Mr Kingan feels it to be proper in now publishing this Report to state explicitly, as he has repeatedly done, that he is satisfied Mr Watson had no connection whatever, directly or indirectly, with the authorship of the anonymous letters.

#

The report had taken three months. As agreed with the journalist, a precis first appeared in the Caledonian Mercury. Now, at the noon of Men's Unclothed Morning, he picked up his package from reception.

At the desk in the anteroom to the bedroom, he opened first his nephew's package. He started with The Scots Times. They were sure to cover the report.

And they did, on the inside page. The full-page article opened:

ALL IN THE WRONG

Kingan vs Watson and Watson vs Kingan—AGAIN!
When men's minds are inflamed with passion, prejudice usurps the seat of judgement and all sense, reason and discrimination are lost—KNOX.
A pamphlet has just now been inflicted on the public respecting the merits of this singular case but for anything that we can discern, the writer, in spite of the zeal and ability he displays, has just left it where it was.

Kingan slumped back, dizzy. He paused until the feeling had passed, then forced himself to read on. Although factually recording the content of the report, the tone of the long article was not pleasant. He had to pause several times. It finished with:

We know that, with the exception of the two families interested in the dispute, it was the conviction of every man, woman and child in the Parish of Govan during the proceedings at the Court of Session that these letters must have been written by a woman; and we likewise know that the conviction reigns throughout the Parish to the present hour.

It is perhaps little complimentary to the penetration of Messrs Oswald, Finlay, Stirling, MacIntosh, Aitken, Watson and Kingan and not least, our acute friend, the Editor of the Herald, that they have been bamboozled by a village politician in petticoats. A lady quite adept at her trade, a clever, quizzical, witty, agreeable woman. About whom the Govanites recite this ludicrous ditty:

A virgin rose of great renown,
whose nose was long, whose hose was blue,
to secrets all she got the clue
by pumping hard each wench and shrew.
Such stories did she so construe
That misery and pain she drew
And held them up to public view.
O Govan Lairds have a' been wud,
And ither Lairds have a' been blin'
Or they wad ne'er hae been sae fooled
By the arts o' Kitty Kittlefin,
Kittlefin, Kittlefin,
The arts o' Kitty Kittlefin.

'What the hell were they talking about?' he asked himself. 'A woman?' He remembered that Jeffrey had said as much during the trial. So had Miss Good, one of his witnesses. But their comments had made no impression on the jury. Nor on him.

He found the text insulting, demeaning. His strategy had completely backfired. He felt like submitting a vituperative missive to the Editor. He rose and paced the room to compose himself. He sat back down and reread the article, then again.

He separated himself from his anger at being mocked and thought about the contents. The claim that Govan knew all along shocked him. 'That's not possible! The maid, that Lily?'

He reread the poem. He knew what *Kittle Corner* was: where the Govan weavers' wives congregated before sunset to exchange the day's gossip. Kittle meant touchy, itchy; Kitty, Catherine. *A virgin rose: a fading beauty. Whose hose was blue.*

'Miss Catherine Hutton!'

He shook his head. He remembered her testimony in court, her tales to Nancy about Watson's comments: the printed gown, little George Oswald, the letter signed Vinegar. Housekeeper to Rowan, she had had easy access to the barn. The letter tied to the slate. She would have known Mary MacLean. He tried to remember if she had been at Miller's ball. The image came back of her, seated at Nancy's side.

He felt crushed by the realisation, 'She was Vinegar.' He sat back, bewildered. Then a chill penetrated his soul as he remembered Nancy's words, 'we share our woes.' It was then the doubt arose which, for the rest of his days, he could not shake: 'Did she know all the time?'

The End